ARLO FINCH

IN THE KINGDOM OF SHADOWS

ARLO FINCH
IN THE KINGDOM OF SHADOWS

JOHN AUGUST

ROARING BROOK PRESS
New York

Copyright © 2020 by John August
Published by Roaring Brook Press
Roaring Brook Press is a division of Holtzbrinck Publishing Holdings Limited Partnership
120 Broadway, New York, NY 10271
mackids.com

Library of Congress Control Number: 2019941007
ISBN 978-1-62672-818-9

Our books may be purchased in bulk for promotional, educational, or business use. Please
contact your local bookseller or the Macmillan Corporate and Premium Sales Department at
(800) 221-7945 ext. 5442 or by email at MacmillanSpecialMarkets@macmillan.com.

First edition, 2020
Book design by Elizabeth H. Clark
Printed in the United States of America by LSC Communications, Harrisonburg, Virginia

1 3 5 7 9 10 8 6 4 2

About the Type

The text is set in **Garamond**, a typeface based on the designs of sixteenth-century French designer Claude Garamond. It has become one of the most popular choices for print, used in everything from novels to textbooks to Field Books. Its crisp lines and even weight make it ideal for reading under the covers by flashlight.

The cover and chapter headings are set in **Cheddar Gothic**. Hand drawn by designer Adam Ladd in 2016, the typeface consists of only uppercase characters—but all twenty-six letters offer variants with extra flourishes. Cheddar Gothic was chosen for its distinctive look and adventurous spirit.

— 1 —

A PERFECTLY ORDINARY CAMPOUT

IT WASN'T TECHNICALLY A LIE.

Blue Patrol really did want to test out their new camp stoves. The annual Pine Mountain Company cook-off was coming up at the end of the month. Green Patrol had won the Golden Spork award the past three times, so for Blue Patrol to have any chance at winning it this year, they would need to practice their recipes on the real equipment.

"Why does it need to be at the river, though?" asked Indra. "Couldn't we just do it in one of our backyards? That's going to be the first thing they ask us."

They referred to their parents. Blue Patrol needed an excuse for why they were squeezing in an extra campout—a campout for only their patrol, no adults or other Rangers invited.

"We can say we need to duplicate real-world conditions," said Wu. "That's plausible."

Connor agreed. "Also, make sure to mention the fire ban. That explains what's different this year versus other years." After a remarkably dry summer, the Forest Service had banned open campfires in the Colorado mountains, which meant all patrols would be using tiny butane camp stoves. With limited fuel and just two burners, the stoves made cooking much more complicated.

"That still wouldn't explain why the campout has to be at the river," said Julie Delgado. "Our parents are going to ask." Her twin brother, Jonas, had the same concern.

"The river's the only campsite we can hike to from town," said Wu. "That way, no one needs to drive us. And if anything happens, we can just walk back."

Arlo Finch shook his head. "We shouldn't even bring up that something could go wrong. That'll just make them nervous. It has to seem like a perfectly ordinary campout."

In reality, it was far from ordinary.

What Blue Patrol had planned for this first Saturday in September was incredibly risky. It involved deception, bargaining, mystical artifacts and a seven-thousand-mile journey. There were a hundred ways it could go wrong.

But Arlo Finch was convinced it was the only shot they had.

A flash flood had destroyed the original town of Pine Mountain over a century ago, leaving behind rubble and ghost stories. This Saturday morning, as Blue Patrol set up their tents along the Big Stevens River, it was hard to believe such a small creek could do such tremendous damage. It was lower than any of them had ever seen it, with dried mud clinging to the exposed rocks. Water striders skittered along shallow, slimy pools.

"It stinks," declared Julie, never one to shy away from stating the obvious. She and Jonas staked their tent farthest from the water. In the three months since summer camp, Arlo, Wu and Indra had been careful to keep the twins involved in the planning, so they wouldn't get too upset when supernatural perils inevitably appeared. They weren't anticipating another hag or troll, but you could never be sure.

As part of those preparations, Connor and Indra set up the wards around the campsite. Indra had nearly completed her Elementary Wards patch, but still needed practice in properly sourcing and stacking the stones to protect the camp from malevolent and mischievous spirits.

If only there were wards to keep people away, Arlo thought. That was one of the biggest question marks in their plan: *what do we do if someone shows up and starts asking questions?*

The dry summer and campfire ban had greatly reduced the number of tourists coming to see the autumn aspen foliage, which meant Blue Patrol didn't need to worry about nosy outsiders. The bigger concern was that one of their parents would decide to stop by for a visit—perhaps a surprise cookie delivery. Diana Velasquez, the company's marshal, might also decide to check in on the patrol.

Connor had said not to worry, that if anyone showed up they'd improvise. Arlo had to trust that his friends could handle it, because he wouldn't be there.

He checked his daypack one last time, confirming it held two water bottles, four protein bars, a box of waterproof matches, an aluminum emergency blanket—and a bowling ball covered with duct tape. Given how full it was, the pack was lighter than one would expect.

He kept his Ranger's compass and the spirit knife in his pockets. He knew he'd want them close.

"Someone's coming!" whisper-shouted Wu, pointing to a shape making its way down the hill from the road. Everyone tensed up until they could confirm it was who they expected.

Arlo checked his watch: 9:19 A.M. His sister was early. She was *never* early.

It was strange to see Jaycee in outdoor gear. She usually wore combat boots and a black high school marching band sweatshirt, but today she was dressed in appropriate hiking gear, including a fleece jacket.

"What are we standing around for?" asked Jaycee. "Let's do this."

Arlo thought it would have been polite for her to at least introduce herself to the rest of the patrol, but suspected his sister was as nervous as he was.

"Send one last text to Mom," said Arlo. "But not a question. You don't want her to text you back."

"Why don't you send her a cat meme?" suggested Wu. "Everyone likes cat memes."

Jaycee stared at Wu through narrowed eyes. Arlo had gotten this withering look from his sister a thousand times and knew to ignore it, but he could see it unsettled Wu. Arlo realized he was going to have to watch out for any tension between Wu and his sister. They had a long journey ahead of them.

"I'll text her that I can't find my charging cable," said Jaycee. "So when I don't answer she'll assume my phone is dead."

Arlo had to admit that was a pretty clever plan. His sister clearly had practice at this. He had marveled at how easily Jaycee had been able to sell the ruse that she would be sleeping over at a friend's house to work on a class project.

How many other not-true stories has Jaycee told over the years? Arlo wondered. He suddenly felt bad about not being honest with his mom about what he was up to this weekend. *It wasn't technically a lie*, he reminded himself. Blue Patrol really would be camping at the river and testing out the new stoves. But Arlo Finch wouldn't be there. Neither would Henry Wu. If everything went right, they'd be halfway around the world with his sister.

Once Jaycee's text was sent and delivered, she turned off her phone. Arlo, Wu and Jaycee strapped on their daypacks and said goodbye to the patrol.

"Don't forget to check in when you get back," said Indra.

"And don't die," added Julie.

Arlo looked to Wu. "You know you don't have to come." While Wu had been instrumental in planning this expedition, it ultimately wasn't his mission. Arlo wouldn't have blamed his friend if he wanted to stay in Pine Mountain.

"You seriously think I'm missing this?" Wu pointed his walking stick into the forest. "Let's go!"

2

THE CITY OF LOST THINGS

THE LONG WOODS GO EVERYWHERE. That was one of the first things Arlo learned upon his arrival in Pine Mountain almost a year earlier.

Indra and Wu had explained that the Long Woods weren't part of the normal world, but rather connected to it at thousands of distinct spots around the globe. Later, Arlo had learned how Connor and his cousin had been drawn into the Woods as children. That cousin—Rielle—would end up living with the mysterious Eldritch, while Connor would emerge from the forest hundreds of miles away in Canada. The strange geography of the Long Woods meant that distances didn't work the same way. You could hike for just a few hours and end up on the other side of the world.

That's what Arlo was hoping to do. But first, he had to figure out exactly where he was going.

As Arlo, Wu and Jaycee left the patrol at the banks of the trickling river, Arlo could clearly picture where they were headed first: the Broken Bridge. Of all the places he'd visited in the Woods, it felt the most familiar. He'd spent many hours there this summer (and another summer thirty years earlier).

Part of the reason they'd chosen the Old Pine Mountain campsite was that it was only ten minutes away from a reliable Long Woods entrance. To get there, they first needed to cross the river, then cross it again.

"Why didn't we just stay on the other side?" asked Jaycee, frustrated to have already gotten her boots soaked from splashing through the water.

"That's not how it works," said Wu.

"But we're headed back where we began!"

"We're on the right path," said Arlo. "You just have to trust me."

Although the Long Woods went everywhere, it wasn't a simple matter to find one's way from point A to point B. Locations within the Woods couldn't be mapped, nor could the passageways in and out. You had to navigate by feel.

Originally, Arlo had relied on the subtle vibrations of his Ranger's compass to find his way, but as he gained more experience, he found himself picking his routes by pure instinct. No matter where he was in the Long Woods, Arlo could picture a familiar location like his house or the Gold Pan diner and feel where they were. Then it was a simple matter to head in that direction.

Well, simple for *him*. It was clear that Arlo had an uncanny ability to find and follow the paths of the Long Woods. Like Rielle, he was a tooble with mismatched eyes and a spirit trapped inside him. This dual nature allowed him to navigate the Woods unlike any other Ranger he'd met—except for the villainous Hadryn. And Hadryn was now a captive of the Eldritch.

Up ahead, an immense boulder rested in a shaft of sunlight. It looked like a stone whale covered in lichen. Arlo reached into a narrow crack along its face and pulled himself up, finding footholds as he went.

"Can't we just walk around it?" asked Jaycee.

"That's not how it—" Wu stopped himself midsentence, frozen by Jaycee's icy glare.

Arlo understood why Jaycee was confused and frustrated. She was used to a normal world of marching bands and standardized tests. Nothing about the Long Woods made sense until you experienced it with your own eyes.

"Where we're going is up here," he said simply.

Jaycee wedged her foot into the crack and hoisted herself up. Arlo took her hand and helped her through the last bit. As they stood atop the rock, his sister let out a small *wow*.

Wow was right. They weren't standing on a boulder at all, but rather one of the fallen stones near the Broken Bridge, a massive structure that extended halfway across a vertical chasm that Arlo suspected was bottomless.

Wu scrambled up behind them. He'd been here before, but the first glimpse of it each time was still impressive.

"You need to keep your voice down," whispered Arlo to Jaycee. "There's a troll who lives under the bridge."

"That's not the only ravenous creature you'll find," said a voice from the foot of the stone. They looked over the edge to find a small man with a handlebar mustache relaxing in a patch of sunlight, gnawing the last bit of meat off the carcass of a freshly killed bird.

It was Fox.

"Figured I should have a meal," he said, licking his fingers, "in case it was my last."

Fox walked so quickly that they had a hard time keeping up with his pace—and his elaborate sentences, which always seemed to double back on themselves.

"Not a spirit in these Woods would take you where I'm taking you, unless they were being taken, too," he said. "It's full of trappers, traders and worse, which is why I'm only taking you a little too far—but close enough that it's much too far for me."

Six weeks earlier, after Jaycee had returned from visiting their father, Arlo had asked Fox for help in finding a path through the Long Woods. The destination? A forest in the middle of Guangzhou, China.

That was the city Arlo's father had been living in for the

past four years, ever since he'd fled the United States after being accused by federal authorities of various computer crimes. Now their father was a fugitive. If he tried to enter the country by plane or ship, he would be arrested immediately.

But Arlo suspected he could sneak his father in through the Long Woods—after all, the Long Woods went everywhere. The problem was that Arlo had never been to that specific forest in Guangzhou, and therefore had no connection to it. No connection, no feeling. No feeling, no path.

Fox had said he couldn't get them to Guangzhou either—his knowledge of the normal world was minimal. "But I know a place that knows all the places. I hear they've got an atlas that'll show you all the ways in and out of the Woods."

That seemed impossible. Arlo felt certain the Long Woods couldn't be mapped. Fox said he didn't know how the atlas worked, but he was convinced it was real. "Somehow these trappers and traders can use it to find where they're going."

If there was a way to get to Guangzhou through the Long Woods, the atlas was their best shot.

"How much further is it?" asked Wu, huffing a bit.

Fox stopped short, his nose twitching. Then he suddenly dropped low to the ground, motioning for them to do the same. Even in his human form, Fox moved like the small predator he was.

Arlo followed Fox's pointing finger to two shapes far in the distance, moving roughly parallel to them. He looked over at Wu, who already had his binoculars out.

11

"It's two guys," Wu whispered. "Hunters, maybe?" He handed the binoculars to Arlo.

They definitely looked human—two burly men in camouflage, each carrying a large backpack. They were talking, but were too far away for Arlo to make out what they were saying, or if it was even English.

"Are they trappers?" he whispered to Fox. Trappers captured forest spirits, selling them to the Eldritch for gold and other treasures.

"If they were trappers, they'd have cages on them," Fox whispered back. "More likely they're traders smuggling something— drugs, money, gold. Dangerous work for dangerous men. That one you call Hadryn, I'm certain he's done it. Man can make a fortune if he's willing to take the risk."

The two men were nearly out of sight. Arlo and his friends had gone unnoticed. They stood up, resuming their course.

"Are we smugglers?" asked Wu. "We're trying to smuggle your dad back into the country."

"We're doing it for a good reason," said Arlo. "That's the difference."

Fox smiled and shook his head. "Humans always think there's a good reason."

After another hour of hiking, Arlo smelled smoke in the air. It wasn't a campfire. The scent on the wind was oily and sulfured, like the diesel generator behind Mitch's garage.

"We're close, aren't we?" Arlo asked Fox.

"I think so," said Fox. "This place puts my fur on edge. Last time I was here, I was just a pup."

"You got trapped?"

Fox nodded. "They were using red squirrels as bait. Those were always my weakness."

"How'd you escape?" asked Wu.

"Sharp teeth and fat fingers. I bit. They dropped the cage. It broke open and I ran. Swore I'd never come back."

As they reached a rise, they found themselves on a bluff overlooking the source of the smoke.

Below them, a city filled the valley, thin wisps of smoke rising from a hundred chimneys. This town was unlike anything Arlo had ever seen, a collection of random buildings from every conceivable culture and time period. Swooping pagodas wedged against squat brick huts with corrugated metal roofs. Hemp ropes ran from a giant black obelisk to support a faded red-and-white circus tent. Near the center of town sat an intact airliner, its massive wings serving as the roof to other small buildings.

"Where did this all come from?" asked Wu.

"Everywhere," answered Fox. "Sometimes things fall through the cracks of your world. Keys and socks, especially, but bigger things, too. Ships, planes. People. Now and then, whole cities have fallen through. And when they do, they end up here."

Jaycee reached down to pick up a black plastic TV remote. It was dirty and wet, but looked relatively modern. The keys still lit up as she pushed the buttons. Arlo could imagine the remote's owner searching the couch cushions in frustration, convinced it had to be somewhere.

But it wasn't. It was in the Long Woods.

"This is Fallpath," said Fox. "It's the city of lost things."

— 3 —

THE OWL AND THE SNAKE

WHERE DO YOU FIND AN ATLAS? It felt like the kind of circular riddle Arlo's dad would propose, like looking up the definition of *dictionary* in the dictionary.

According to Fox's sources, the atlas was somewhere in Fallpath. Beyond that, all Fox could tell them was that the atlas was apparently protected by an owl and a snake. But were they literally an owl and a snake, or spirits of some kind? Fox wasn't sure.

"Maybe it's a chimera," said Wu. "A creature that's half owl and half snake." That gave him an idea: "They both eat rats, so maybe we could feed it one and that's how you get past it. I bet we can find a rat somewhere."

Jaycee had no patience for Wu's theories. "What are you talking about? We'll just ask. Someone will know where it is."

"What if they don't want to tell us?" asked Arlo.

Jaycee shrugged. "Then we'll deal with it. We can't just stand around worrying about things that haven't happened yet." With that, she started walking down the hill into Fallpath.

In planning this expedition, Arlo had wondered how Jaycee would handle the challenges of the Long Woods. Would she be overwhelmed? Could she keep up? He hadn't considered how much preparation his sister had already had. Like him, she'd always been the new kid at a new school, figuring out the rules on the fly. She might never have been in this magical forest, but she'd found her way around Philadelphia and Chicago. She'd flown by herself to China. She'd seen more of the real world than Arlo had.

"She's right," Arlo said to Wu. "We'll figure it out."

Arlo and Wu thanked Fox, then followed Jaycee down the path into the city. When Arlo looked back, Fox was already gone.

The main road running through Fallpath was a narrow stripe of mud. Ramshackle buildings of two and three stories leaned into the street, in some places joined together by plank bridges. Electrical cables connected creaking rooftop windmills and duct-taped solar panels. On either side of the road, carts and tables were stacked with food, weapons and scavenged items. Arlo spotted manual typewriters, iron daggers, roasted pigs, potion jars, medieval lutes, an abacus, dolls, fidget spinners and an Atari video game cartridge for *E.T.: The Game*.

The vendors and buyers all looked to be human, of every

conceivable ethnicity and background. Many had animals with them: dogs, chickens, two-headed lizards on leashes. Most of the haggling seemed to be happening in English, but based on the accents, it wasn't everyone's first language.

"Do these people live here?" asked Wu.

"Some of them, I think," said Arlo. In what little he could find written about the Long Woods, Arlo had learned about the distinction between Longborn—people who were native to the Long Woods—and those who came later in life, called Drifters. Fallpath was apparently the only permanent settlement in the Long Woods, so it had become the nexus of trading—legal and otherwise.

As they headed deeper into the town, it got so crowded Arlo could barely see his boots.

"Watch out for pickpockets," warned Jaycee.

Arlo felt a tug on his backpack. He spun around to see a small, white-haired woman with brown teeth that pointed in nine directions. She lunged at him, sniffing his jacket.

"You've been near a spirit!" she hissed. "A furry one. I can smell it on you." Her eyes were mismatched colors, green and brown, just like his. *She's a tooble, too*, Arlo realized.

Jaycee pushed her way between them. "Go away! Shoo!"

The crone didn't back off. "It's on you, too. Still warm! Must be close. Where is it?"

Arlo quickly glanced back down the road to the hill above the city where they'd left Fox. The old woman followed his gaze. She smiled, then whistled through her teeth. Two younger women in filthy hooded sweatshirts—*Her daughters?* Arlo wondered—were suddenly at her side.

"Get your cages, girls! We've got quarry." With that, the three women pushed their way through the crowd, headed out of town.

"Should we warn Fox?" asked Wu.

"He said he wasn't going to stick around," said Arlo. "He'll be fine." Arlo said it with confidence he didn't really feel. "C'mon. We need to find the owl and the snake."

"I can take you," said a thin voice behind him. "The owl and the snake. I can take you."

The voice belonged to a young girl, one so short Arlo hadn't seen her at first. She couldn't have been more than five. She was wearing cartoon-cat pajamas, purple rain boots and a knit Cleveland Browns hat that covered most of her straight black hair.

"You know where they are?" Arlo asked. "The owl and the snake?"

Before the girl could answer, Wu asked, "Is it a chimera? Half owl and half snake?"

Now the girl seemed confused.

"Listen," said Jaycee. "If you can take us to them, we'll give you a candy bar." Jaycee pulled an energy bar from her jacket pocket. The girl's eyes lit up.

"It's really more like a protein bar than a candy bar," said Wu.

Jaycee glared at Wu, who quickly added, "They're good, though. They really taste like candy bars."

Arlo focused on the girl: "Can you take us to the owl and the snake?"

The girl grabbed Arlo's hand, leading the way. She moved fast, weaving effortlessly through the crowd. Several times Arlo glanced back to make sure Jaycee and Wu were keeping up.

They left the main road, ducking into a narrow alley. Greasy cooking smoke stung Arlo's eyes. Suddenly, the girl stopped in front of a door hanging loose on its hinges. They'd gone less than a hundred feet.

"Here," she said, pointing.

"This is where the owl and the snake are?" Arlo asked. "We can find them in here?"

This couldn't be right. The building looked seedy, even by the standards of Fallpath. A heavily tattooed man with vomit in his beard was propped against the wall, unconscious. Several human teeth lay in the mud beside him. Arlo could hear music spilling from behind the door, and rowdy men arguing.

Arlo had expected to find the owl and the snake at some sort of shrine or temple or mystical library, not a backwoods bar. As Wu and Jaycee caught up, Arlo broke the bad news: "I don't think she knows where she's going."

"She does," said Jaycee. She pointed to a hand-painted sign above the door:

THE OWL AND THE SNAKE

They're not animals or spirits, Arlo realized. *It's the name of a place.*

Jaycee handed over the promised protein bar. Arlo expected

19

the girl to tear off the wrapper and devour it, but instead she tucked it under her hat. Then she pushed the door open and stepped inside.

Arlo, Jaycee and Wu leaned to get a quick glance before the door swung shut again. It was definitely a bar, complete with beer taps, neon signs and sawdust on the floor. A jukebox played the kind of country rock that Mitch the mechanic liked.

"Why would the atlas be in a bar?" asked Wu.

"Let's find out," said Jaycee, pushing past them. Arlo and Wu followed her in.

Despite not even being noon, the patrons of the Owl and the Snake had clearly been here for hours drinking and gambling. Instead of money or poker chips, they seemed to be wagering with something more valuable: spirits. Arlo recognized the lantern-sized devices he'd seen the Eldritch use when they descended upon the Summerland.

"They're trappers," he whispered to Wu. "Those things are cages."

One man showed his cards, evidently winning his hand. As he went to collect his winnings, his opponent suddenly flipped the table over. Arlo, Wu and Jaycee pressed back against the wall as a full-on brawl broke out, among not just the two men but half the bar.

"You!" shouted a female voice from across the tavern. Arlo looked over and saw an Asian woman in her forties wearing leather pants and an army-green canvas jacket. She was standing with the young girl and holding the protein bar. "Why are you giving my kid candy?!"

She was headed their way, mostly ignoring the fighting around her. When a burly man stumbled into her path, she deftly spun him around, then kicked him back into the brawl. Then her focus returned to the trio.

"It's actually a protein bar," said Wu.

The woman was now directly in front of them. Even in heeled boots, she was barely taller than Arlo, but she was incredibly intimidating. "My daughter has a soy allergy."

"So do I," said Arlo. "There's no soy in it. You can check the ingredients."

The woman locked eyes with Arlo, dubious. Like him, her irises were two different colors: one blue, one brown. Then she turned her attention to the protein bar, finding the ingredients list. One of the drunken fighters slammed into the jukebox. It shattered and sparked. The music died. That finally crossed a line for her.

"Enough!" she shouted. She then twirled one finger above her head.

Suddenly, a massive wind rose up in the bar, lifting each of the troublemakers off the ground. The door opened, then one by one, the brawlers were flung screaming out into the street. Once the last one was out the door, the woman dropped her hand. The wind stopped. The bar was now eerily quiet.

The woman tossed the protein bar to the young girl, who

had been waiting on the other side of the room. The woman said something to her in Chinese that Arlo guessed might be *half now, half after dinner.* The girl whined in response, but the mother wasn't giving in. Ultimately, the girl skulked out of the room.

The woman surveyed the damage to the bar. In addition to the broken jukebox, tables and chairs were overturned, shattered beer steins everywhere.

"Do you want us to help you clean up?" asked Arlo, hoping to get on her good side.

"No," she said dismissively. "This happens all the time." The woman knocked three times on the bar. Arlo watched as tables and chairs began rolling and righting themselves, like animals getting back up after a fall. Invisible hands scooped up the shards of broken steins, which mended themselves in midair. They then floated back to a shelf behind the bar, neatly arranging themselves in rows. In less than thirty seconds, the bar had been largely reset.

Even Jaycee was impressed by this display of practical magic. "Can you do that?" she asked Arlo.

Arlo couldn't, but he was pretty sure he knew how it worked. "Does everything have a spirit bound to it?"

"Not everything," the woman answered, pointing to the jukebox. "That'll be a hassle to fix. Might just have to replace it." She then looked at Arlo more closely, intrigued. "I'm Zhang. What's your name?"

Whether Arlo should use his real name had been debated

within the patrol from the early planning stages. It seemed likely that Arlo's name had been mentioned by Hadryn and others. *You don't know who you can trust*, warned Indra.

"Daniel," he said. (Daniel was in fact his middle name.)

"What's your deal, Daniel?" asked Zhang. "You're a tooble, but you're clearly not Longborn."

"How do you know?"

"Because you seem amazed by things you would have seen your whole life. You're obviously tourists."

Jaycee had grown impatient. "We're looking for an atlas."

Zhang feigned surprise. "And why do you think there'd be an atlas here?"

"A friend said you had one," said Wu.

"Did your friend tell you how expensive it was to use the atlas? Because for first-timers, the fee is fifty thousand dollars cash."

"We don't have any money," said Arlo.

"Then we don't have anything to talk about." Zhang took a rag from her belt and began wiping down the tables.

"We have something better than money," said Wu.

"Don't say Bitcoin."

Arlo took off his daypack. "It's an upscale. A big one."

That got her attention. "Really? Let's see it."

Arlo unzipped the pack, awkwardly extricating a duct tape–covered bowling ball. While solid, it was also remarkably light, as if just a plastic shell. Arlo could easily hold it in one hand as he started peeling back the tape to reveal an edge of glinting red-gold coatl scale. It strained against the tape, inexorably tugged upwards.

He peeled back a little more. With a rip, the ball suddenly fell, just missing Arlo's feet. Still holding one end of the tape, Arlo nearly had his arm yanked off as the scale shot upwards. Upscales were like helium balloons, but much stronger. They were what made it possible for coatls to fly.

"Where'd you find it?" Zhang asked.

While Fox had pointed Arlo and Blue Patrol in the right direction, actually obtaining the coatl scale had required an exhausting trek through the Long Woods to a cavern halfway up a jagged mountain peak. Once inside, it had taken hours to get the scale down from the roof of the cave, with Arlo climbing up a human pyramid. They'd gotten out of the coatl's nest just moments before the huge flying serpent returned.

Arlo didn't want Zhang to know any of that. "In a cave," he said.

"So, can we see the atlas?" asked Jaycee.

Zhang took the scale from Arlo, admiring its pearly iridescence. Judging by her reaction, it was clear the upscale was worth more than the fifty thousand dollars she'd asked for.

"You've got a deal."

— 4 —
THE ATLAS

AT PINE MOUNTAIN ELEMENTARY, Arlo and his friends had frequently consulted *Culman's Bestiary of Notable Creatures*, a book of supernatural lore the librarian kept locked away in her cabinet.

Arlo was picturing something similar for the atlas: a hardcover tome listing locations around the world. It would probably be oversized, perhaps with an embossed leather cover. The pages might be edged in gold.

He could not have been more wrong.

At the end of a short hallway, Zhang unlocked a heavy iron door. She then reached inside to flip a light switch. Row after row of dusty bulbs slowly flickered to life, revealing just how immense this space was. It was bigger than the school gymnasium. Maybe even bigger than the entire school.

Rough wooden shelves ran in maze-like rows, with each

spot on the shelves marked with a letter and number. The labels seemed to correlate to the object stored there: a rusted bike, a broken bottle, a graveyard angel.

"It's like the warehouse at Ikea," said Wu. "If it was super, super creepy."

Arlo suspected this giant room was still within the small footprint of the Owl and the Snake. Distances in the Long Woods were unpredictable. It seemed reasonable that powerful enchantments could squeeze extra square footage into a building.

Zhang switched on a desk lamp at a cabinet with dozens of small drawers. "Where exactly are you trying to go?" she asked.

Arlo turned to his sister, who knew all the details.

"It's a park on the north side of Guangzhou," said Jaycee. She handed over a few sheets of paper she'd printed from the internet with a map of the city and the park circled in red.

"And you've been there?" Zhang asked. "Is there an actual forest? Not just a tree or two. It needs to be pretty wild."

"I was there two months ago. And yeah, if you get off the main path you wouldn't know you're in the city at all."

Zhang seemed satisfied. She pulled out a drawer in the cabinet and began flicking through index cards, searching for something.

Meanwhile, Arlo and Wu started examining the nearest shelf. Each object on it had its own tag, a stub of yellowed paper attached with waxed string. For a plastic kazoo, Arlo read the handwritten description:

1/20/87 northwest of a broken stone wall

Wu showed Arlo the tag on a moldy stuffed dinosaur:

8/4/70 an island in the middle of the river

"What are these things?" whispered Wu.

Arlo had no idea. There wasn't any obvious connection between the objects, and none of them seemed at all valuable.
So why were they labeled? Why was the door locked?

"Maybe it's a museum," Arlo whispered back.

"Or maybe she's some kind of weird hoarder."

Zhang looked over at them. "Don't touch anything!" she
yelled.

"Sorry!" they both yelled back.

But what's the big deal? Arlo wondered. *Why doesn't she want
us touching it?* He decided there was no harm in asking: "What
is all this stuff?"

"Wow, you really are tourists." Zhang pulled a card from the
drawer, evidently the one she'd been looking for. Then she gestured with her hand to indicate the entire room. "This is the atlas."

Arlo was as confused as Jaycee and Wu. "I thought the atlas
was a book."

"How could it be a book? You can't map the Long Woods.
You can only navigate between known places."

That made sense to Arlo, but— "Then how can you navigate
to a place you've never been?"

27

He couldn't tell if Zhang was more annoyed or amused. "Daniel, my man. That's why you're here, isn't it?" She held up the card from the catalog. "Follow me."

Zhang led the way through the shelves, snaking left and right to arrive at a dark section, the overhead lights having burned out. She sent up three snaplights in quick succession, giving her enough light to make out the labels: "R17. R18. R19."

She reached in to pick up a Rubik's Cube. It was scrambled, and at least one of the colored stickers had peeled off. Zhang checked the tag, comparing it to the index card. "Yup. This is your park."

She handed Arlo the cube. He was confused. "Do I have to solve it?"

"I can solve it," offered Wu. "I can do it in three minutes."

"No. It's not like that at all." She took the cube back. "This Rubik's Cube, it's a marker. For whatever reason, it ended up near one of the entrances to the Long Woods. Maybe someone dropped it—whatever. And it sat there long enough that some of the energy from the Long Woods seeped into it."

Zhang sent up three more snaplights in different directions, illuminating the shelves. "Everything here came from some place in the world. And they all carry a little piece of the world with it. If you focus on it, you can feel where it came from and use that to find your way there."

She handed Arlo the cube again. He stared at it, trying to concentrate on it the way Superman did with his heat vision.

"Not like that. Wow. That's ridiculous." She cupped her

hand under Arlo's. "Don't think about the thing itself. Think about what's around it. Where does it want to be?"

Arlo was pretty sure he knew what she was getting at. Finding your way in the Long Woods was less about *trying* than *reacting*. You couldn't force it. You had to follow the path that was already there.

As the snaplights fell, Zhang faded into darkness. Arlo kept his eyes and his mind open. He could feel the cold plastic of the Rubik's Cube in his hand. He heard his breath. He felt the weight of his body.

The air stirred. It was cold.

A distant bird trilled. Water trickled.

He felt the ground holding him up. Just inches below, worms were chewing through the earth.

How do I know this?

One of his stickers was loose. Dew slipped into the gap.

It was night. The trees towered over him. Beyond them, the moon. Everything was blue.

"Are you there?" asked Zhang. He couldn't see her, but could feel her hand under his. He must still be back in the warehouse, he realized. *The atlas.*

"I'm here," he answered. "There. Yes."

"Look closely. Make sure you really know it. Feel it. You have to make it familiar."

Arlo shifted his attention to the nearest tree, studying its rough bark. Then he explored the tiny spring burbling a few feet away, a silver ribbon that slipped back into the rocks.

He could smell the wet earth and rotting leaves and distant car exhaust. He felt the weight of the birds on the branches.

"Hey!" It was his sister's voice. She was nearby, but also distant. "Are you okay?"

"I'm fine."

"You don't look okay." There was a tone in her voice he'd never heard before. "Whatever you're doing, stop it."

"She's right," said Wu. "Your skin's really cold."

If they were touching him, he didn't feel it. Instead he felt the cold soil beneath him, and the raindrops pelting down, and the blazing hot sun he couldn't escape. His sticker was peeling more and more each day and night and day and night and day and

now he was falling
falling through
falling into

He gasped. It was dark. Something was smothering him. He struggled and fought, desperate for air. His heart was pounding so hard it hurt his ribs.

He sat up, bracing himself on his elbows. Jaycee and Wu were on their knees. His sister was crying.

"What are you doing?!" he asked. His voice was hoarse.

Jaycee grabbed him, hugging him tight.

"Dude, you passed out," said Wu. "Your eyes rolled back. Totally white. And then your heart stopped. We've been doing CPR for a couple of minutes."

Jaycee swatted her brother. "I thought you were dead!"

"I'm fine," he said. "I promise." It was weird to see his sister so concerned about him. In thirteen years, he had never seen anything like it.

Arlo looked past Jaycee to Zhang, who looked neither happy nor disappointed he had survived. "What happened?" he asked.

"I told you to look at the area *around* the object, not *become* the object." She held up the Rubik's Cube. "This is just plastic. It's not alive. If you put yourself inside it, you're not gonna live long."

Zhang put the cube back on the shelf, making sure the tag was visible.

Wu and Jaycee helped Arlo back to his feet. He was a little woozy, but also confident.

"Guys, I know where we're going."

5
TOMMYKNOCKERS

A CAMPOUT WITHOUT A CAMPFIRE JUST FELT WRONG.

It was nearly eight, the night was dark and the remaining Blue Patrol members were sitting around three electronic candles Indra had brought from home. The orange LEDs flickered in a way that was fairly convincing, and yet—

"This is terrible," Julie declared. No one disagreed.

Just like the make-believe campfire, the make-believe campout had largely been a bust, beginning with the test run for the company cook-off. The butane stoves were efficient at boiling water for the rotini pasta, but left everything else charred or raw. It was like cooking on a blowtorch. The patrol had ultimately decided to just eat the pasta plain and bury the half-cooked sauce under a distant dead tree.

"At least we know the sauce won't kill it," said Connor.

Even the s'mores had tasted wrong. "It's the smoke that

makes them good," opined Jonas. "Without that, they're just gooey candy bars." They'd only eaten one apiece, rather than their usual three or four.

The dishes had been washed. The food was strung up in a tree to keep it out of the reach of bears. All the chores were finished, but the statewide fire ban meant that they couldn't spend the next few hours poking at a proper campfire. The night wasn't particularly cold, but without a fire there was nothing to focus on. The silence was uncomfortable.

Indra checked her watch. "They should be in Fallpath by now," she said. "Maybe even on their way to Guangzhou." They had deliberately not talked much about Arlo, Wu and Jaycee, just in case anyone wandered into the camp.

"Are they going to let us know when they get to China?" asked Jonas.

"Not unless there's an emergency," said Connor. "Wu's not even supposed to turn his phone on."

"What if we need to get ahold of them?" asked Julie. "What if something goes wrong on our side? They'd have no idea."

"They've got enough to worry about," said Indra. "They just have to focus on finding Arlo's dad and getting back."

A digital watch beeped. Connor switched it off and retrieved a pill bottle from his jacket pocket.

"How long do you have to keep taking those?" asked Jonas.

"Not sure," said Connor. "Maybe forever."

Connor had been airlifted from summer camp with a severely infected spleen that had had to be surgically removed.

While he was mostly recovered, he needed to be extra-careful to avoid germs, and wasn't supposed to lift heavy objects until the doctors gave him the okay.

"How much did the surgery cost?" asked Jonas.

Indra was offended on Connor's behalf. "You can't ask that. It's rude."

"How is it rude? I'm curious. Plus, the helicopter. Did your parents have to pay for that?"

Indra interjected again: "He probably doesn't even know!"

Connor swallowed a pill with a swig of water from his bottle. It took a second try to get it down. "It cost a lot. Insurance covered some of it, but I know my parents had to pay, too."

"Good thing your family's rich," said Julie. The silence got even more silent.

The Cunningham family's wealth was an oft-discussed topic in Pine Mountain, but never in front of them. While they weren't ostentatious, Connor and his brother always had the latest outdoor gear. Their family had a new SUV every year, and went skiing at resorts where valets helped you in and out of your boots.

Much of the talk about the Cunninghams wasn't about how they spent their money, but where it came from. The family owned more than a hundred acres around the valley, but according to someone on the town council, ten years earlier they had fallen behind on taxes and had been in danger of bankruptcy.

Then their fortunes had changed dramatically. Some speculated that they'd made a deal to store nuclear waste in one of the long-abandoned mines on their property. Others suggested that they'd found a new vein of gold and were secretly extracting it. But no one had dared directly inquire until Jonas Delgado posed the question that everyone else had been quietly whispering for a decade:

"How'd your family get its money, anyway?"

Indra was about to object that it was nobody's business, but Connor held her off. Clearly, he'd been thinking about it for some time.

Connor took a long moment to figure out the best way to begin. "So, remember how I told you that Katie and I got lost in the Long Woods?"

They nodded. As a young boy, Connor and his cousin Katie had wandered away from a family campout at Highcross and found themselves in the Long Woods. They'd been lured there by the hag—the same forest witch the patrol had faced in the Valley of Fire. After three weeks, young Connor had eventually made his way back to his family. But his cousin Katie had stayed with the Eldritch. She now called herself Rielle. She visited her parents in Pine Mountain twice a year, but otherwise lived in the Realm.

"When Rielle comes to visit, she brings stuff with her," said Connor.

"What kind of stuff?" asked Jonas.

"Gold mostly. Silver. Sometimes diamonds." Connor let the words sit there in the darkness, not elaborating or explaining.

Indra wanted to make sure she was hearing him correctly. "Your cousin brings you gold from the Realm?"

"Apparently, that was part of the deal they made with the Eldritch."

Indra kept pressing: "The deal *who* made with the Eldritch?"

"Her parents, my parents. Everyone." Connor was clearly uncomfortable saying this out loud. But he also seemed relieved to not be keeping the secret to himself anymore.

"So your parents have met the Eldritch?" asked Indra. "Don't you think you should have told Arlo? They could have information about what the Eldritch are actually after."

Connor was defensive. "No. I don't think anyone in my family has actually met the Eldritch. I mean, other than Rielle."

"Then who made the deal?" asked Jonas.

"Remember, I was really young. I wasn't any part of that. But from what I understand, there are people—human people like us—who work with the Eldritch. Like, negotiators. I think they're with the government."

This idea intrigued Jonas. "A secret government agency that deals with aliens from the Realm."

"They're not aliens," said Connor.

Jonas was undeterred. "They're literally extraterrestrial. I think it counts."

Meanwhile, Julie was still catching up with the revelations. "Wait, so your family *isn't* storing nuclear waste in the mines?"

Connor smiled. "No."

Indra wasn't ready to move on from the issue of Rielle. "To be clear, your family is getting paid by the Eldritch for your cousin. That's crazy."

Connor downplayed her objection. "It's not like she's there against her will. She wanted to stay."

"She was four! How could she know what she wanted when she was four?"

"You don't understand! Katie—Rielle—she wasn't normal. She was always strange."

Indra was so agitated she stood up. "So what, you give her to the Eldritch, let them deal with her? Why don't we just give them all the strange people?"

"I didn't do this, Indra!" snapped Connor. "It wasn't my choice!" Embarrassed to have lost his temper, he restated things in a calmer tone: "Look, I didn't make the decision—the adults did. But I understand why they did it. Sometimes you have to choose between two bad options."

"What, keeping your daughter or going bankrupt?"

"Me, okay? They chose *me* over *her*. The Eldritch had both of us, and the only way my family could get me back was to let her stay." Connor wiped away tears. "That's what happened."

Everyone was silent for a long moment. This was another moment when a campfire would have been helpful, giving them all something to stare at.

"I'm really sorry, Connor," said Indra. "I can't imagine what it's been like to carry that secret all these years."

"It's not your fault," said Julie.

Jonas agreed. "You were just a kid."

Connor half-smiled. "It's weird that my family is rich because my cousin's gone. It's like when someone dies and there's insurance money. It's bad and good at the same time."

Jonas held out his hand, stopping the conversation. "Do you hear that?"

They listened carefully. From somewhere in the dark came a thumping sound, followed by creaks. Was it a creature? Was it simply wind in the trees?

Then they heard tiny giggles and immediately knew—

"Tommyknockers," said Julie with a groan.

Tommyknockers were mischievous spirits often encountered in the Rockies. A century earlier, miners blamed them for fatal collapses, but according to the Ranger Field Book, they were largely harmless. At most, they were apt to steal tools and untie ropes.

"We're fine," said Connor. "The wards should keep them out."

As if in response, there came a crash followed by more giggles. All four members of Blue Patrol realized at the same time what it had to be: "The food!"

They had hoisted the bag with all the food and cooking supplies high in a tree well away from the campsite, as per Ranger guidelines. Unfortunately, that placed it outside the perimeter of the wards.

All four Rangers charged to defend their food. The moon was nearly full, so it wasn't hard to spot the tiny creatures as they jumped from tree to tree, giggling. They looked like hairless monkeys with pointy ears. One wore a cooking pot like a massive helmet. It crashed into tree stumps, unable to see. Two others were stuffing themselves with marshmallows.

Throwing pine cones and snaplights, Blue Patrol managed to scare off the tommyknockers, but it took nearly fifteen minutes to recover the food they'd scattered. Bites had been taken out of their apples, and the eggs for breakfast were dripping from the carton.

"Should we maybe just cook them now?" proposed Jonas.

"I could eat," said Indra. After the disappointing pasta, a second dinner sounded like a great idea. They carried the bag back to their campsite.

When they got there, a young woman their age was standing in the candlelight. She was wearing an embroidered silk coat, silver earrings and a thin jeweled headpiece. Like Arlo, she had mismatched eyes: one green, one brown.

Indra had never met this girl before, but immediately realized who she had to be: "You're Rielle, aren't you?"

"What are you doing here?" asked Connor. He didn't greet her like a cousin, or even a friend.

Rielle seemed confused to see only the four of them. "Where's Arlo?"

The members of Blue Patrol exchanged glances, a silent conversation. They deferred to Connor, who was clearly suspicious. "Why do you need him? What's going on?"

"He's in danger. I'm just here to warn him." Rielle seemed to intuit that Arlo wasn't at the campsite. "Can you at least get a message to him?"

"What's the message?"

"It's Hadryn. He's escaped."

39

— 6 —

THE WALL

THERE WAS SIMPLY NO WAY FORWARD. After four hours of hiking across the Long Woods, through narrow chasms with water up to their knees and meadows of deep purple flowers that smelled like grape soda, Arlo had led the trio to a dead end. They were standing at the foot of a vertical cliff of white limestone hundreds of feet tall. It faintly glowed in the moonlight.

To both the left and the right, the white band continued to the horizon, an endless wall.

"Maybe we can go back and try a different route," suggested Wu.

"How far back?" asked Jaycee. "We're not going to that city again."

It wasn't just that she was exhausted—they all were—but the urgency of time. According to the schedule laid out in their plan, they should have already gotten to China. Blue Patrol anticipated them back in Pine Mountain in under twelve hours. More importantly, their families were expecting them to return from their respective campout and sleepover. There simply wasn't time to retrace their steps.

"I know we're close," said Arlo. "I can feel it. It's just ahead."

"But we can't climb that," said Wu, pointing to the limestone cliff. "Maybe if we had the right gear, but even then I'm not sure."

Arlo wasn't giving up without really investigating the situation. He shed his pack and walked right up to the cliff face. It was as white as chalk, and just as soft. He scratched his fingernail against it. The white stone crumbled.

Wu was right; it couldn't be climbed. Every handhold would simply break away.

Frustrated, Arlo sat down to think, leaning back against the cliff wall. Wu and Jaycee also took a breather, drinking from their water bottles and eating protein bars. They all needed a break from the long day, from the Long Woods, and from each other.

Arlo stared up at the cliff. *If only we still had the upscale*, he thought. *We could float up to the top.*

His dad called that kind of if-onlying "counterfactual." Clark Finch wasn't a fan. *You can't change the past. You can only change what you do next.*

But at this moment, Arlo Finch had no idea what to do next. The best option seemed to be bailing on the plan and just heading back to Pine Mountain. Jaycee would understand. Of the three of them, Wu would probably be the most disappointed. He had lobbied hard to be included on the expedition, arguing that they might need him to speak Chinese once they got there.

Arlo wondered if that was the real reason Wu had wanted to come. At summer camp, it had been Indra, not Wu, who had accompanied Arlo on most of his adventures. Wu might have seen this as his chance to reestablish the primacy of his friendship with Arlo.

Arlo noticed his boots had a bright purple stain from walking through the flowers. He wondered if he could rub it off.

As he brought his foot to his hand, Arlo suddenly fell backwards in a reverse somersault that surprised him. Sitting up, he felt disoriented, but soon made it to his feet. Oddly, the sky was in the wrong place: behind him, not above him. *He was standing on the cliff wall.* Gravity had somehow shifted, turning "sideways" into "down."

He tried walking. The white limestone beneath him seemed utterly unremarkable. If he closed his eyes, it felt no different from walking on the ground.

"That's so cool!" shouted Wu, who ran towards the cliff and awkwardly jumped-slash-fell onto the vertical surface. He stuck there, firmly planted, before getting up. He brushed the white dust off his jacket.

"Bring my pack!" Arlo shouted to Jaycee.

Jaycee sighed, but retrieved it. She stopped at the edge of the cliff wall, not wanting to fall as clumsily as Arlo or Wu. She put her right boot on the wall and simply shifted her weight until she was standing horizontally.

She tried to play it off like it was no big deal. "So which way do we go now?"

Arlo pointed to the right. "It's not much further." He led the way, happy to have been wrong.

There *was* a way forward. It was just sideways.

7
HADRYN

ALVA HADRYN THOMAS WAS BORN in a small town in Texas forty-three years earlier. In the weeks after summer camp, Indra had found his birth announcement online, confirming he really was human.

There had been doubts because Hadryn was a shape-shifter. He could convincingly appear to be anyone by altering his face, his body and his voice. At Camp Redfeather, he had impersonated nearly every member of Blue Patrol at one point or another, although he spent most of his time as Thomas, a visiting Ranger assigned to their patrol.

He was charming, clever and extremely dangerous. He hadn't just broken the Ranger's Vow; he seemed to have no moral code whatsoever. He bragged about the people he'd killed over the years, mostly in the pursuit of powerful magic and mystical knowledge.

Sociopath was the term for someone without a conscience, and that seemed to fit.

Hadryn had a particular obsession with Arlo Finch, a mix of jealousy and vengefulness going back to their first meeting. In their last encounter, he had threatened to kill everyone close to Arlo unless he agreed to help recover more arcane artifacts. Hadryn was ultimately captured by the Eldritch, who had been keeping him as a prisoner in the Realm.

Until tonight. Now he was free.

"What do we do?" asked Julie after Rielle had left. "Is he going to come after us?"

"He might," said Indra. "We need to figure out a system so he can't impersonate us again."

"I'm more worried about him killing us," said Jonas. "We can't stay here tonight. We should go home."

Indra scoffed at the idea. "He can google. He can easily figure out where we live, or where we go to school."

"Those are the same for us," said Julie, who never missed an opportunity to point out she and her brother were home-schooled.

Connor tried to be the voice of reason. "Look, Rielle said the Eldritch are looking for Hadryn. That means he has to be careful. He's probably lying low for now."

"Still, we have to warn Arlo," said Indra.

Everyone agreed. They decided to text Wu's phone. If he turned it on when they got to China, he'd get the message.

Everyone crowded around Connor as he typed:

Rielle came. She says Hadryn escaped

The Eldritch don't know where he is. She says you're in

danger

"You can't just leave it like that," complained Julie. "It's too scary. You have to be a little positive."

Indra and Jonas agreed. Connor typed one more text:

Good luck!

— 8 —
THE FAR SIDE
OF THE WORLD

"WE'RE IN THE WRONG PLACE," said Wu. "This is bad. This is really bad."

He was consulting the brick-like GPS unit he'd been carrying in his pack. The device was at least twenty years old. Wu had found it at the back of a shelf in his family's garage, its batteries covered with a salty crust. Unlike the maps on a modern cell phone, it didn't rely on a data connection, so it could be used offline.

But it wasn't completely intuitive, either. It came with a thick manual set in small type.

"Maybe you're not using it quite right," said Arlo, trying to be gentle.

In fact, Arlo was certain Wu was dead wrong. This patch of sunny forest was exactly as Arlo had seen it in the atlas. Every tree and every rock was just where it should be. Even the bird songs were correct. It was thrilling, like waking from a dream and realizing it was real.

Wu showed Arlo the device's tiny pixelated screen. "See, we're here." He pointed to a blinking dot. "And we're supposed to be there." He pointed to a red X.

"How far off are we?" asked Jaycee. "Are we even in China?"

"Yeah, I mean, we're on the north side of Guangzhou, but it's the wrong park. We're six miles away from where we want to be."

Arlo had to stifle a laugh. "We just came seven thousand miles and you're worried that we're off by six?"

"We had a plan! We knew which buses to take. I don't know how to get us to your dad's apartment from here."

"We'll figure it out," said Arlo. "We're fine."

Wu was unconvinced. "Should I use my phone? We can get maps and directions."

They all knew the stakes. The moment Wu or Jaycee switched on their phones, they would connect to the local wireless network. It would show up on their monthly bill as a roaming charge. There would be no way to conceal that they'd somehow been to China. Only by staying offline could they sneak in and out undetected.

"Don't turn on your phone yet," said Arlo. "It's not an actual emergency."

Arlo Finch had no idea that there were three text messages waiting to tell him just how much of an emergency it was.

Twenty minutes later, they found themselves on a wide dirt path flanked by towering columns of green bamboo. The afternoon was hot and incredibly muggy. After a year in Colorado, Arlo had forgotten the suffocating closeness of humidity. The back of his T-shirt was soaked with sweat.

"Which way?" he asked Wu. "Left or right?"

Wu consulted the GPS. "I think right? I'm not really sure."

Then, under the wind and birdsong, Arlo heard voices. Someone was singing. Wu and Jaycee heard it, too.

"There!" said Jaycee, pointing down the path. A group of hikers was approaching, singing a song in unison. They were kids—three girls and three boys—and looked to be between ten and fourteen years old. As they came closer, Arlo saw they wore khaki uniforms with bright red neckerchiefs.

"I think they're Rangers!" said Wu.

This felt like a good omen. "Ask them where we are," said Arlo.

They met up with the group in the middle of the path. Gesturing to himself and Arlo, Wu spoke Mandarin to the girl who seemed to be the patrol leader.

"Rangers!" she said with a big smile. The patrol saluted, putting their hands over their hearts. Arlo and Wu saluted back.

Although he couldn't understand a word of what they were saying, Arlo caught the gist. He watched as the Chinese Rangers unfolded maps and discussed routes. One boy held out his water bottle to Arlo, asking if he was thirsty.

"Can I refill mine?" Arlo asked, pantomiming the action. The boy nodded vigorously. The patrol also shared packaged buns with bean paste.

"These are good," Jaycee said. "I've had them before."

Wu reported what he'd learned from the map discussion: "They say there's no good way to get where we're going by bus. They say we should take a taxi."

"How much will that cost?" asked Jaycee. They only had the one hundred Chinese yuan she had brought back from her trip, the equivalent of twenty dollars. They had estimated it would be plenty for bus fare, but not much more than that.

Wu asked the patrol about the cost of the taxi. The answer wasn't good. "It's going to cost everything we've got."

"It doesn't matter," said Arlo. "We have to go for it."

After shaking hands with the Americans, the Chinese Rangers headed on their way, singing the same song. Arlo envied their afternoon hike. He and Blue Patrol hadn't had the chance to do normal Rangers things for a long time.

——•◦•——

Another twenty minutes of walking got them to a small hotel near the edge of the forest, where a single taxi was waiting out front, its driver smoking a cigarette in the shade. He was in his late forties, and wearing a collared shirt and dark slacks despite the heat.

After a brief discussion with Wu, the driver snuffed out his cigarette and gestured for them to get into the taxi. Being the smallest, Arlo took the middle seat, his pack on his lap.

"Are you sure he knows where he's going?" asked Jaycee, leaning across to Wu.

"He seemed to know what part of town it was in," answered Wu. "I don't think he really speaks much Mandarin, but we sorted it out." In planning for the trip, Wu had warned them that people in this part of the country spoke primarily Cantonese, which was considerably different from what Wu had grown up speaking.

A few turns later they emerged from the forest on a road descending from the mountains. Arlo leaned over his sister to get his first view of Guangzhou.

He had never seen a city of this scale. Skyscrapers seemed to be in a battle over which one could reach the highest. Many of them were basic glass rectangles, but a few were unique, with rounded edges and delicate tapers. One tower reminded him of the spirit knife in his pocket, a dark cylinder with elaborate designs.

"It's crazy, isn't it?" said Jaycee. "Just this city alone has more people than most states in the U.S."

Wu leaned forward to ask the driver a question. "He says it's going to take forty-five minutes," he reported back. "Nothing to do now but wait."

After twenty hours of constant movement, it felt odd to simply be a passenger, to have your fate completely in someone else's hands. Soon their exhaustion, combined with the vibration of the car, had each of them resting their eyes for longer and longer stretches.

Arlo suddenly slumped to his left, falling into Wu. The taxi was exiting an expressway. *When did we get on an expressway?* he wondered. Had he fallen asleep?

Wu and Jaycee were both out cold. Even sitting up, Wu's trademark snore was pronounced. Arlo smiled. Jaycee had her head propped against the window, her lower lip dangling.

On the dashboard, the taxi meter was at 86.95¥ and climbing. Arlo caught the driver watching him in the rearview mirror. It could have been simple curiosity, but it wasn't hard to read it as something more suspicious.

Arlo nudged Wu awake. "Can you tell if we're going the right way?" he whispered. He pointed out the window to the road signs.

"I can't read Chinese," Wu reminded him. "I can only speak it."

Wu checked the GPS unit in his lap. He couldn't get it to turn on, so he flipped it over, checking the batteries.

Meanwhile, Arlo carefully tapped Jaycee's shoulder. He'd been on the receiving end of her waking anger too many times before. Gradually, one eyelid opened. Jaycee glared at him with a single pupil.

"Do you think we're in the right place?" Arlo asked. "Does this look familiar?"

Jaycee straightened up, peering out the window. Just based on her shoulders, Arlo could tell she recognized something.

"This bridge! I know it," she said. "We're close."

They had crossed over a river onto an island. The buildings here were much shorter—six to ten stories at most. Amid the cars and trucks, three-wheeled bicycles carted wrapped bundles, their riders talking on cell phones while they pedaled. Shoppers crossed the street in the middle of blocks. Their driver made liberal use of his horn.

The taxi slowed, then turned onto a much narrower street with tiny shops on both sides and bundles of electrical cables hanging overhead. Arlo was surprised to see that not everyone looked Chinese. There were African men with colorful shirts and Indian women in full sarongs. Some of the hand-printed signs were in English: *T-SHIRTS! PHONE CHARGER! BEST SALE!*

Jaycee suddenly grabbed Wu's arm. "Tell him to stop. I know where we are!"

After paying the driver all one hundred yuan, the trio weaved their way through a dizzying maze of narrow streets and alleys. Jaycee seemed to know exactly where she was going. They passed smoky barbecue stands, phone repair stalls and butchers' shops with pig carcasses dangling by their hooves.

They arrived at the base of a six-story cinderblock building. The steel mesh door was painted sea green. Jaycee pressed one of the forty buttons beside the door. It buzzed.

And then they waited. As five seconds became ten seconds, Wu was the first to ask—

"What if he's not home?"

In all their weeks of planning, they hadn't prepared for that possibility. They had assumed Clark Finch would be in his apartment, because where else would he be? He was a fugitive in China without a job.

Jaycee pressed the buzzer again.

"Are you sure that's the right one?" asked Arlo. "Because they all kind of look the same." Notably, none of them said *Finch*.

Annoyed—and maybe doubting herself—Jaycee pressed the buttons directly above and below the original one. Still no answer.

"We can call him," said Wu. "I mean, I don't know how long we can wait. It's already 11:30. We're way behind schedule."

Jaycee agreed. "I should call him from my phone. He'll recognize the number." She unzipped her pack, digging out her phone.

Arlo stopped her just as she was about to switch it on. "Wait," he said. "Just one more minute."

"Why?"

He couldn't really explain, at least not in a way that seemed rational. Maybe it was the exhaustion. Maybe it was the crush of colors and people and smells. But Arlo was convinced that turning on their phones was a mistake. A concession. A betrayal.

After making it all the way to China, all the way to their dad's apartment, it felt like cheating to rely on modern technology for this last part. It was like getting a car ride across the finish line of a marathon. It felt like giving up. Like surrender.

For the past six weeks—for the past three years—Arlo Finch had held out hope that he would be reunited with his father. He had envisioned this encounter a specific way, with their dad opening his door to find his son and daughter waiting for him. Astonished, he'd say—

"Jaycee!? Arlo!?"

Wait. That voice was real.

They turned to find their father standing halfway down the street.

Clark Finch was wearing cargo shorts, sandals and a gray T-shirt. He carried a bag of groceries. He was shorter than Arlo remembered, and thinner—the kinds of details one doesn't see in a video call. Jaycee dropped her pack and bounded over to him.

Arlo hadn't felt his feet moving, but somehow arrived next to them. Jaycee stepped aside so Arlo could have his turn. His father scooped him up, squeezing him tight. Arlo recognized the press of his bony shoulders, the scratch of his beard, the smell of his skin. It was really him.

"What are you doing here?" his father whispered.

"We're here to bring you home."

— 9 —

ENEMIES OF THE STATE

THEIR FATHER'S APARTMENT WAS SO SMALL you could touch both walls at the same time.

Jaycee had described it after her visit that summer, but Arlo had assumed she was exaggerating. If anything, she had been underselling just how tiny it was—more of a cell than a proper apartment, with just a bed, a desk and a shelf under the window to hold a microwave and rice cooker. The bathroom was down the hall, and shared with all the units on the floor.

Arlo, Jaycee and Wu watched from the doorway as Clark Finch quickly packed his laptop and a few hard drives into a canvas pack. Outside, a thunderstorm had begun.

"We didn't turn on our phones," said Arlo. "We didn't want to leave a digital footprint."

"That's good," said Clark. "Did anyone ask your name, or want to see ID?"

"No," said Arlo. "I mean, we talked to some Rangers in the park, but I don't think we told them our names." He looked to Wu for verification.

"We just said we were from Colorado," said Wu.

Scanning the family photos taped to the cracked walls, Clark yanked one down and handed it to Arlo. "Is this online anywhere?" The photo showed Blue Patrol from the winter Court of Honor, when Arlo had received his Squirrel patch. Arlo had labeled his friends' names so his dad would know who he was talking about.

Arlo sighed. "Yeah. It's on the company website, I'm sure." It wouldn't be hard to individually identify them.

"It wasn't just the Rangers in the park, though," said Jaycee. "There was also the taxi driver."

This seemed to worry Clark. "Did he use a navigation system? Did he ever punch in this address?"

Arlo tried to envision the taxi's dashboard. He could see the meter, and the driver's cell phone in its holder. But was there a map on it? He couldn't remember.

"I don't think I ever told him the address, just the neighborhood," said Wu.

"Why does it matter, though?" asked Jaycee. "I thought it was only the Americans who were after you."

Clark opened the microwave, loading it with small electronics and flash drives. "I'm not worried about me. The three of you are in the country without visas, without any documentation. The authorities could arrest you and there'd be no way to get you out. They could deny they even had you in custody."

"It'll be okay," said Arlo. "Seriously. We just have to get back to that park, then I can take us through the Long Woods."

Clark Finch shut the microwave door. "I still don't understand what you mean by 'Long Woods.' Is that a group or a ship or what? I need to know where we're going."

Jaycee took her father's arm. "Look, Dad, I don't get it either. But I also don't understand most of what you do with computers and stuff. I just know it's real and it works. You have to trust Arlo. He can do this."

Arlo felt a flush. He'd never heard his sister talk about him this way.

Clark twisted the timer knob on the microwave. Almost immediately, the contents began sizzling and popping as the delicate electronics melted. There would be no way for authorities to ever read the data they held.

He looked over at Arlo. "Okay then. Let's get to those woods."

———•◦•———

The back staircase ended at a steel door leading into a narrow alley. Clark motioned for the other three to hold back while he poked his head out to look. He quickly ducked back, pulling the door shut.

"There are police on the street."

"Are they here for us?" asked Wu.

"It could be something else. We should—" The squawk of a siren cut him off. A motorcycle engine rumbled up the alley. A rain puddle reflected its red-and-blue lights under the door.

The metal door rattled as the unseen officer yanked on it, finding it locked. Then, a burst of Chinese on a walkie-talkie, to which the officer responded. Wu and Clark listened carefully.

"Two American boys and a girl," Wu whispered, translating. "They know we're here."

"Is there another way out?" whispered Arlo to Clark.

"Just the front. But they'll have that covered, too." Clark moved them back into the stairwell.

Wu leaned into Arlo. "You could use a slipknaught. We could sneak past them."

"I can't," said Arlo. The last time he'd used a slipknaught, he'd nearly died. The silver cord connecting his spirit to his body had stretched so thin it almost snapped. Besides, Arlo wasn't sure he could even tie a knaught this far from the Long Woods.

Clark was typing on his phone. "I think we can get past them," he said. "I've been working on something just in case. Kind of an escape hatch. I just have to set some variables." Arlo watched as his dad swiped through screen after screen of inscrutable code. The software on his phone was entirely custom, and likely made no sense to anyone other than Clark Finch. "Let's see if this works."

Suddenly, sirens began blaring. It wasn't just the fire alarm, and it wasn't just this building. They could hear different buzzers and horns wailing in every direction.

"It's the national early-warning system," explained Clark. "I faked a major earthquake four hundred kilometers north of the city. There's a protocol for all public safety officers."

As he said this, they heard the motorcycle suddenly roar off. Clark waited a few seconds, then carefully opened the door to check that the alley was clear. "Let's go!"

The neighborhood streets were teeming with shoppers, workers and families, all panicked about the imminent temblor. As they spilled out of the buildings, officers herded them towards approved safe zones. Amid the confusion, the crowd, the sirens and the thunderstorm, no one noticed the four Americans walking single file down the sidewalk with newspapers over their heads.

Across the street, Arlo spotted their taxi driver standing beside his cab. He was being interviewed by a man and a woman with umbrellas. They were wearing suits rather than uniforms.

Arlo quickly turned away, worried the driver might recognize him. *Keep walking*, he told himself. *Don't look back.* He was last in line. They'd be out of sight in just a few seconds.

Then, a shout. Arlo looked back.

The driver was pointing directly at him. The woman with the umbrella was running after them, while the man was talking into a radio, no doubt reporting that the Americans had been spotted.

"Run!" Arlo shouted.

Even after twenty hours of exertion, Arlo was relieved to find he still had adrenaline left. He felt fast and nimble as he zigzagged through the crowd behind his dad, Jaycee and Wu. Where the sidewalks were too packed, they ran in the road. Electric trams, which had been automatically stopped by the earthquake alert, were blocking the intersections, letting the group weave between honking cars.

They reached a more prosperous-looking street with modern glass buildings facing the river. Clark led them down a ramp into an underground parking garage. The attendant's booth was empty, but a TV screen showed giant Chinese characters that Arlo suspected meant "Emergency" or "Alert."

Ducking behind an SUV, they watched and waited to see if anyone had followed them down the ramp.

"How far away is this 'Long Woods'?" asked Clark.

This wasn't the time to explain why that was a silly question. "We need to get to a park north of the city," said Arlo. "It's about twenty miles."

"Won't they be waiting for us, though?" asked Jaycee. "That taxi driver knows where he picked us up."

Arlo realized Jaycee was right. By the time they got back to the park, the police would have the roads staked out.

"Wait," said Wu. "Why do we need to go there at all? That park was just the place Zhang had in the atlas. There's got to be other ways to get into the Long Woods. We just need to find a forest somewhere."

Arlo turned to his dad and sister. "Where was the place you went to this summer? You said it was really natural and isolated. Some park or forest."

"Dafushan," said Clark. "It's south. It's about an hour by train."

"But we can't take one," said Jaycee. "They'd find us."

"All the trains are stopped because of the fake earthquake anyway," said Clark. He was back on his phone, swiping through more screens of gibberish. "But if that's where we need to go, I can drive us."

"Wait," said Arlo, confused. "You have a car?"

"Well, not yet. Let's see if we get a hit." Clark tapped a button on his phone. Nothing happened. Then, one by one, headlights began glowing on cars around them, until nearly a quarter of the garage was lit up.

"Modern cars are basically computers," he said with a smile. Then he added, "But you shouldn't steal cars in general. This is a special case."

They picked a white sedan with dark tinted windows. Just to be safe, Arlo and Wu crouched in the back seat until they'd crossed the third bridge, out of the city center. Then they sat up, watching the skyscrapers recede.

Shafts of sunlight broke through the storm clouds. Guangzhou looked impossibly modern, like something out of a sci-fi movie.

"If we make it out of here, we should come back sometime," said Wu. Arlo agreed.

— 10 —
DAFUSHAN

AFTER DITCHING THE CAR IN A NEARBY PARKING LOT—and carefully wiping off their fingerprints—they merged with a busload of American tourists at the entrance to Dafushan Forest Park. The tour leader was a young Chinese woman who spoke flawless English. She carried a pole topped by an orange pom-pom so her group could always spot her.

"In this park, you will see a fish that is very special to the Chinese people," she said. "Who can tell me what a koi fish is?"

A potbellied man with a fancy camera yelled, "It's like a giant goldfish!"

"Yes! And does anyone know the story of the koi fish?" This time there were no takers, so the young woman continued: "An ancient story tells of a school of golden koi fish. They swam up the great Yellow River until they reached a waterfall and could go no further. But one fish did not stop. It tried to swim up the waterfall to reach the very top.

"Again and again it fell. For one hundred years it kept trying to swim and jump up the waterfall. Until one day, it succeeded. It reached the top. The gods saw this and rewarded the fish for its perseverance, transforming it into a great dragon. The koi are a symbol of hard work and achieving the impossible."

Wu leaned over to Arlo. "Anything?"

Arlo shook his head. He didn't feel any pull towards the Long Woods. But this wasn't surprising in such a busy area, with its concrete paths and park benches. "We need to get someplace without people."

The four of them drifted away from the group to examine a large painted map of the park.

Dafushan Forest was shaped like a heart—the lumpy organ in your chest, not a construction-paper valentine. Bike paths connected a series of small green lakes, with shrines and monuments scattered throughout.

Clark pointed to an area at the southern edge of the park. "Over here is where we went hiking this summer. It's pretty secluded, but it's not like we could hide out there if that's what you're thinking." Arlo realized his dad still didn't understand the next part of the plan, or what they meant by the Long Woods.

In a low voice, Jaycee said, "Don't all look, but I think that guy's on to us."

Arlo casually glanced back to see a uniformed man talking into his radio. He was old and heavyset, more like a mall security guard than an actual police officer. Still, he was clearly keeping an eye on them. This wasn't good.

"Should we run?" asked Wu. "He doesn't look fast."

Jaycee scoffed. "That's not going to look suspicious at all."

"He's calling it in," said Clark. "He's not sure it's us. Just keep looking at the map."

To his right, Arlo spotted a second security guard holding out his phone to take a picture of them. This guard was younger, and no doubt faster. He would be harder to outrun. "We have to do something."

"Excuse me! Family!" said the tour leader, beckoning them. "Let's stay together now." While they'd been at the map, the tour group had been outfitted with bright green rental bikes from a nearby stand. They were waiting for the four of them to join.

Clark smiled. "Sorry! C'mon, kids."

In planning this journey to China, Arlo had never envisioned he'd be riding a three-speed touring bicycle with a group of sweating American tourists, but here he was. After the countless miles they'd hiked, it felt like the height of luxury to pedal on asphalt paths. He could do this for hours.

But this wasn't a pleasure trip. They needed to get somewhere less traveled in order to find an entrance into the Long Woods. And there was still the worry that the security guards had alerted the authorities.

Clark gestured for them to take an upcoming fork to the right. They were already at the back of the group, so there was a good chance no one noticed when they split off. They pedaled hard until they were out of sight.

This trail was narrower, leading into an older part of the forest. The trees were less majestic, their knobby and twisted branches scratching at the gray sky.

"Can you find an entrance . . . while you're on a bike?" asked Wu, huffing.

"Don't know," Arlo said, also winded. "Never tried." When he first began crossing into the Long Woods, he'd needed absolute quiet and concentration to find a path. But over the months, he'd become able to do it while walking—or even running away from a massive troll.

Jaycee stopped her bike. She cocked her head, listening. "Do you hear that?"

Arlo did. It was a helicopter. And it was approaching. Fast.

"Get off the trail!" Arlo shouted, leading the way. These bikes weren't meant for off-roading, but the forest was relatively flat. As long as no one tried anything too extreme, they'd hold up.

The helicopter was getting closer. Closer.

It roared directly overhead. The shaking leaves sounded like rain. The chopper kept going, following a straight line.

"They didn't see us!" shouted Wu, gleeful.

Or maybe they were just going too fast, thought Arlo. *They could circle back.* He veered right, then left, heading down a slope. With no actual destination in mind, he just wanted to get as deep into the forest as possible. He was moving on pure instinct, brushing close to trees and swerving around rocks. It was all too fast to be scary.

He glanced over his shoulder to make sure the others were keeping up. And then—

THUNNNNNK!

Arlo was suddenly flying over his handlebars. Time slowed as he swam against the air.

He covered his face as he hit the dirt, rolling in the dry leaves. It was so surprising, so unexpected, that he didn't even have time to feel the impact. He sprang back up on his feet, staring at the bicycle ten feet away, its front wheel badly bent. He'd hit a log covered by leaves.

Arlo stared at his palms. They were scraped raw, covered with white flecks of rough skin that were just starting to bleed. They didn't feel like they were part of his body.

And then the pain hit. It was like a wave crashing into him. His hands, his face, his knees. They were all burning hot.

"Arlo!" His dad ditched his bike, running to him. Wu and Jaycee were right behind.

Arlo squinted in the sunlight. Why was it suddenly so bright?

His dad knelt down in front of him, checking his face. "Are you okay? Are you dizzy? Is anything broken?"

"I don't think so. I'm okay." Arlo started to cry.

It wasn't from the pain, not really. The tears came because

his father was there to tend to his injuries. Arlo hadn't had that for years. He leaned his head against his father's shoulder. For just that moment, he felt safe and protected.

Wu climbed off his bike, letting it drop. "These aren't going to get us any further."

Arlo was confused why until he turned around to see a vast desert, immense dunes of dark sand stretching to the horizon like a frozen ocean. They weren't in China anymore.

"You did it," said Jaycee, ruffling his hair.

Clark Finch stood up, just now realizing something was off. He looked back at the forest behind them and then to the endless dunes ahead. "Where are we?"

Arlo smiled. "The Long Woods."

11
BLACK SANDS

IT WAS LIKE WALKING ON ANOTHER PLANET. The sand was coarse and crunchy, small beads of volcanic glass that shimmered in the moonlight. The sky was filled with thousands of stars. They felt much closer than they did in the normal world, like holes poked in a domed ceiling.

Arlo focused on the stars to take his mind off his aching feet. They'd been walking for hours. Every part of him was exhausted, but his feet had it the worst. The sand slipped into every crack, scraping his ankles and toes. There was no point trying to get it out. It would be like toweling off underwater.

As he reached the top of another dune, Arlo waited for Wu, Jaycee and their father to catch up. Jaycee was clearly the most fatigued. She kept stopping for water, or to retie her boots, or to ask a question that didn't need an answer. At times, she'd take her dad's hand for support. But she was equally likely to refuse it.

Arlo could tell Jaycee was just *done*. Unfortunately, they were only halfway there.

The ever-changing geography of the Long Woods made it impossible to predict how long a trip would take at the outset. Even when traveling between familiar places, Arlo only knew the direction of the path, not the length. But he could always feel when he was halfway to a destination, and then three-quarters, and then seven-eighths. The pull became stronger the closer he got.

Sounds like gravity, his dad had said. *It's proportional to the distance and the mass of the object. The nearer two things are, and the bigger they are, the more they're drawn together.* Arlo admired how his dad could explain mysterious things in ways that didn't diminish them.

Reaching the crest of the dune, Clark nodded at Arlo. "Maybe we can take a break for a few minutes? I need a breather." He clearly didn't, but Jaycee did.

"Sure thing," said Arlo.

Jaycee plopped down, leaning back against the dune. Wu dropped to his knees, sloughing off his pack to grab his water bottle.

Clark took Arlo's chin, turning his face to get a better look at his scrapes. "How's it feel?"

"It hurts, but it's okay." Arlo wondered how bad it actually was. Without a mirror, he could only gauge based on their reactions.

Clark tugged at a bandage. "This one's coming off. Let me swap it out." He took a spare one from Arlo's first-aid kit. As he peeled open the wrapper the paper flew from his hand, swept up by a sudden gust.

The wrapper spun in the air, caught in an invisible eddy. Clark tried to grab it, but it kept dodging him. He laughed in disbelief. "Crazy. Have you ever seen anything like this?"

Yes. Arlo had seen something just like this.

Arlo reached into his pocket for the spirit knife. The moment his fingers touched the hilt, he could see the force that was spinning the wrapper. It was a sparkling cloud of energy with no fixed form. An elemental. An air spirit.

Back at Camp Redfeather, Arlo had encountered Big Breezy: a powerful, sentient wind that had led him to Giant's Fist, where the spirit knife was hidden. When the Eldritch attacked, Arlo had cut Breezy free from her restraints, resulting in an explosion that destroyed the Summerland campsite.

The spirit in front of him now looked like Big Breezy—and maybe it was. Spirits didn't seem to have distinct boundaries. When asked, Fox had said he was "all the foxes." Maybe Breezy was all the winds.

Whatever this spirit was, it was definitely trying to get his attention. It ruffled his hair before descending the dune.

"Stay here," Arlo said to his father, following the spirit.

"Where are you going?!"

"I think it wants to show me something." Arlo half slid down the dune, trying to keep up with the spirit.

Clark turned to Wu and Jaycee. "Do you know what that's about?"

"Not really," said Wu, shrugging. "But it's fine."

The spirit hovered at the base of the dune, waiting for Arlo to catch up. Then it began to swirl, blowing back the sand. As the grains tumbled away, the moonlight revealed something buried underneath: a pillar lying on its side, at least twenty feet long.

Arlo reached down to touch it. It was wood, smooth and cold. At first, he assumed it was a fallen log. But then he saw the metal bolts. This was something man-made.

"What is this?" he asked out loud. "A telephone pole?"

As if to answer, the wind grew stronger. Now the sand wasn't being pushed as much as lifted, a cyclone suctioning the dune away. Arlo had to shield his eyes and step back to keep from getting pulled in. Through his fingers, he watched as more and more of the hidden object was exposed.

The pole was connected to a much larger wooden structure. *A cabin?* Arlo wondered. *A barn?* Whatever it was, it had been completely buried in the next dune. The building had a flat face and a curve to its roof.

The spirit was evidently finished. It floated to the side, waiting.

Wu shouted down: "What is that?!"

"I don't know!" Arlo yelled back.

The darkness made it hard to see into the building. Arlo sent a snaplight arcing past it. He could make out wooden crates and barrels arranged haphazardly, as if they'd been tossed around. There was also an entrance, though it seemed strangely positioned ten feet off the ground.

Arlo carefully approached, ready for something terrible to rush out. He had read enough scary books to know that buried things tended to be buried for a reason, and that one should be careful when digging them up.

He was so focused on the building that he didn't look where he was walking. He caught his toe on something hard and heavy in the sand and nearly tripped.

The object was metal, rusted iron, and nearly as long as he was tall. Using the toe of his shoe, he started scraping away the sand. The air spirit joined in, quickly exposing the rest of it. Once it was revealed, Arlo stood back, confused by what he'd found.

It was an anchor.

He then looked at the structure, suddenly realizing what he was staring at: a huge sailing ship on its side, like the *Mayflower*, or a pirate frigate.

What was a ship doing in a desert?

12
CALYPSO

THERE WAS NO WAY TO TELL HOW LONG THE SHIP HAD BEEN BURIED.
There were no markings, no dates stamped into the iron bands
along the fallen mast. Most of the vessel was still embedded in
the dune, with the entrance to the cabin ten feet up the sloping
deck.

Jaycee, Wu and Clark joined Arlo, staring up at the immense
ship.

"There could be treasure inside, like gold or gems or artifacts," said Wu, his energy supply having suddenly rebounded.
"We definitely have to go in."

"Or we could just, you know, *not*," said Jaycee. "You guys
could come back here some other time with ropes and stuff and
not get us all killed tonight."

Jaycee had a point. With more time and better equipment,
Arlo and the patrol could properly explore the ship. But there

was no guarantee he'd be able to find this place again. Locations in the Long Woods had a habit of vanishing. While the Broken Bridge seemed constant, he'd never made it back to the Valley of Fire. For all he knew, it didn't exist anymore.

"The spirit wanted to show me this," said Arlo. "I should at least figure out why."

"If you two want to check it out," Clark said, "Jaycee and I can wait out here. What would you think about building a fire first, so we can rest up for a few?"

Everyone liked that idea. Breaking open some of the wooden crates, they found shattered porcelain vases packed in bone-dry straw. Wu made quick work of building a fire. As the orange flames crackled, Arlo realized just how much the temperature had fallen since the sunset. The fire warmed their hands and thawed Jaycee's icy gaze.

Now it was time to explore the ship.

The deck was sloping at a steep angle. Luckily, the planks had separated a bit, offering handholds and footholds. It was a tricky climb, but Arlo and Wu managed to make it to the cabin door, its frame perpendicular to the deck. The door itself was hanging precariously on a single hinge. With the slightest touch it fell off, sliding down the deck and crashing in the sand right beside Jaycee.

"Sorry!" Arlo yelled. Jaycee glared at them.

Arlo and Wu climbed through the doorway into what they assumed was the captain's quarters. With the boat lying on its side, they were technically standing on a wall. Above them to the left, a table was bolted to the floor. The chairs that went with it were at their feet, along with a leather-bound book.

As Arlo took a step towards it, the planks creaked. The wall they were standing on wasn't particularly solid.

"I'll hold onto you," offered Wu.

With Wu holding his left hand, Arlo reached out with his right, straining to touch the book. He finally got his fingertips on it, pulling it into his grasp. He straightened up and examined it.

While the cover was sturdy, the pages inside the book were incredibly delicate, more like dried leaves than paper. They held columns of numbers and words written in fancy script.

"I think it's a captain's log," said Wu. "It's like a journal, a record of where they went and what happened."

It was impossible to read by snaplight, but Arlo could clearly make out the word embossed on the spine of the book: "*Calypso*. That must be the name of the ship."

"Do you think it's from our world, something that fell through? Or was it always in the Long Woods?"

"I don't know," said Arlo. "All this sand could have been an ocean at some point."

They sent more snaplights into the edges of the room. In the far corner, there was a reflection from not a mirror, but some sort of metal object. It was definitely intriguing. The only question was how to get there. It would mean walking across the none-too-sturdy wall.

Wu thought it was doable. "If you stay close to the deck and distribute your weight, it should be fine." Sensing Arlo's un-asked question, he added, "I mean, I could do it if you want. But you weigh less."

Arlo knew Wu was correct, but only barely. "I maybe weigh five pounds less than you."

"This could be a five-pound situation," said Wu. "But if you want me to go . . ."

"No, it's fine." Wu wasn't being cowardly, just appropriately cautious. Also, Arlo didn't have a better idea.

Keeping one hand touching the deck, Arlo walked a nar-row line along the base of the wall. With each step, the wood creaked and shuddered underfoot. Arlo wasn't sure if the sound came from the boards themselves or the nails holding them in. He carefully climbed over the fallen chairs.

A louder creak. Something shifted, then a thin ribbon of sand began falling from the ceiling. Arlo sent a snaplight ahead to see where he was going. From this angle, he could clearly make out the metal object, a brass cylinder roughly the shape of a lantern. He knew exactly what it was.

"It's a spirit cage!" he yelled back to Wu.

"Is there something in it?"

Arlo reached into his pocket for the spirit knife. With it, he could see a faint glow spilling from the seams of the cage. "Yeah! I'm pretty sure."

"Maybe that's why the wind wanted you. So you could get it."

That idea made sense to Arlo. In his experience, spirits were capable of giant things like knocking down a forest, but struggled with smaller tasks. The wind spirit who pushed aside the sand dune likely couldn't reach inside the ship to get to this cage, and wouldn't be able to open it anyway.

Arlo wasn't sure he was going to be able to get to the cage, either. The boards ahead were splintered in places, with iron nails hanging free. Arlo decided to lean back against the deck floor, hoping it would carry some of his weight. Slowly crossing foot-over-foot, he made it the last few feet. He was carefully reaching down to grab the handle on the cage when he felt another shudder. A creak.

He froze, waiting. A second stream of sand slipped through a crack overhead, spilling onto his head and down the back of his shirt. It was like standing inside an hourglass—and time seemed to be running out. With squinted eyes, Arlo picked up the brass cage, which was lighter than he'd expected.

Now all he needed to do was make it back to Wu. He reversed course. He had just made it to the chairs when he heard cracking, a series of bright brittle pops. Arlo and Wu traded a look. They both knew this was bad.

"The table!" shouted Wu.

Arlo dropped the cage, scrambling over the fallen chairs. He jumped, grabbing ahold of a table leg as a deluge of sand crashed down. He couldn't get "under" the table, but it protected him from the worst of the impact as several tons of sand smashed through the walls. Arlo struggled to hold on, and to breathe.

After ten seconds or so, the sand slowed to a trickle. Arlo looked down past his boots to a new opening in the floor-slash-wall, through which his dad and Jaycee were looking up at him.

"Are you okay?" Clark shouted.

"Fine," shouted Arlo. He looked across to the cabin entrance, where Wu was holding on to the doorframe. "We're good."

It took a few minutes to climb down, and a few more to dig out the spirit cage. Once Arlo had retrieved it, the wind began swirling around him like a dog waiting for a treat.

Clark asked to see the cage, inspecting its fittings and mechanical parts. "It's some kind of storage device, isn't it?" he asked. He pointed to an opening at the base. "This looks like a connection port."

"They hold spirits," said Arlo. "For power, I think. They're like batteries."

"Or hard drives," said Clark. "From what you describe, spirits sound like they're both energy and information."

"How do we get it out of there?" asked Wu. "Just smash it open?"

Arlo took the cage back. "I think there's a knaught that's binding it shut." With the knife in hand, he could just make out a glowing filament that wrapped around the device several times. "I bet I can cut it."

Wu looked wary. "Isn't that how you destroyed Summerland?"

"Sort of. But Big Breezy was really angry. That's mostly what did it."

"I'm just saying that maybe this spirit won't be super relaxed after being locked in that thing for however long."

It was a fair point. Arlo decided to walk fifty feet away from the group just in case it exploded. He looked back at his dad, Wu and Jaycee at the campfire. They were watching him, but also seemed ready to run.

With the wind whipping through his hair, Arlo slid the translucent blade of the knife into a narrow groove along the edge of the cage. The shimmering thread was no thicker than kite string. It wouldn't take much to cut.

He exhaled. Then he sliced through it.

The cage sparked. Arlo was thrown onto his back, the device at his feet. Sitting up on his elbows, he watched as something inside slammed against the brass, denting it. The metal bands buckled. Fasteners popped.

Then a thin spray of water erupted from the seams, like a leaking soda can. The hiss grew louder, climbing in pitch like a tea-kettle whistle.

Arlo flipped over onto his belly, covering his face as the cage exploded in a giant thunderclap. Suddenly the air felt wet and smelled like rain. As he looked past his fingers, he saw sand crystals beginning to float, electrified by the spirit's energy.

Uh-oh.

He held the spirit knife firmly and turned back over to see what was happening. The original air spirit was swirling to-gether with the just-released water spirit, which had the form of a massive storm cloud. At first, Arlo thought they were fighting,

80

but their interaction seemed more friendly than combative. They rose up together, filling the sky.

Lightning struck a nearby dune. Then another. The thunder was deafening.

Then came the rain. It poured down in sheets, blown almost horizontally by the wind. As he got to his feet, Arlo was drenched. He looked back at Wu, Jaycee and his father, who were huddled together for protection. The campfire was struggling to stay lit.

Arlo yelled at the sky: "Hey! Knock it off!"

The storm continued to pound down. Then, just as quickly as it had begun, the rain stopped, like a faucet turned off. The last drops splashed into puddles that drained into the sand. The clouds faded, revealing stars again.

Arlo watched as the two spirits flew off, disappearing behind the dunes. He hadn't expected a *thank you* exactly, but a little gratitude would have been nice.

Walking back to the group, Arlo tucked the spirit knife back in his pocket. "Do you want to rebuild the fire, or should we keep walking?"

They all looked at Jaycee, whose vote was the only one that mattered.

She shrugged, resigned. "Let's go. The sooner we're home, the better."

13
DAYBREAK

CELESTE BELLMAN FINCH HAD ALWAYS BEEN A LIGHT SLEEPER.

As a young girl, even the slightest noise would wake her. In particular, she had an uncanny ability to hear the front door open, no matter how quietly the task was performed. When she and her brother were kids, she had caught Wade sneaking in or out on multiple occasions. Now that she was a mother, her focus had turned to Jaycee, who several times that summer had tried to meet up with friends long after pretending to go to bed.

So it wasn't surprising that Celeste was able to hear the front door quietly opened that morning just after dawn. The question was, who was coming or going? Wade was rarely up before noon. Arlo was off on a campout, and Jaycee was staying over at a friend's house. Most likely one of her children had come home early. But which one? And why?

She tied her robe as she made her way down the stairs. That was when she saw the first thing that unsettled her: the front door was wide open.

Maybe it was the wind, she thought. Since that winter, it hadn't latched quite right. When she'd asked Wade about it, he had grumbled that it was as fixed as it could be, which felt like an admission that he'd been part of how it had gotten broken.

As she went to shut the door, she saw the second unsettling thing. There was fresh blood on the doorknob. It came off on her hand.

Her heart began pounding. She couldn't help but think of terrible things: accidents with cars or knives or encounters with wild animals.

"Arlo?! Jaycee?!" she called. "Are you here?"

There was no answer.

She forced herself to count to three, to not panic more than was warranted. In the worst-case scenario—a stranger in the house, a stranger who had bled on the doorknob—at least her kids weren't home. Plus, she wasn't alone.

"Wade!" she yelled. "Wade, can you come downstairs now?!"

That's when she heard the water running. Someone was in the kitchen, using the sink.

Unlike his younger sister, Wade Bellman had always been a heavy sleeper. Their mother often had to shake him awake to get him to school in the mornings. As an adult, he'd slept through thunderstorms, fireworks and heavy winds that ripped off a section of the house.

So it was remarkable that he heard his sister yelling: "Wade!"

He opened one eyelid. The morning light hit him square in the face. He'd forgotten to close the curtains.

"Wade, can you come downstairs now?!"

Was she angry? Had he done something, or not done something he was supposed to do? While there were plenty of things that met those criteria, Wade couldn't think of any that would merit scolding him before breakfast.

If she wasn't yelling *at* him, maybe she was yelling *for* him. The emotion in her voice could have been fear rather than anger. He sat up halfway in bed.

"What do you need?" he yelled back, then coughed. It was hard to shout before coffee.

She didn't answer.

He hadn't expected any specific response—*I've told you to stop putting dead squirrels in the freezer!*—but rather a restatement of the request to show she was serious. Something like, "Just come down here now!"

But no answer? That was strange. That was worth investigating.

Wearing ratty slippers, sweatpants and a Flying Spaghetti Monster T-shirt, Wade made his way down the stairs. The front door was partway open. It hadn't latched right since the Night Mare had smashed it open while trying to kill Arlo the previous winter. Was that what his sister was so upset about?

"Celeste!" he yelled. "Where are you?"

She didn't answer, but Wade could hear her talking quietly in the kitchen. He figured she might be on the phone. It could be something about Arlo or Jaycee, who were gone for some reason. Wade didn't keep track of them.

He found his sister sitting at the kitchen table with her back to him. There were dishtowels streaked with blood on the floor. The side door was open.

"What's going on?" he asked, worried. Celeste didn't respond.

As Wade stepped closer, he saw a coin on the table spinning on its edge. His sister was completely transfixed by it.

Wade reached in and picked it up. It looked to be an ordinary quarter. He knelt down beside his sister, gently shaking her out of her stupor.

She looked over at him, confused. "What are you doing?"

"You yelled for me to come down. You were talking with someone."

"I was just sleepwalking," she said. "I do that sometimes."

"No you don't. You've never sleepwalked in your life. There was someone here and you were talking with them."

She gathered the towels from the floor. "You're crazy.

Everything's fine." She walked to the sink and began rinsing the blood out of the towels. She didn't seem to know what she was doing, or why. The water ran pink.

"Arlo should be back soon," she said. "They're camping down at the river, the site of the old town. You can't miss them."

— 14 —
GHOSTS

BLUE PATROL WAS JUST GETTING SET UP FOR BREAKFAST when they heard a vehicle pull off the main road. It drove as far as the barricade, then the engine died. A door squealed open and slammed shut.

"Arlo!" shouted a man's voice. "You here?"

Jonas looked to Connor, who looked to Indra. *Who is it?*

"I think it's his uncle," she said. "Wade."

Julie, who was sitting in the doorway of the tent tying her boots, rolled back inside and zipped the flap shut. She wanted no part of what was about to go down.

"What if it's not his uncle?" asked Connor. "What if it just *looks* like him?"

"Either way, we just say that Arlo's not here," said Jonas. "That's the truth."

"Arlo went on a hike," suggested Indra. "With Wu."

Connor was skeptical. "Why would they go on a hike at dawn?"

"For their Hiking patch!" shouted Julie from the tent. "They both need their Hiking patch."

Wade emerged from the trees. At least, it looked like Wade. He was wearing sweats, slippers and a down vest over a T-shirt. More importantly, he wore the same aggravated expression they had seen many times before.

He pointed at Indra. "Where's Arlo?"

"He went on a hike," she said. "For his Hiking skill patch."

"He went with Wu," added Jonas. It all sounded a little forced. None of them were sure whether Wade bought the excuse, or if he was even Wade.

"Which way did they go?"

They exchanged glances, trying to coordinate their answers, then pointed in three different directions.

Wade wasn't amused. "Look, we need to find Arlo. He's in trouble."

"What kind of trouble?" asked Connor.

"Somebody came to the house just now. Someone missing a few pints of blood. I wager they're looking for Arlo."

"Hadryn," said Indra. They all felt a shudder. Rielle's warning was coming to pass.

"Who or what is a Hadryn?" asked Wade.

"You knew him as Thomas," said Indra. "He was in Yellow Patrol with you at Redfeather thirty years ago."

Wade remembered the name. "The kid from Texas. Arlo

said he showed up at your camp this summer, like he hadn't aged a day."

"He's a shape-shifter," said Jonas. "He's really dangerous."

"Did you see him?" asked Connor. "Did you talk to him?"

Wade shook his head. "He was gone before I got there. And like I said, I think he's hurt. He's bleeding. But Arlo's mom, he did something. Hypnotized her, maybe. They were talking. That's why I figure he's on his way. He knows Arlo's here with you."

"He's not, though," said Julie. She unzipped the tent, stepping out. "Arlo's safe. He's seven thousand miles away."

"What is that girl talking about?" asked Wade.

Indra explained. "Arlo and Jaycee went to China to get their dad."

"Wait, what? They flew to China?"

"No, they went through the Long Woods," said Julie.

"The Long Woods?" Wade's eyes drifted up, like he was trying to summon a distant memory. It never came. "That's one of those things I used to know and I don't anymore, right?"

"It's normal," said Jonas. "It's because of the Wonder."

"And also because you're old," said Julie.

A *ding!* Connor checked his pockets, then his pack, searching for his phone.

Indra sorted through the potential scenarios. "If they're in China, they're okay, because Hadryn wouldn't know they're there. But if they're in the Long Woods, they're not safe. Hadryn could find them, and the Eldritch wouldn't be able to do anything. It sounds crazy, but Arlo is actually safer here in Pine Mountain, because the Eldritch are probably watching us right now."

"Guys!" said Connor, excited. "Wu just texted." He showed them the message on his phone.

"They're back."

— 15 —
HOMECOMING

IT STILL DIDN'T LOOK LIKE A PROPER HOUSE. The doors and windows were mismatched, with cracked glass patched with packing tape. The paint was peeling and the porch roof sagged from carrying too many snows.

But after a year living in Pine Mountain, this not-quite-house had become home. Arlo Finch was glad to be back.

"Her car's here," said Jaycee, pointing at the station wagon. "Let me go in first and warn her. I don't want her to drop dead from shock." As she headed for the house, Arlo noticed his uncle's truck was missing. It was odd for him to be up so early.

"Last time I was here was before you were born," said Clark. "It was your granddad's funeral. We had about two hundred people out here afterwards. Everyone in town loved him."

"There's a picture of him in the diner," said Arlo. "He helped dig out the road after a giant snowstorm."

"Yeah, he loved to tell that story. It's crazy how isolated this town can get. Like you're in a cul-de-sac at the edge of the world."

"I like it, though," said Arlo. "It's nice that it's small."

It suddenly occurred to Arlo that his father might not like Pine Mountain. He'd always lived in big cities with trains and museums and professional baseball teams. *What if he wants to leave?* They had moved to Pine Mountain out of necessity. Maybe it wasn't a necessity anymore.

Wu had been texting. "Connor says your uncle is at the campsite."

"Why would he be there?" asked Arlo.

"Maybe you better read from the top." He handed him his phone. Arlo read the message thread in chronological order.

Rielle came. She says Hadryn escaped

The Eldritch don't know where he is. She says you're in

danger

Good luck!

We're back.

Arlo's uncle is here. He says Hadryn was at Arlo's house

this morning

Says Hadryn's hurt. But dangerous

Are u ok?

We're ok. Maybe don't go to Arlo's house

                                        Already here.

As Arlo was reading, a new text came in:

Be careful!

"Everything okay?" asked Clark.

"Fine," said Arlo. "Just checking in with the patrol." As he handed the phone back to Wu, they exchanged a worried glance.

The front door opened. Celeste Finch stepped onto the porch, Jaycee right behind her.

For Arlo, everything seemed to shift into slow motion. Clark began walking up the driveway. Celeste spotted him and reacted in disbelief. Then she moved across the porch and down the steps. The sunlight hit her. She seemed to glow.

Clark dropped his pack. Neither was running the way couples do in movies. If anything, they seemed wary, as if not believing this moment was real.

They met in the front yard, just past the rusted iron fence. Arlo couldn't hear what they said, but they were looking directly at each other. Clark took Celeste's hands. She smiled. And then they kissed.

Arlo Finch wasn't a fan of kissing at all. It was gross and made weird wet sounds and mostly just exchanged spit and germs.

But on this occasion, he was fine with it. His parents had been apart for a long time, so if they wanted to smoosh their lips together to celebrate, he wasn't going to stand in their way.

"Arlo! Jaycee!" called their dad. "Get over here."

They joined them in a hug. It was strange to be holding both parents at once. Strange but nice.

"Thank you," Jaycee whispered to Arlo.

Arlo smiled. For the first time in three years, the Finch family was back together.

16
THE DECISION

IT WAS IMPOSSIBLE TO EXPLAIN TO THE ADULTS how they'd gone to China and back. Even Clark, who had gone with them through the Long Woods, was still confused on the details.

"Wait, you were in another city *before* you came to Guangzhou?" he asked. "Why?"

"We needed to use the atlas, which it turns out wasn't a book at all, but a place," said Arlo. "That's where Zhang had the Rubik's Cube that let me find the park. Which was a different park than the one we left from." Arlo omitted the detail about his heart stopping, which would have worried his parents even though he was fine.

Wu had gone home, and Jaycee was taking a shower, so Arlo was left on his own to get his mom, dad and uncle up to speed on what had transpired over the last twenty-four hours.

"How did you get scraped up?" asked his mom.

"He fell off a bike," said Clark. "I was there for that part."

Arlo took this opportunity to remind them that the expedition had been well planned. "We had a first-aid kit. We were prepared."

His mom was still bewildered about exactly how her husband had traveled seven thousand miles, and across an ocean. But he was sitting beside her on the couch, so however it had happened, she couldn't argue with the results.

After his shower, Arlo found Wade waiting for him in the kitchen. He was finishing an energy drink. "Your parents went upstairs. Jaycee's asleep in her room."

"Did you tell them about Hadryn?"

"No. And I don't think your mom remembers that anything strange happened this morning. He mesmerized her or something."

Hadryn had performed the same spinning-coin technique on Arlo at the start of the summer. Arlo's memory of that conversation had come back only in fragments, sometimes as dreams.

"Your mom could have gotten hurt," Wade said.

"I know." It scared Arlo to think of Hadryn in his house, in this kitchen, sitting across from his mother. "I didn't know he'd escaped from the Eldritch. If I'd been here, I could have protected her."

"How exactly would you have done that?"

"I don't know. I would have figured something out." He

thought back to his last encounter with Hadryn, on a cliff over-looking Camp Redfeather: *I know where you live, Arlo Finch. I know your family, your friends, your school, your patrol. And I'm guessing you'd rather they be alive than dead. So you'll do exactly as I tell you.*

Arlo didn't want to admit it, but had he been in the house that morning, he would likely have agreed to help Hadryn in order to protect his family.

Wade stood up from the table. "I've got my buddy Nacho coming over to see if he can put up some extra protections in case that guy comes back."

"Hadryn's not supernatural, not really," said Arlo. "So normal wards won't work. It's not like with the Night Mare."

"Nacho will have something." Wade threw his empty can into the recycling. "I held on to some of the towels with blood on them. Figured there might be something useful to do with that."

Arlo had never met Nacho, but he apparently spent a lot of time on obscure websites dealing with arcane knowledge. As his uncle was headed out, Arlo asked: "Are you scared?"

Wade stopped, considering the question. "I'm just worried that what you've done is going to get someone hurt."

━━•◦•━━

Arlo woke up just after sunset to the click of his bedside lamp. His dad was sitting on his bed. He was smiling, but Arlo didn't buy it.

"Hey, buddy."

Arlo sat up halfway. His mother pulled over a chair from the desk.

"So your mom and I have been talking, and we're worried that the authorities are going to come looking for me. They're going to know I'm not in Guangzhou anymore. They had people keeping tabs on me, just like the Chinese did."

"They won't know you're here, though."

"But they're going to check anyway," said his mom. "They'll search the house."

Arlo was ready for this. "There's a hiding spot in the basement behind one of the chests. I can show you!"

Clark shook his head. "I can't stay here, Arlo. They'd find me. And if they discovered that you and your mom and your sister are hiding me, you'd all be in trouble."

"It's okay. We're already in trouble."

His mom took his hand. "Arlo, you can't have both of your parents in jail. Plus, Jaycee is sixteen. They could charge her as an adult."

"That's fine," said Jaycee. They all looked to the doorway, surprised to find her standing there. "I don't care."

Clark tried to get them back on track. "What the two of you did was so impressive. So amazing! When you showed up at my apartment, I couldn't believe it. I knew I needed to get you out of China to keep you safe. That was my priority. But I shouldn't have gone with you. That was a mistake."

Arlo pulled away from his parents, climbing out on the far

side of the bed. He had a sense where this was headed. "I'm not taking you back there!"

"That's not what we're asking," said Celeste.

Clark dismissed the notion. "I couldn't go back to China anyway. But if you can get me to an island, or somewhere in South America . . ."

"No!" said Jaycee, almost shouting. "Do you know how hard it was to bring you here?!"

"I do, honey," said Clark. "And I love that you did it, but I can't stay here."

"Yes you can!" shouted Arlo. "You're just afraid. Both of you are scared. But I've seen so many scary things that you don't even know about. Actual monsters, not government lawyers."

Jaycee tried a different approach. "If you leave again, I will never forgive you. Either of you."

Her threat hung in the air. Arlo felt his heart pounding.

Celeste broke the silence. "I love you both. I know why you're upset. But this is not your decision to make."

"You're wrong," said Arlo. "It *is* my decision."

Arlo understood exactly what they were asking him to do. He understood why it was a sensible choice. But it wasn't the choice he was making.

"I'm the only one who can take you through the Long Woods," he said. "And I won't. You can't make me. We brought you here and you're staying. That's my decision and it's final."

— 17 —
A COMPROMISE

ARLO AND JAYCEE SPENT THE NEXT TWO HOURS in her bedroom, the only room with a lock on the door. They didn't discuss the argument or what their next steps should be. Instead, Jaycee finished her homework. Arlo was content to lie on the floor, staring up at the ceiling.

They figured their parents would have to come to them eventually. They were right. The knock came just past ten P.M.

Jaycee unlocked the door. Arlo sat on her bed.

Celeste and Clark Finch looked calm but focused. Arlo was happy to see the two of them together, even if it was in opposition to him and his sister.

"So we have a new plan," said Celeste. "It doesn't involve you or the magic forest or anything."

Arlo resisted the temptation to correct her on *Long Woods*.

"The simple fact is, I can't stay in this house," said Clark. "I guarantee they'll search it and they'll absolutely be watching."

Celeste stopped Jaycee before she could object. "But we think we've found a way for him to stay in Pine Mountain. At Mitch's shop, there's a storage room behind the office. We've talked to Mitch, and he's agreed your father can stay there. At least temporarily."

Arlo had spent many afternoons at the Pine Mountain Garage while his mom handled paperwork for Mitch Jansen, the owner of the shop. Arlo knew exactly which room his mom was describing. It was small—but honestly, not much smaller than his father's apartment in China.

"Why would Mitch agree to that?" asked Jaycee. "He'll be putting himself at risk."

"Because he's a friend," said Celeste. "And he knows we need help."

"From what your mom says, no one's ever back in his office," said Clark. "I'll stay quiet. I can sleep during the day and come out at night when it's all shut."

"When are you going?" asked Jaycee.

"Right now. Mitch is on his way over."

This was all happening too fast. Arlo hadn't even gotten to have breakfast with his dad in the house. He wanted to negotiate an extension until morning at least. But he had nothing more to bargain with. The plan had been set in motion without him.

All he could do was hug his father before he left. "Will we be able to see you?"

Clark smiled. "We'll figure out a way, I promise. I love you both so much. I want to hang out with you, to do normal dad stuff that doesn't involve national security and the big woods."

"The Long Woods," corrected Jaycee.

"See! I want to know that. I want to know everything about you guys. But we can't do everything at once. We have to be smart about this. Just like you had a plan for getting me here, we have to have a plan for *keeping* me here."

After his father left with Mitch, Arlo sat on the stairs for an hour. Although he knew his dad hadn't meant it as a criticism, Arlo heard it as *you didn't really think this through*. And the truth was, he hadn't. He'd been so focused on getting his father home, he hadn't considered what would happen afterwards. He'd only thought about the actions, not the consequences.

The situation he found himself in wasn't caused by the Eldritch or other extra-dimensional forces. He only had himself to blame.

· 18 ·
SEVENTH GRADE

IT WASN'T SUPPOSED TO BE LIKE THIS. Pine Mountain Elementary was set up to run from kindergarten through eighth grade. Last spring when he finished sixth, Arlo had expected to be back in the fall with all his classmates. He'd have a new teacher, but little else would change.

For the first time in years, Arlo Finch would attend the same school for successive grades. He wouldn't have to start over again.

Then, at some point in early August, a pipe in the ceiling of Pine Mountain Elementary had broken. With no one at the school to notice, the water had run unchecked for a week. The resulting flood had badly damaged several classrooms. In the end, the school district had decided it would be cheaper to bus Pine Mountain's seventh and eighth graders to Havlick than to repair the ruined wing of the building.

So now Arlo had to get up twenty minutes earlier every morning so he could catch the school bus to Ramos Junior High in Havlick.

Everything about junior high was complicated and frustrating.

Instead of a desk to hold his things, he had a narrow locker that he shared with a wrestler named Bryce, who smelled like day-old french fries. After deciding who got which shelf, they had barely spoken three sentences to each other.

Instead of one teacher, Arlo now had seven, each teaching a different subject. He rotated among his classes according to a schedule that changed every day. If it was an "A" day, he had math first. On "B" days, it was English. On "C" days, it was band.

He hadn't intended to join band, but when he got his schedule at the start of the year, it was already printed there. Arlo chose clarinet simply because Jaycee had played it before switching to drums, so they already had one in the house. He'd gotten over the weird wooden taste of the reeds and could consistently play from low G to middle G without a squeak.

The band teacher, Mr. O'Brien, was the bearded Warden from the previous year's Alpine Derby—the one who was so proficient in firecraeft. Two weeks into the school year, Arlo hadn't said anything about Rangers to Mr. O'Brien, but it was nice to know there was an adult with such skills nearby.

The biggest change from elementary school was how much less he saw Indra and Wu. Their schedules didn't overlap with his at all. For one thing, they had placed into honors math, while

Arlo was in the basic track. For his elective, Wu was taking art, while Indra had woodshop.

So on Monday, the bus ride and lunch period were the only opportunities they had to discuss what had gone down in China and make plans for dealing with Hadryn.

"We need to come up with a secret handshake," proposed Wu. "One that he couldn't know. Then every time we meet each other, we have to do the handshake, and that's how we'll know he's not impersonating one of us."

Arlo and Indra agreed with Wu's idea, but actually implementing the handshake proved difficult. It required a sequence of squeezes and taps, and if both parties did the same thing at the same time, it was hard to feel whether the other one had done it properly. Ultimately, they arrived at a system that used the Morse code from the Field Book to encode their names. The person whose name came first alphabetically would start.

Arlo: .− .−. .−.. −−−

Indra: .. −. −.. .−. .−

Wu: .−− ..−

A dash was a squeeze, while a dot was a tap with a finger. By the end of lunch, they had it mastered.

"We'll teach the rest of the patrol at the meeting," said Indra.

Arlo wondered how feasible it was for them to be shaking hands every time they met, but kept his reservations to himself.

Likewise, Arlo didn't say anything about his father staying at Mitch's garage, nor did his friends ask. The fewer details they knew, the fewer lies they'd need to tell if asked.

While Arlo didn't share any classes with Wu and Indra, there was one Pine Mountain classmate who had his exact same schedule: Merilee Myers.

She sat next to Arlo in every class except band, and then only because as first-chair flute she was in the front row.

Merilee seemed to think they were friends. They were not. Arlo found her deeply exhausting, whether she was talking about her pets, her penny collection or her puppet theater.

In biology, they were assigned as lab partners. For the dissection unit, Merilee had named their frog Frank even though it was clearly a female, given its belly full of black eggs. She wrote up a detailed history of Frank's adventures before arriving at Ramos Junior High and made Arlo read it while she watched.

On the bus to and from school, Arlo made sure to take a window seat by Wu so Merilee wouldn't sit next to him.

"You guys are always together," she said one afternoon. "You're like peanut butter and jelly."

From that day forward, whenever she saw Arlo without Wu, she'd say, "Where's jelly?"

Arlo secretly wished Merilee would catch a cold—a mild one,

just enough to keep her out of school for a few days—so he could get a little peace and quiet.

And at the same time, part of him was happy to have Merilee around. As odd as she was, Merilee was also thoroughly normal, and completely unconnected to the Long Woods and national security. He didn't have to worry that she was secretly Hadryn in disguise; no one could possibly imitate her.

Merilee was unbelievably annoying, but she was also un-questionably on his side. In times when he didn't know who he could trust, he could count on her. Even if they weren't actually friends.

19

SER Y ESTAR

THERE WERE TWO VERBS IN SPANISH THAT BOTH MEANT "TO BE," which was one of the many reasons why the language was impossible.

In his two weeks in Spanish 1A, Arlo had learned the alphabet, including how to roll his double r's. He knew his colors from *azul* to *verde*. But aside from a few stock sentences like *Me llamo Arlo Finch* and *Buenos dias, Señora Veracruz*, he was completely unable to generate an original idea in Spanish.

He actually liked his teacher quite a bit. Señora Veracruz was warm and bubbly and wore sequined athletic shoes, a different color each day. She never scolded them for butchered pronunciation. Rather, she chirped the way the word was supposed to sound, bracketed with *¡Sí, sí!* and a smile. Any attempt to repeat the word back would be greeted by an enthusiastic *¡Muy bien!*, no matter how little progress had been made.

Every noun in Spanish had a gender, masculine or feminine. For no good reason, shirts were female (*las camisas*) and books were male (*los libros*). You had to remember which gender each word was in order to pick the proper form of *the* to go with it. The whole thing struck Arlo as unnecessarily complicated, but at least the rules were consistent.

Then came *ser* and *estar*.

This was the main topic of fifth period that Monday, Arlo's first day back after his secret trip to China.

According to the textbook, you used *ser* whenever you were talking about a permanent condition, like your profession or your nationality. You used *estar* when you were talking about temporary things, like your location or your mood.

But isn't everything temporary? wondered Arlo. In Rangers, he was a Squirrel, but he wouldn't always be that rank. So was it *ser* or *estar*?

Arlo was annoyed by Merilee Myers, a condition that would fall under the "mood" criteria for *estar*. But he had always been annoyed by her, which suggested *ser* instead.

Time itself, the most temporary of phenomena, used *ser*. But not all time followed that rule. According to Señora Veracruz, in Spanish it wasn't possible to *be* an age. Instead you had to *have* an age, as if you carried time around with you in a backpack.

The only comfort Arlo could take is that the rest of the class seemed just as flummoxed by the distinction. He also felt a pang of sympathy for his mom and her confusion over how they'd gotten to China and back.

Perhaps *ser* and *estar* were like the Long Woods. You couldn't really understand them until you'd traveled through them.

There was a knock at the classroom door. Everyone looked over as Principal Brownlee stepped in, beckoning to Señora Veracruz. He whispered something to her. Arlo couldn't hear any of it, but felt his stomach dropping. He wasn't at all surprised when Señora Veracruz looked over at him.

"Arlo, I need you to go with Principal Brownlee."

Arlo stood up and started walking to the door. He didn't want to make eye contact with anyone in his class.

"Take your things," said the principal.

As Arlo circled back to his desk, he felt the stares of his classmates. There was some whispering, no doubt speculation on exactly what was happening. He collected his Spanish book, notebook and pencil.

"Do you want me to take notes?" whispered Merilee.

Arlo shook his head and quickly walked to the door. He was relieved when he was finally out in the hallway.

Principal Brownlee had bright white hair that he kept perfectly combed. Arlo had never spoken to him, but recognized him from the first-day assembly.

He had a vaguely Texas accent, which made it sound like he was holding a chopstick between his teeth. "We're headed to the office."

"Is something wrong?" asked Arlo.

"An FBI fella wants to talk to you. So yeah, I'd say something's definitely wrong."

Arlo took a seat across the table from a heavyset man with droopy eyes who was wearing a navy-blue suit. He had a yellow notepad and a manila file folder, which he shut as Arlo sat down. Arlo caught a glimpse of a photograph inside.

"I'll leave you to it," said Principal Brownlee, shutting the conference room door. The room had no windows. It was incredibly quiet inside, probably the most silent space in the entire building.

The man in the navy suit smiled. "Hello, Arlo. My name is Agent Sanders. How are you doing today?"

"I'm good." *Would that be* ser *or* estar? he wondered.

"Do you know why I'm here today?"

Arlo shook his head. He could guess, but he knew it was best not to.

"I work for the FBI. As you probably know, our job is to help keep the country safe, and to protect American citizens wherever they are. I need to ask you some questions today, Arlo. And I hope you'll be able to help me, because I suspect you want to be able to keep people safe, too."

Arlo knew where this was going.

"You're in Rangers, is that correct?"

The man's question blindsided him. He hadn't been expecting that at all.

"Yes," said Arlo.

"And what rank are you?"

"Squirrel. I'm mostly done with the stuff for Owl, though. I just have my board of review."

Sanders took a note on his pad. "That's great. I made it up to Ram. Never got to Bear."

"Where were you in Rangers?"

"Georgia, just outside Athens. My company went to camp in Virginia, though. A place called Allen's Peak. Have you heard of that?"

"Of course!" Arlo had read about it in the Field Book. It was one of the first Ranger camps in the country and was famous for its extensive caves.

"I loved being in Rangers," said Sanders. "All the outdoor stuff, for sure, but also the principles. Things like the Ranger's Vow. 'Loyal, brave, kind and true.' So important, don't you think?"

Arlo's smile faded. He recognized exactly what Sanders was doing. He was trying to use the Ranger's Vow to get Arlo to confess. *But to what?* Arlo wondered. *How much does he actually know? And what photograph does he have in the folder?*

"What do you think about honesty, Arlo?"

"I think it's good."

"Even when it's sometimes not easy to tell the truth, right?"

"Sure."

Sanders seemed to sense that Arlo was on to him. "When was the last time you talked to your dad, Arlo?"

Arlo exhaled, then spoke the sentence he'd been practicing for the past three years: "I would like to speak to my attorney."

Sanders acted surprised. *Acted*, noted Arlo. The way he raised his eyebrows. The low "Hmm!" It was all a performance. "Why would a thirteen-year-old kid need an attorney? I'm just asking you some simple questions."

"I would like to speak to my attorney," repeated Arlo in the same level tone.

"Your dad could be in real trouble. Not just with us, but with China. Don't you want to help him out?"

"I would like to speak to my attorney."

After his dad had fled to China, lawyers from the organization defending him had trained Arlo, Jaycee and their mom on how to handle questions from the government. They had practiced answering with the same eight words for hours, until it had become as natural as breathing. By law, the government couldn't force you to answer questions without your lawyer present. Arlo wasn't going to tell Sanders anything.

But maybe Sanders would inadvertently tell Arlo something.

"Your dad, well, he's missing. Obviously, we know he's been living in China. A city called Guangzhou—am I pronouncing that right?"

Arlo didn't answer. Sanders continued: "We've been keeping an eye on him, making sure he's safe. We don't want anything bad to happen to him. So when we learned that the Chinese authorities had gone to his apartment, and then he's missing, well, we just want to make sure no harm's come to him. He is an American citizen after all."

Do they think the Chinese have him in custody? wondered Arlo.

Sanders tapped the manila folder. He seemed to be weighing a decision. "There was something I was going to show you. But if you're not talking, I guess it's pointless."

He's fishing, thought Arlo. *Don't bite.*

Arlo shrugged like he didn't care. They both knew it was an act. Sanders stood up, straightening his jacket. He took a business card from his pocket and placed it in front of Arlo.

"My cell number is on there. You call me if you want to talk, or if you feel like you're in any kind of danger."

Danger. It was such an odd way to end a sentence. So intriguing. *Probably just bait*, thought Arlo. Still . . .

"I like to look at photos," he said.

Sanders chuckled. "Oh, so you can say other things. Here I was thinking you only had one sentence in you."

Arlo smiled. He didn't mean it.

Sanders opened the folder, keeping it to himself. He was still debating whether or not to show its contents to Arlo. At least, he wanted to make it look that way.

"One of the main jobs in any investigation," he said, "is figuring out how two things are connected. Did that car just happen to be in front of the bank during the robbery, or were they the lookout? Sometimes, it's *How did the killer know the victim?* You can go crazy trying to figure out the answer. Sometimes, you're just stumped. The pieces don't fit."

Sanders took a piece of paper from the folder. He set it down in front of Arlo.

It was a photograph, black and white, evidently from a security camera. It showed a man staring straight ahead, a wicked gleam in his eye.

It was Hadryn.

Arlo's heart began racing. Palms sweating. He felt the urge to flee, but he managed not to react visibly. At least that's what he hoped.

Sanders tapped the photograph. "This here is a very, very dangerous man. And for some reason, he knows you, Arlo Finch. I would love to know why."

Arlo shrugged. "Sorry. I can't help you."

20
TROUBLEMAKER

ARLO WASN'T ALLOWED TO GO BACK TO CLASS, even though he could have made it in time for seventh-period gym.

Principal Brownlee said that had it been up to him, Arlo would be expelled for refusing to cooperate with Agent Sanders, but that the school district was too scared of bad publicity. "Don't think I'm going to let you off easy. I read up on who your dad is and how he's hurt this country. If you try any of that computer hacking stuff on this school, I'll bury you in the soccer field myself."

On the bus ride back to Pine Mountain, Arlo caught up with Wu and Indra. After exchanging their agreed-upon handshakes, they spoke in low voices. Arlo was relieved to learn that neither of them had been pulled out of class for questioning. That suggested the authorities didn't suspect that they were in any way involved in Clark's disappearance.

"If they had security footage of us in China," said Wu, "they would have definitely been asking me questions, like 'How the heck did you get there and back?'"

For Indra, the most intriguing question was why the FBI had a photo of Hadryn. "I mean, yes, he's probably broken all kinds of laws. He could have robbed banks or killed people. So it's not surprising that he'd be on a most-wanted list—but how would they know to connect him to Arlo?"

"Hadryn said he'd been looking for me for thirty years," said Arlo. "He found me by googling me. Maybe the FBI got his search history."

Wu had a more conspiratorial suggestion: "Or maybe somebody in the government is talking with the Eldritch."

Arlo had assumed that Agent Sanders mentioned being a Ranger to establish common ground, a shared interest. *What if it was more than that?* he wondered. *Does Sanders know about the Eldritch, and why they're interested in me? And if so, whose side is he really on?*

Arlo arrived home to find Uncle Wade sitting in a lawn chair on the driveway, watching as a team of six agents packed up gear in a white van. They were wearing latex gloves and disposable booties over their shoes.

"They got here about noon," he said. "Went through everything, including the trash. I'm making sure they don't take anything they're not supposed to. They seem disappointed in how few electronic devices we have." Wade smiled, a bit smug.

"What about fingerprints?" asked Arlo in a low voice. "Dad could have touched stuff while he was here."

"I wiped down and vacuumed everything when you went off to school. Doubt there's any trace of him left."

"Did they look in the secret hiding place in the basement?" It didn't matter, really. Arlo was just curious.

Wade scoffed. "Kid, they checked *everywhere*. They had blueprints of the house I'd never seen." He leaned in closer. "Also, my buddy Nacho came by. He's working on something to stop that Hadryn guy from coming around. Says it won't be a ward per se, but more like an alarm. We'll at least know he's here."

By the time Arlo's mom and sister got home, the agents had gone. The house had clearly been thoroughly searched, but nothing was damaged or destroyed.

Arlo and his family were careful not to say anything important inside the house, since it was possible the agents had installed surveillance devices. In case someone was listening, they spoke as if they had no idea where their father was, or what was really happening.

"I just hope he's okay," said Jaycee, a little louder than she needed to. "I'm really worried about him."

"Me too," said Arlo. *Was that enough? Should I say more? It didn't feel like quite enough worry.* "I hope he calls us and lets us know where he is."

"I'm sure he will if he can," said Celeste. "You know what

might make us feel better? A little hike before dinner. Who's up for it?"

Walking through the woods with Jaycee and his mom, Arlo learned that Agent Sanders had interviewed all three of them that afternoon. He'd gone first to the Gold Pan diner to question Celeste, then to Havlick High to talk with Jaycee.

In each case, they had told him nothing and demanded to speak with their attorney.

"I don't think the FBI knows much at all," said Jaycee. "The guy kept asking about when I went to visit Dad over the summer. I'm pretty sure he thinks Dad gave me something to bring back from that trip, which he definitely didn't."

Celeste had spoken to the attorney representing their father's case. The lawyer said there was nothing to suggest that the FBI visit was out of the ordinary. "She said they're just checking all the boxes. They probably think the Chinese authorities have your dad and they want to know if he's contacted us."

Celeste hadn't told the attorney that Clark was back in the country—it would be too hard to explain. But assuming nothing changed, she said Arlo and Jaycee could visit their dad in a week or two. "Maybe it's time you got an after-school job, Jaycee. You should learn how to change oil at Mitch's garage. And Arlo, you can come with me when I'm doing the accounting."

The hike had started as an excuse to get away from potential eavesdropping by federal officers, but by the end of it, they were just enjoying the walk. They saw three deer and a dozen fat squirrels getting ready for winter. They listened to the birds in the trees and distant dogs barking. After a stressful few days, the hike was calm and ordinary. It was a relief.

Arlo decided not to tell his mom and sister about Hadryn. They had enough to worry about.

----•◦•----

Since the beginning of the school year, Arlo had felt largely invisible in junior high. This was a significant change. Most years, he had been the new kid joining an existing class. At Ramos, he was just an ordinary seventh grader, indistinguishable from his classmates.

Until now. Heading to his locker that Tuesday morning, Arlo felt like he was wearing a flashing neon sign. Kids he didn't know would pause in their conversations to watch him as he walked by. He caught snippets of their whispered conversations:

"I heard his dad murdered a bunch of people . . ."

"The police made him take a lie detector test . . ."

"My brother said he's going to get deported . . ."

Reaching his locker, he was surprised to find all his books stacked on the floor in front of it. Bryce was waiting for him.

"I don't want your stuff in my locker anymore," he grumbled. It was the most words Bryce had ever said to him in a row.

"It's my locker, too," said Arlo. As he dialed the combination, he could feel the weight of a dozen kids staring at him. He went slowly, wanting to get it right on the first try. It would be embarrassing if he messed it up.

He lifted the latch. The door opened.

Then Bryce slammed it shut again. "I said, keep your crap out of my locker."

Bryce was standing square-shouldered, puffing out his chest to make himself look bigger. Arlo recognized the posture and the growl. It was all an act. Arlo had seen Russell Stokes give the same performance in Rangers.

"What are you going to do?" said Bryce. "Run and cry to the principal? I hear Brownlee wants you out."

Everyone was staring. *What do they want?* Arlo wondered. *An argument? A fistfight?*

He spotted Merilee Myers in the crowd. He dreaded what annoying thing she would say as she forced her way into the confrontation. Everyone would be talking about how Arlo Finch was saved by some weird girl from his elementary school.

But Merilee Myers said nothing. She just watched.

The bell rang for first period. *Show's over*, Arlo thought.

He bent down to pick up his books. Bryce kicked them as he walked away. One of the binders opened up, math pages flying out.

Everyone headed off to class. Only Merilee stayed to help him with his books. "I'm fine!" Arlo snarled. "Just go!"

Merilee left him. As he collected his papers, Arlo thought back to the various monsters he'd faced over the past year, his many brushes with death. He longed for the simplicity of an enemy who could be escaped or defeated.

Seventh grade was an endless struggle, an unwinnable competition.

It wasn't a battle. It was an ordeal.

21
NEWCOMERS

AFTER A ROUGH DAY IN JUNIOR HIGH, that night's Rangers meeting was a welcome relief.

The basement of the First Church of Pine Mountain was a swirl of activity, with patrols in each corner of the room checking gear and planning for the next campout. But for Blue Patrol, this was an especially notable meeting because they were adding two new members. No longer would they be the smallest patrol.

Wyatt and Sarah were both sixth graders at Pine Mountain Elementary. While Arlo had never spoken to either of them, he had seen them around enough to feel confident this wasn't another Hadryn-as-new-patrol-member situation.

Sarah Fitzrandolph was the granddaughter of the elementary school librarian and shared her grandmother's obsession with Scottie dogs. She'd won the school spelling bee three years in a row, coming just one word from making it to the state championship each time. Sarah wore her red hair in a thick braid that went halfway down her back.

Wyatt Stokes had had a girl's name up until third grade, when he transitioned to being Wyatt. He was Russell's younger brother. Normally siblings were put in the same patrol, but Wyatt didn't fit the Red Patrol vibe. His passion was animals, not sports. He was raising his own dairy cow named Florence and felt certain that she could add a lot to Blue Patrol. "We can have fresh milk at every campout!"

Connor patiently explained a few of the reasons they didn't pack milk on campouts: it was heavy; they had no way to refrigerate it; if it leaked it would make a mess.

"But it's worth it, you'll see," said Wyatt, undeterred.

Arlo admired Wyatt's confidence. At Arlo's first meeting a year ago, he'd barely spoken, afraid to look foolish.

Still, it was funny to realize how little Sarah and Wyatt knew. Not only were they unfamiliar with camping basics, they didn't know the Ranger's Vow or how to salute properly. They couldn't even tie a basic square knot.

For a change, Arlo Finch was not the youngest, smallest and newest member of Blue Patrol. Instead of learning how to do things, he could teach.

Connor's brother, Christian, was back in Pine Mountain after spending his summer completing the requirements for his Bear rank. He had returned looking noticeably older, in part because of his scruffy beard.

The actual details of Christian's training, called the Vigil, were a highly protected secret, but Arlo knew it involved elemental techniques like firecraeft and stonecraeft, along with nature skills like tracking and camouflage. Never one to shy away from wild speculation, Wu believed the Vigil consisted of a series of trials designed to test a Ranger's physical, mental and moral discipline. "And if you fail, they wipe your memory so you can't remember what they've taught you. That's how they keep it secret."

As much as Arlo had picked up in his forays through the Long Woods, there were still whole areas of lore he hadn't even begun to learn. That was exciting.

After the meeting, Connor brought Christian over to talk privately with Arlo, Wu and Indra. "I told Christian about Rielle coming to the campsite, and her warning that Hadryn had escaped."

"In the Vigil, do they teach you anything about the Eldritch?" asked Wu. "Do you even go in the Long Woods?"

Christian smiled. "You know I can't answer that."

"You could nod though," offered Wu. "Or blink."

Christian didn't nod. He eventually blinked, but it didn't feel like a conscious choice.

Indra tried a different approach. "We know Hadryn was a Ranger, and that he probably got his Bear, so he would have been through the Vigil. We ought to have a sense of exactly what he can do. We already know he can smokejump and shape-shift."

"Can you shape-shift?" Wu asked Christian.

"Seriously, I can't tell you."

Arlo reminded Wu of what he'd learned in their confrontation. "Hadryn said he could shape-shift because he ate a doppelgänger's heart."

Christian was confused. "Wait, so he can make himself look like a specific person? Not just turn into a wolf or something?"

"You do that?!" asked Wu, excited. Again, Christian wasn't going to answer.

"Hadryn could impersonate any of us," said Indra. "And he did. A lot."

"I can promise you that's not something we learn in the Vigil," said Christian. "And nothing we do involves killing a creature or eating its heart. What you're describing sounds like bloodcraeft."

Wu asked Christian to confirm that the word was spelled with the special *ae*. It was.

"That's so cool."

"Something's been bugging me about that morning," said Indra. "Hadryn went to Arlo's house, and from his mom, he found out that we were camping by the river. But then why didn't he try to impersonate one of us? Like Wu or Arlo?"

"He wouldn't have known that Wu and Arlo were in China," said Christian.

"Then he could have come as Arlo's mom, or a police officer, or anyone. It just seems weird he didn't try."

"Maybe he can't shape-shift for some reason," said Arlo. He had only had the faint edges of a theory, but felt he might be able to flesh it out if he said it aloud. "Christian, you said what Hadryn was doing with the doppelgänger heart is bloodcraeft. When he was at my house, he was apparently bleeding a lot. He got hurt somehow escaping from the Eldritch. Would that have weakened him?"

Christian nodded. It sounded plausible. "Again, they don't teach us bloodcraeft. But from what I know of it, it's like you're infusing your body with all these toxins and mystical bits you take from other creatures. The whole thing is kind of vampiric. You're stealing their energy. So if you were to suddenly lose a lot of blood, it makes sense that you'd lose power, too."

Arlo was intrigued by the notion that Hadryn was weakened. It would help explain why Hadryn hadn't come directly after him for the past two days. There had been so many opportunities, particularly at school, yet Hadryn had stayed in the shadows. *He isn't just hiding from the Eldritch*, Arlo thought. *He's getting his strength back.*

At some point, Hadryn was certain to return. Arlo vowed to be ready.

22
AFTERNOONS

"SO WHAT DO YOU THINK OF MY SECRET CLUBHOUSE?"

"I like it," said Arlo. "But you need more pillows. And maybe an air freshener."

They were sitting on the hard floor of his father's tiny room—a closet, really—in the back of Mitch's automobile repair shop. Clark Finch had been living there for two weeks, and things had settled into a routine.

He slept most of the day, then woke up in the afternoon. (The tiny room had no windows, which made his inverted schedule easier to maintain.) After rolling up his sleeping bag, Clark ate two granola bars and worked on his laptop. He masked his internet traffic inside the movies Mitch kept constantly streaming on the office television.

"The thing is, Mitch was watching stuff around the clock

already," said Clark. "So it's not even suspicious that he's downloading hundreds of megabytes an hour."

Just in case someone was watching, Clark didn't interact with Mitch at all. There were no whispered conversations, no notes slipped under the door. They wanted nothing to suggest that there might be someone other than Mitch in the garage.

Each night at about eight o'clock, when the shop was closed, Clark would unlock the door and walk in circles to get some exercise. "I can do push-ups and sit-ups in here, but there's no quiet way to get blood moving in your legs," said Clark.

After his workout, he'd eat the food Mitch or Celeste left for him in the refrigerator. He couldn't risk using the microwave oven—it put out fields of magnetic energy visible even to satellites—so it was strictly cold meals for him.

Nights in the office were also his chance to use the bathroom and wash up. "I've got a bucket just in case," said Clark, pointing behind Arlo. "But I hold it if I can."

Well before dawn, Clark Finch would carefully wipe down everything he'd touched to get rid of the fingerprints and retreat to the closet to sleep.

To Arlo, the whole process felt like reverse camping. Rather than going outside, you were going deeper inside. You weren't trying to see new things; you were trying to not be seen.

It was now five o'clock in the evening. Arlo's mom was just outside the door, doing accounting work at Mitch's desk, with a war movie playing on the TV. Arlo and his dad could talk without worrying that anyone could hear them. Arlo detailed the previous weekend's Ranger campout, and how Blue Patrol had come in second place in the cooking competition, collecting the Silver Spork for their chili pie. In a shocking twist, Green Patrol had come in third with their gummy pad thai; Red Patrol took gold with their beef stew.

The conversation drifted from camping to school to the geography of Pine Mountain.

"I've been thinking a lot about the Long Woods," said Clark. "And knaughts as well. What's crazy to me is that I can't find anyone talking about these things online—except for a few people who seem genuinely wackadoodle. Which makes me think maybe I'm the wackadoodle."

Arlo explained the Wonder as best he could, and why people seemed to forget about the Long Woods the further away they got from them. He also told him about the Night Mare, the hag, Fox, the grisp, Rielle and the Eldritch. He was about to dive into the time travel that resulted in his becoming a *tooble* with a spirit trapped inside him when his mom gently knocked on the door.

"It's time, Arlo," she said. "We need to go."

Arlo couldn't believe it had already been an hour. He hadn't even started to explain the Broken Bridge, much less Hadryn.

"Don't worry about it," said Clark. "You can tell me on Friday."

And that was the truly remarkable thing: for the first time in years, Arlo Finch could count on seeing his father in person. Every Monday and Friday afternoon, he'd meet his mom at the diner and walk over to Mitch's garage with her. He'd chat with Mitch and pet his fat orange cat before heading back to the office to "do homework."

Once there, Celeste would shut the door. Arlo would knock three times on the closet. Clark would step out and give them each a big hug before he and Arlo retreated back into his hiding space to discuss Rangers, science, dogs, friends, baseball, books and everything. Sometimes they just played Uno or checkers.

School was still awful. He had recurring nightmares about Hadryn, the FBI, the Eldritch and Principal Brownlee. He also had pimples and what he was pretty sure was athlete's foot.

But for two afternoons each week, none of it mattered. He had his dad back.

On the first Friday of October, Clark Finch had news.

"I have a theory, and I need your help to test it."

Arlo was excited to do whatever his father proposed, be it drinking a mysterious glowing substance or shooting an experimental ray gun.

Clark continued: "So: knaughts. I've been reading up on things that might help explain them. There's actually a whole field of mathematics called topology that deals with knot theory—the normal kind of knots, not your special kind."

Arlo admitted it was confusing that the two words sounded alike.

"The world we experience has three dimensions. And in three dimensions, it would be impossible to tie slipknaughts like the ones you describe."

"But you could in four dimensions," said Arlo. "That's what Wu said the first time I tied one. It's like I pushed the rope through another dimension."

"Exactly. And I think that dimension is basically what you call the Long Woods. At least, it's an aspect of the Woods."

That matched with Arlo's experience. "When you're inside a slipknaught, it's like you're in a spirit realm. You can see them, and they can see you."

"You also said something about a glowing cord?"

Arlo recapped what Fox had told him about the silver cord that kept a person's spirit connected to his body. Arlo added that he had seen a similar phenomenon with both the Eldritch lashes and the tether that had kept Cooper the ghost dog in the front yard for decades.

"All the things you're describing sound like they're related to knaughts. They're all about tying things down or together. And that cage thing you found in the ship—the one with the spirit in it—you said you cut through a cord with your knife to set it loose. It was literally bound to the device."

Arlo was eager to hear his assignment. "Do you need me to tie a new kind of knaught? Or cut one? I'll do it."

Clark smiled. "My theory is that knaughts are a form of quantum entanglement. I can't explain it in a way that totally makes sense, at least not any more than you can explain the

Long Woods. But the idea is that two things can be linked together in a way that's completely different from what we're used to."

He handed Arlo a paper clip and held one in his own hand. "Let's say these two paper clips are atoms, and they're entangled on a quantum level. If I turn my paper clip"—he twisted it ninety degrees in his palm—"yours would turn, too. And instantly."

"How is that possible?" asked Arlo.

"Because on a quantum level, they're the same paper clip. They act as one thing even if they're hundreds or thousands of miles apart. Einstein called it 'spooky action at a distance.'"

"That's cool," said Arlo. "It sounds like the Long Woods."

"It does, doesn't it? Scientists have been writing about quantum mechanics since the 1920s, but it's really hard to actually do anything with it. It happens at a microscopic level, and then only at extreme temperatures. But in theory, a quantum computer could break codes billions of times faster than any normal computer. A lot of my work is simulations to show what could happen if we were ever able to build a functional quantum device."

"Can you do that?"

"I don't know." Then he added with a mischievous smile, "But maybe I just did."

From behind his rolled-up sleeping bag, Clark pulled out his phone. There were now extra wires dangling off it, connecting it to a separate device that looked like a calculator.

"I had to scavenge a bit, but it should work well enough. If you're up for it, I'd like you to take it to the Long Woods—"

"I'll do it!"

"—and run a program on it. It should only take twenty minutes or so. It won't do anything exciting, but it should let me know if my theory is at all workable."

"You want to test your hypothesis."

"Spoken like a true scientist." Clark handed Arlo the phone and showed him how to run the program. All the wireless connectivity had been disabled, so it was basically just a tiny computer.

"What if it works?" asked Arlo. "What will you be able to do?"

"It's not about what I'd be able to do. If this works, it could be the biggest discovery in science since the atom."

23
CONNECTIONS

THE LONG WOODS HAD A SHORTAGE OF TREE STUMPS.

When hiking in the regular forest, Arlo could reliably find a stump to use as a chair or table. Of course, that was because of forestry; tree stumps were mostly the result of someone cutting down a tree. The Long Woods had no Long Woodsmen with saws and axes to leave tree stumps where you wanted them. Trees simply grew and fell without any consideration for convenience.

Arlo was looking for a place to set his father's device so it could run undisturbed. With no tree stumps available, he settled for a flat rock at the edge of a vast meadow filled with intensely blue flowers.

Following his dad's instructions carefully, he powered on the phone and made sure all the cables were securely connected. Once it had booted up, he tapped the icon for *primes_qntm_woods.r.*

The screen filled with gibberish, then a progress bar appeared with a number over it: *1%*.

Arlo watched and waited.

He'd been to this spot in the Long Woods twice before on previous excursions and had mentally bookmarked it. He liked how the field of flowers looked like the ocean, complete with tiny waves as the breeze rushed across it. The air smelled of cinnamon and honey. It reminded him of the candle store at the mall back in Chicago on that day when his mom took him shopping for new dress shoes for the school play. He'd wandered into the store while his mom took a phone call. The woman at the counter smiled and said, "I know what you're looking for." Then she handed him a box wrapped in golden foil. As he started to peel it open—

That was odd.

Standing at the edge of the forest, Arlo wasn't sure what had just happened. He had been remembering a visit to a candle store in Chicago when the memory suddenly changed. On that day in Chicago, there hadn't been a woman at the counter. She certainly hadn't spoken to him, or handed him anything. *Was I remembering, or imagining?* Arlo wondered.

He looked down at the device. *2%*.

This was going to take a while.

He tried to mentally go back to the candle store, to picture it clearly. But it was gone. Lost. He couldn't find it anywhere in his mind, just as he couldn't find the Valley of Fire anymore. All paths had been erased.

Maybe the scent could lead him there. He inhaled deeply through his nose, hoping to smell more of the intense cinnamon-honey aroma. But he'd already become desensitized to it. He couldn't single out that smell anymore.

But he did hear something: running water. Not a trickle, but a sizable stream. It was like the static on the radio between stations. Which was odd, because he didn't remember any rivers anywhere nearby.

As he looked out across the field of blue flowers, he saw an object fall from the sky. It didn't seem to have originated from anywhere. There were no clouds, no helicopters, no hot-air balloons. The object had simply sprung into existence, then plummeted.

Arlo checked the device: *3%.* He had time.

As he walked through the meadow, his shoes stirred up trails of pollen that shimmered in the sunlight. Flower petals tinkled like bells.

He stopped in the middle of the field. At his feet lay a fat fish nearly a meter long. It was wriggling and wet, its gaping mouth chewing the air. Its scales were iridescent shades of red and yellow and orange. Its eyes were open, searching, confused.

"It's like a giant goldfish!" said a man's voice.

Arlo turned to discover he was back at Dafushan Park in China, standing near the guide who was leading the group of American tourists. Arlo looked at the pole she was holding. Instead of an orange pom-pom, it was now topped by a paper dragon that swirled in the breeze.

"An ancient story tells of a school of golden koi fish," the woman said. "They swam up the great Yellow River until they reached a waterfall and could go no further."

Arlo reached down and picked up the fish. It was slippery and nearly slid out of his hands. He pressed it against his chest. It smelled like rain.

"But one fish did not stop. It tried to swim up the waterfall to reach the very top."

Arlo began walking, headed towards the sound of the water. The koi fish's whiskers tickled his cheek. Its sharp fins scratched his arms.

"Again and again it fell," said the woman's voice. "For one hundred years it kept trying to swim and jump up the waterfall."

The sound of a river kept getting louder. Then a spray of water hit Arlo in the face. He squeezed his eyes shut.

"Until one day, it succeeded."

When his eyes opened, Arlo wasn't in the meadow anymore. He was standing at the base of a roaring waterfall, by a pool of crystal-blue water that swirled around jagged rocks. Sunlight caught the spray, resulting in a pale rainbow. The trees were bright green and tropical, with the wind whipping their fronds.

Like the eye of a hurricane, this place was deafening yet peaceful, turbulent but calm. In his year of traveling through the Long Woods, Arlo had never seen anything like it.

The fish struggled in his arms. Arlo had forgotten he was holding it.

He knelt down and let it plunk into the water. The fish quickly swam away, disappearing into the churn.

"Where are we?" asked a female voice.

Arlo turned to find Rielle standing next to him on the bank. She was wearing a white tunic and trousers. Her hair was pulled back with an emerald-green ribbon that matched her belt. Delicate chains connected the rings on her fingers to engraved silver bracelets.

"I've never been here before," said Arlo. Most of his interactions with Rielle had been in this odd middle space where time and geography didn't seem to flow logically. They'd met first in a reflection, then on a snowy road. At a bonfire one night, he and Rielle had found themselves side by side, watching a fiery dragon.

"It's about the dragon, isn't it?" asked Arlo.

"Mirnos," said Rielle. "That's what the Eldritch call it. They'd captured a spirit and were bringing it across the bridge into the Realm when it broke free. It turned out it was actually twin spirits, Ekafos and Mirnos . . ."

"Time and space," said Arlo, remembering what Fox had told him at the Broken Bridge. At Camp Redfeather, Ekafos had pulled him across the lake—and back in time to thirty years earlier.

"Ekafos swam to a place beyond time," said Rielle. "And Mirnos hid deep in the Long Woods."

"Is that where we are?" asked Arlo. "Does he live by this waterfall?"

"What waterfall?" Rielle turned to him. "What do you see?"

It was an odd question to ask a person standing next to you. "A waterfall. Trees. Sunlight. Why, what do you see?"

"It's dark," said Rielle. "And cold. But I do hear water."

Arlo watched as she raised her hand and cast a snaplight. The sunlight was so bright that Arlo could barely make out the faint glow as the snaplight arced over the river.

Rielle gasped. She was seeing something very different. Something frightening. "It's Mirnos," she said. "It's waking up."

Then Arlo heard an insistent beeping. As he turned to find the source, the forest swirled around him. Sunlight strobed dark-light-dark-light. Arlo stumbled, dizzy.

It took a moment to find his bearings.

He was back at the edge of the forest. His father's device was beeping. Arlo looked at the screen.

100%. Test complete.

24
HALLOWEEN

BECAUSE THE HOUSES IN PINE MOUNTAIN were spread so far apart along steep roads without sidewalks, conventional trick-or-treating simply wasn't practical. So instead, every Halloween the kids walked along Main Street, visiting each of the stores in town, where the shop owners would hand out candy.

While Arlo missed the tradition of ringing doorbells, he liked that Pine Mountain's solution meant you got to see everyone's costumes at once.

Arlo was especially proud of his this year. With Uncle Wade's help, he had fashioned an astronaut uniform out of a plastic fishbowl, a white painter's jumpsuit and two full rolls of duct tape. The helmet featured twin air hoses, but the plastic quickly fogged over, so Arlo decided to carry the helmet under his arm as if he were walking to his rocket.

Indra was dressed as Harry Potter, complete with robe, scarf, thick-rimmed round glasses and a zigzag drawn over her eye. Nearly everyone she passed, kid or adult, asked why she wasn't going as Hermione Granger instead. "Because that's not who I want to be," she said matter-of-factly.

Wu went as a character from *Galactic Havoc 2*, with blue-and-white face paint and a giant double-bladed sword made from cardboard. "It's actually a specific Geodomo skin you can only get by finishing the ten-gauntlet challenge," explained Wu. Arlo nodded as if he understood, but he had still never played the game, so he didn't know who Geodomo was or what his default skin looked like.

The trio had met up just after dark in front of Peterson Hardware at the west end of Main Street. Their plan was to walk east and finish at the Gold Pan diner, but rumors of full-size candy bars at the Pine Mountain Realty office sent them running there first. The line was twenty kids deep by the time they arrived, and it seemed to be barely moving. Every few seconds, a flash of light would spill from the doorway. It was clear they were taking photos, but why?

"Maybe it's to make sure no one is circling back," said Wu. "That happens a lot when you offer full-size bars."

Sarah and Wyatt, the two new Blue Patrol members, stepped out of the office. They were dressed as Thing 1 and Thing 2 from *The Cat in the Hat*.

"What's with the photos?" asked Arlo.

"It's some kind of advertising thing," explained Sarah. "There

142

are props and stuff like that. They won't give you the candy unless you take the photo."

"What kind of candy is it?" asked Indra.

"Three Musketeers," said Wyatt. "It's full size, but you also have to bring home this real estate brochure for your parents."

Arlo traded a look with Wu and Indra. Was it worth it? It was widely agreed that Three Musketeers was the worst major-brand candy bar, but at least they'd be getting a lot of it.

"I mean, it's *full size*," said Wu. "You're not going to get that anywhere else, even if it's Three Musketeers."

It took nearly ten minutes to make it in the door, where two costumed fourth graders were posing by a hay bale in front of a mountain backdrop. The photographer, a bald man who looked like Santa's cowboy brother, barked orders about how to stand and where to look. "Closer! Like you like each other!"

Only after he was satisfied with the shot were the kids given their candy bars, a brochure rubber-banded to each one.

The photographer pointed at Arlo. "You three. You're up."

The man had Arlo sit on the hay bale while Wu and Indra flanked him with their respective sword and wand raised. Arlo was certain it looked ridiculous, but just wanted to get the candy and go.

After a few flashes, a thin woman with angel wings leaned in and whispered to the photographer. He nodded, then pointed to Arlo. "Let's do a few without the astronaut."

Arlo happily stepped aside.

"Wait!" said Indra. "Why don't you want him in the photo?"

The photographer looked over at the angel-winged woman, who pretended she hadn't heard. Indra repeated her question: "Excuse me! Why don't you want my friend in the photo?"

Arlo waved her off. "I don't care. It's okay."

"It's not okay!" said Indra. By this point, several third graders were leaning in to look, curious about the commotion. "Why did you tell him not to take Arlo's photo?"

"This is a family business," said the woman, gesturing at the tiny office. "We can do whatever we want."

"It's because of who his father is, isn't it?"

The woman scoffed. "It's Halloween. Just take your candy."

"We don't want your candy!" said Indra. Which wasn't true at all. Arlo definitely wanted his full-size Three Musketeers. The long wait had made him crave its milky sweet blandness. "We just want you to admit the truth!"

The angel-winged woman had had enough. "Fine. I don't want that traitor's kid associated with my business."

Arlo felt a palpable blow to his chest. He looked down to see if he'd somehow been shot with an arrow, but the wound was strictly emotional.

For the past few weeks, Arlo had noticed whispered conversations in town. Even at the weekly Rangers meeting, he sensed he was being discussed. But outside of school, no one had said anything to his face. This was the first confirmation that strangers knew who he was. And that they didn't like him.

"Let's go," said Indra, headed for the door.

Arlo followed her, avoiding eye contact with everyone. On his way out, Wu took three candy bars from the basket. He pulled off the sales flyers and tossed them in the recycling can.

The Three Musketeers ended up being a perfectly adequate candy bar now that Arlo had devoured it in four bites. He struggled to swallow.

"You okay?" asked Indra.

"I'm fine," he finally choked out, trying to get the nougat off his teeth.

"That woman is awful," said Indra. "It's not your fault who your father is."

"And your dad's actually really cool," added Wu. "Mine wouldn't have been so up for trekking across the Long Woods."

"Do you want to keep trick-or-treating?" asked Indra.

"Definitely." Arlo wasn't going to let one mean real estate agent stand in his way of a sugar coma.

Thirty minutes later, they'd hit every store on the street and begun sorting through their haul at a booth in the Gold Pan diner. Arlo's mom was waitressing—she was dressed as a 1980s Valley girl—and the restaurant was busy with a dozen families. Jaycee was helping out in the kitchen.

Arlo went behind the counter to refill their water pitcher. He was allowed, because he'd been officially trained that summer.

"How'd you make out?" asked a gravel-voiced man at the last stool. He was dressed in a trench coat and fedora, his face covered by a piece of white fabric with symmetrical dark splotches. Arlo was immediately suspicious. He didn't recognize the voice.

"Who are you?" he asked.

"I'm from *Watchmen*. It's a comic, but you're too young to read it. Your mom would kill me."

Arlo smiled. It was his father under that disguise.

Clark kept up his sinister voice. "I figured if there was any day I could wander out of the garage, it'd be today."

"Do you want to meet my friends?" asked Arlo.

Clark shook his head. "Too risky. But I wanted you to be the first to know that the experiment you ran for me in the Long Woods? It worked."

"What does that mean?"

"That device was able to do quantum calculations faster than anything that's ever been built."

"How much faster?" asked Arlo, even though he had no frame of reference.

"A billion times. More than that, probably."

"So you're happy?"

"More than happy. There's still a lot of work to do, but if we can replicate these findings, it's a game changer."

Arlo wanted to hug him, or high-five. But that would look suspicious. So instead he just refilled his dad's water glass.

"How about you, Arlo? You having a good Halloween?"

"Great," he lied. "All good." With that, Arlo carried the pitcher of water back to his friends, who were still sorting and discussing their candy. He saw Clark tip his hat as he walked past, headed back to his hidden closet in the garage.

— 25 —
HALLOWEEN, PART TWO

ARLO WAS AMAZED THAT HIGH SCHOOL KIDS managed to talk so much without actually saying anything. When gathered in a group, every utterance was met with "Definitely" or "That's so crazy" or "I know, right?" It was a circle of constant affirmation about boring things like algebra teachers and dating and college applications.

In contrast, when Arlo was hanging out with Indra and Wu, there was forward motion to the conversation. Topics were debated. Plans were decided upon. It wasn't just treading water.

He had been sitting in the passenger seat of the station wagon for at least five minutes while Jaycee talked with a group of high school kids that included Benjy, her sometimes-boyfriend who was dressed up as Spider-Man, and Christian Cunningham, who wore a fuzzy Chewbacca suit minus the head. *What could they possibly need to discuss?* Arlo wondered. They had just spent all day together at school. They would be seeing each other again in ten hours.

They were still in the parking lot of the diner. Their mom needed to close up, so she had asked Jaycee to drive Arlo home. He wondered if it would be just as fast to walk—but then the time he'd already spent waiting would be wasted.

Arlo reached over to the steering wheel and hit the horn. It was louder than he had expected. Jaycee glared at him but finally said her goodnights. She shut the door and started the car. "Impatient much?"

"What were you talking about?" asked Arlo.

"Nothing."

"Then why did it take so long?"

"Because it's high school. You'll see."

As they pulled out of the parking lot, Christian waved goodnight. His beard had grown in, which made him look more like a folk singer than a Ranger.

By Colorado law, Jaycee's provisional driver's license didn't allow her to drive with anyone under twenty-one in the car, unless they were a family member. That meant it was legal for her to drive Arlo, but not her high school friends. While Jaycee hadn't had a single accident, Arlo remained hypervigilant whenever she was at the wheel, tensing up at every turn and stop sign.

"Do you know where Christian went over the summer?" she asked, definitely not keeping both hands on the steering wheel.

"I think somewhere in New Mexico. Why? Are you into Christian or something?"

"No! He's a senior anyway." She turned off Main Street onto Wirt Road, not switching off the blinker as quickly as Arlo would have liked. "You should only date someone in your own grade or one away."

Is that a rule? Arlo wondered. *Is it a dating regulation, like driving with a provisional license?*

Jaycee continued: "I just wondered if he'd been in the Long Woods or not. I know he's super into Rangers, so I figured that's where he was all summer. He doesn't talk about it."

"He was doing his training for Bear. It's all really secret."

The car suddenly died. It wasn't a jolt; the engine simply went quiet. The station wagon drifted to a stop.

"What did you do?" asked Arlo.

"I didn't do anything!"

"You stalled it."

"No I didn't! I wasn't going slow enough to stall." She turned the key in the ignition. The engine *click click click*ed but refused to start.

Arlo knew something was very wrong. He had spent many winter mornings warming up the station wagon, and this was a different sound. A different problem.

That's when Arlo saw him: a man walking into the headlights' glare. He was lean and wiry, dressed in a tattered duster coat, his face turned away from the light. He held his right hand up, fingers curled.

Firecraeft, thought Arlo. *He killed the engine. The spark plugs won't ignite.*

"Stay in the car," said Arlo.

"Why?" asked Jaycee. "Who is that?"

The man slowly turned to face them. His face was haggard, his eyes sunken. He looked ten years older than when Arlo had last seen him. Still, he recognized him immediately.

It was Hadryn.

26
OLD FRIENDS

ARLO STEPPED OUT ONTO THE DARK ROAD. He left the car door open, the chime dinging over and over. "Stay inside," he warned Jaycee again.

The night air was bracingly cold, with wind stirring the treetops. Owls hooted in the distance.

Arlo avoided looking directly at the man standing ten feet in front of him.

"What are you supposed to be, anyway?" asked Hadryn. "A janitor?"

Arlo had forgotten he was wearing a costume. "An astronaut," he said. "My helmet's in the car."

"Show me." There was a smile to his voice. Almost friendly.

Arlo reached back in to retrieve it off the passenger seat. He whispered to Jaycee: "Keep trying to start it."

"Who is that?" she whispered back. There wasn't time to explain.

Arlo held up the helmet for Hadryn to see. The engine kept *click click click*ing as Jaycee turned the key.

"Put it on," said Hadryn. "Let's see the whole thing." His voice sounded older. Weaker.

Arlo reluctantly lowered the helmet over his head. Inside, everything echoed, distant and hollow. The plastic was already fogging over. He began to hyperventilate.

Hadryn still had his hand raised. "Tell your sister to throw the keys out the window."

"No," said Arlo. He suspected Hadryn had to concentrate to keep the engine from sparking. Arlo wanted to keep him occupied.

"What's that!?" Hadryn apparently couldn't hear him.

Arlo took off the helmet. "I said no."

Hadryn shrugged. "Suit yourself." He clenched his hand into a tight fist. The engine suddenly sparked, flames shooting out from under the hood. Arlo could smell rubber burning. Steel clanged as metal warped from the heat.

"Get out of the car!" shouted Arlo.

Jaycee quickly obeyed, stepping out on the far side. Hadryn released his fist. The flames kept burning, just not as intensely.

"Who are you?" Jaycee asked.

"Me? I'm an old friend of Arlo's. We go back, what, thirty years?"

"What do you want?" demanded Arlo.

"The knife, for starters. I don't know why the Eldritch let you keep it."

"I don't have it with me. It's at the house." This was true: Arlo kept the spirit knife hidden in his clarinet case, which was currently in his bedroom. "I'll take you there," he offered.

He wanted to get Hadryn away from Jaycee. Plus, the protections that Wade's friend Nacho had installed around the property might give Arlo an advantage.

"Oh, I know what you did at your house. Blood magic? Booby traps? That's not very Ranger-like of you, Arlo Finch."

"So it was your blood?"

"It was. I lost more than just that." Hadryn shed his jacket, revealing that his left arm ended at the elbow. The stump had been tied off with a tourniquet. "No more thunderclaps for me." He said it like a grim punch line.

"The Eldritch kept me shackled to the wall by this arm. They thought that would be enough to stop me."

Arlo realized then what Hadryn must have done: "You cut off your own arm."

"Of course not. I didn't have a knife. I just had my teeth." He smiled. His teeth were pointed like a crocodile's. "I sharpened them on a rock, one by one."

Arlo glanced over at Jaycee. She had one hand in the pouch of her hooded sweatshirt. *Is she on her phone?* he wondered.

Hadryn moved closer to Arlo, towering over him. He smelled foul, a combination of sweat, smoke and rotting meat. He whispered into Arlo's ear. "You're going to bring me the knife, or I'll kill your sister right here on the road. You'll never forget the sound of her screams."

The fire under the hood of the station wagon kept crackling.

Arlo considered his options. He could try to run, but Hadryn was certainly faster. He could yell for help, but the nearest house was half a mile away. *He picked this spot carefully*, Arlo realized.

And yet Hadryn was vulnerable, too. At Camp Redfeather, the Eldritch had quickly caught him once Arlo broke the leather necklace that had been keeping him cloaked. *He's shielding himself somehow*, thought Arlo. *Otherwise, they'd already be here.*

"It'll take twenty minutes to walk to my house," said Arlo. "And another twenty to get back. Someone will definitely be by and see this." He gestured at the burning car.

"You'll meet us at the Broken Bridge in half an hour. If you're not there, she's dead."

Arlo looked over at his sister. She had her arm at her waist, trying to conceal the phone in her hand, its screen glowing. Then a faint female voice said: "Nine-one-one, what's your emergency?"

Hadryn was suddenly moving. Arlo tried to block him but was easily pushed aside. Jaycee backed away, no longer trying to hide the phone.

"You really think the police can protect you?"

"No," she said. Then she held out the small can of pepper spray she always kept on her key ring. She doused Hadryn directly in the face. The liquid burned his eyes. He gasped and coughed, stumbling towards her even as she continued to spray. He finally fell to the ground, screaming as he clawed at his eyes.

The spray can now empty, Jaycee shouted: "Run!"

Ditching the helmet, Arlo ran at full speed. They headed back in the direction of town. The road sloped downhill, which made each step feel like two. Faster and faster, nearly falling, Arlo had to focus on keeping his feet in front of him to avoid tumbling.

Jaycee was right beside him. Neither one risked looking back, but they didn't hear any footsteps behind them. Coming around a curve, they could see the lights of Main Street. In less than a minute, they'd be there. They just had to keep running.

Then a hunched shape stepped out of the shadows onto the road ahead of them. Arlo and Jaycee stopped short, hearts pounding.

The figure moved into the moonlight. It was Hadryn. He was coughing and wheezing from the pepper spray.

"How did he—" asked Jaycee, too winded to finish the question. Arlo was wondering the same thing. *How could he get ahead of us?* There was no time to look for an answer.

"Come on!" Arlo led Jaycee over the edge of the road, half sliding down the slope of dirt and pine needles. They could still make it to town. Main Street wasn't far away.

Then, thirty feet ahead, Hadryn stepped out of a tree. Not from behind it, but from *within* it. The bark glowed with the outline of his body.

Treestriding. Arlo had read about it in *Culman's Bestiary.*

Forest nymphs called *dryads* could teleport between trees, crossing vast distances in seconds. Apparently Hadryn had acquired this ability as well, likely through very dark means.

Arlo moved in front of Jaycee.

Hadryn laughed. "You can't protect her, Arlo. You can't protect any of them. In the end, you'll see: it's every man for himself."

Just then, a shape sideswiped Hadryn, knocking him down. By its size and fur, it looked to be a bear, or possibly a gorilla—the details were lost in the darkness. It had Hadryn pinned on the ground, clawing at him.

Whatever this beast was, it gave Arlo and Jaycee another chance to escape. Racing through the trees, Arlo avoided the temptation to look for a way into the Long Woods. He knew Hadryn could follow them there, and they'd be in even more danger.

They scrambled up a small gully to reach the rough asphalt of Main Street. They were just out of the center of town. Headlights were coming their way.

Arlo and Jaycee both waved their arms, trying to attract the car's attention. As it came closer, they recognized the vehicle, a tow truck.

"It's Mitch!" said Jaycee.

The truck's headlights blinked, its roof lights switching on. The truck was pulling off to the side of the road.

Their mom rolled down the passenger window. She'd evidently been getting a ride home from the diner. "What's going on? Where's the car?"

"We have to go!" said Arlo. "We have to get out of here!"

"Why? What's wrong? Are you okay?"

The truck's engine suddenly died. The silence was jarring.

"What the hell?" asked Mitch, confused. He cranked the ignition, trying to restart it.

"Don't!" said Jaycee. "He'll fry the engine."

Arlo agreed. "He's here somewhere."

"Who?" asked Celeste. "Who are you talking about? Is this some kind of Halloween prank?"

From the edge of the woods, a furry shape stumbled into the light. It was the creature that had tackled Hadryn. Arlo realized now that it wasn't a bear or a gorilla. It was a Wookiee.

"Christian!" shouted Arlo. "Are you okay?"

Christian Cunningham was holding an arm across his ribs, but he didn't seem to be bleeding. His headless Chewbacca costume was ripped and tangled with broken leaves and twigs.

But it didn't add up. The creature they'd seen in the forest was much more ferocious than Christian. It wasn't simply a teenager in a costume. *Can he shape-shift?* Arlo wondered. *More important—*

"How did you know we were in trouble?"

"I didn't," said Christian. "But I could feel an aberration. You develop this sense when someone's using strong magic."

"Do you know where he is?"

Christian shook his head. "He jumped into a tree. He could be anywhere."

Celeste got out of the truck. "Seriously, someone here needs to tell me what's going on." Mitch climbed out as well, pulling a wooden baseball bat from under the seat.

"There was a guy on the road," said Jaycee. "He set the car on fire because he wanted some knife that Arlo has."

Celeste turned to Arlo. "You have a knife?"

"Not a normal knife," said Arlo. "It's magic, sort of."

"Is this the guy from summer camp?" asked Christian. "The one who tried to kill you?"

Arlo nodded. "Hadryn. The Eldritch are after him. I don't know why they can't find him."

"Wait, Arlo!" His mom turned him around to face her. "Someone tried to kill you at summer camp?"

Seeing the confusion and fear in her face, Arlo felt a pang of regret. *She has no idea*, he thought. *The hag. The Night Mare. Various trolls. Hadryn. She thinks Rangers is all just hikes and campouts.*

He took her arm, trying to reassure her. "I'm fine, Mom. I'll be fine."

"Don't lie to your mother!" The gravelly voice seemed to come from all around them.

Arlo turned to see Hadryn standing in the middle of the street. His shirt was torn open, revealing dozens of arcane symbols seared into his skin. Arlo guessed they were wards of some kind, perhaps shielding him from detection by the Eldritch. Hadryn had taken some serious damage in the fight with Christian, most noticeably a gash in his shoulder. His sleeve was soaked with dark blood.

Mitch pushed past Arlo, readying the bat. "You stay right there."

Hadryn smiled with his crocodile teeth. "Mitch Jansen, look at you, all grown up. In thirty years, I've barely thought of you. That's how little of an impression you made."

Mitch didn't recognize him. "I don't know you, fella."

"They made you forget. But you never knew much to begin with."

Then Hadryn paused, sensing something. Arlo felt it, too, and Christian. It was a sudden change in pressure, like standing in an elevator descending too fast. Their eyes went up to the sky, where strange lights began to glow within the clouds.

"NO!" shouted Hadryn. He looked down at his chest, frantically checking the various symbols on his skin. Only as he pulled back his shirt did his fingers reveal an unnoticed wound—a cut that ran right through one of the arcane glyphs.

The lights in the sky divided, then divided again.

"What is that?" asked Jaycee. "What's happening?"

"It's the Eldritch," said Arlo. "They're coming for him." In a few seconds, shadowy tentacles would reach down and pluck up Hadryn, carrying him away to the Realm.

Hadryn pointed at Arlo. "You're gonna bring me that knife. You won't have a choice."

With that, Hadryn brought his wrist to his teeth and bit through a beaded bracelet. With a sliding flash, he suddenly vanished, leaving only a dozen wooden beads bouncing and rolling on the pavement.

Arlo looked up at the clouds. With their prey gone, the expected tentacles never materialized. Instead, a shaft of emerald-green light descended on this small section of Main Street. It flooded every nook and shadow, a sparkling radiance that overwhelmed and confused all senses. It sounded like honey, felt like a rainbow and tasted like music.

While their minds were trying to understand what they were experiencing, the light was unwinding thoughts. This was how the Eldritch kept their activities in the normal world a secret: by erasing every memory of their presence.

Arlo had encountered the Eldritch light twice before and seemed better able to resist it each time. As the glow faded, he could recall most of what had happened that night. He remembered trick-or-treating, the rude woman at the real estate office, and seeing his dad at the diner. He remembered Hadryn on the road, running through the forest, and Christian's sudden rescue.

But the others? They were standing dumbstruck on the side of the road, waiting for someone to tell them what had happened, and why they were there.

Arlo turned to his mom and Mitch. "The station wagon broke down," he said. "Thanks for coming to get us."

— 27 —
FIELD TRIP

ON THE BUS TO SCHOOL THE NEXT MORNING, Arlo filled in Indra and Wu on what had happened the night before.

"Wait, you're saying Hadryn *chewed through his arm*?" asked Wu. "How do you even do that?"

"Coyotes will chew through their legs if they're caught in a trap," said Indra. "It's either that or die."

That wasn't what Wu was asking. "I mean, literally, how do you do it? You can't bite through bone. Plus, think about it: the angle would make it really tough to reach." Wu demonstrated the difficulty of gnawing on one's own elbow. Indra agreed, speculating that perhaps Hadryn had had help, or had even made up the story about sharpening his teeth to seem more menacing.

Arlo grew frustrated that his friends were focused on the

wrong things. "His arm doesn't matter! The point is, Hadryn's back and he tried to kill me last night."

"Sorry," said Wu. Indra said she was sorry, too.

"The good news is, I don't think Hadryn can shape-shift at all right now," said Arlo. "Or if he could, he'd still be missing an arm. So at least he won't be impersonating any of us. And it seems like the Eldritch can find him, which means he'll probably be hiding in the Long Woods where they can't reach him."

"So just don't go into the Long Woods," said Wu.

"For how long?" asked Indra. "Forever? Arlo's going to need to go back eventually."

Wu wasn't so sure. "Why? Most Rangers never set foot in the Long Woods. As long as he stays here, he's safe."

"He's not safe," said Indra. "He hasn't been safe for a really long time."

"She's right," said Arlo. "Even if I never went back in the Woods, bad stuff would still come after me. Think about it. First it was the wisps, then the Night Mare, then the hag. Now Hadryn. I'm tired of waiting for the next thing to come out of the Long Woods. I'm tired of running away."

"Then what do you want to do?" asked Wu. "You can't go after him."

"Why not? Either I go after him or he comes after me, and you, and my family—"

"He'll kill you!" said Indra, far too loudly. Several kids on the bus looked over at them, including Merilee. Indra lowered her volume but not her conviction: "He's too strong."

"Maybe," said Arlo. "At least if I go after him, I'll have the advantage of surprise."

"And then what?" asked Wu. "Let's say you find Hadryn. What do you do? You wouldn't kill him, because you're not a killer. That's the difference, Arlo. Hadryn doesn't care who he hurts. You do. You're good and he's evil."

Arlo shook his head. "It's not that simple."

"It is, though," said Indra. "You follow the Ranger's Vow. You have principles."

"Principles aren't going to protect my family."

"No," said Indra. "They'll protect you from becoming him."

After first period, Arlo left school on his second bus ride of the day. The band was headed on a field trip to Rockwell Elementary, nearly an hour away.

The band teacher, Mr. O'Brien, said the purpose of the concert was to give younger kids firsthand exposure to instrumental music. "They need to see that music isn't just something you play on your phone. It's something you make with your hands and with your friends."

Arlo admired Mr. O'Brien's passion for music education but wondered about the timing. With only a few weeks of practice, the band could barely get through the three pieces they'd learned so far. Arlo himself had a hard time following both the sheet music and Mr. O'Brien's waving hands as his teacher struggled to keep the band on tempo.

Still, the field trip meant that Arlo would be away from school for the rest of the day, and for that, he was grateful.

On the ride, most of the kids were playing games on their phones. Since he didn't have one, Arlo pulled out his library copy of *The Lion, the Witch and the Wardrobe*. He'd read it once before, back in Chicago. This time through, Arlo found himself paying less attention to the Pevensie children than to the native inhabitants of Narnia: the mighty lion, Aslan; the villainous White Witch; and the various fauns, giants and talking beavers. They lived in a world full of magic, yet they all seemed to be waiting around for the non-magic heroes to arrive, as had been foretold in a prophecy.

To Arlo, it felt like a lot of hope to be pinning on kids from another dimension.

An aluminum water bottle rolled along the floor. Arlo stopped it with his foot and passed it back to Russell Stokes. In addition to being a Ranger, Russell was second-chair trumpet.

"Thanks."

"No problem."

These were the most words they'd exchanged since the last day of summer camp, when Arlo had removed the parasitic grisp from Russell's shoulder. The slimy supernatural creature had slithered off into the woods, and taken with it any reason for Arlo and Russell to interact. Still, their not-talking was a vast improvement over the previous year, when Russell had never passed up an opportunity to mock and belittle "Arlo *Flinch*" in front of his Red Patrol buddies.

Arlo and Russell would never be friends, but at least they were no longer enemies. When you were used to being bullied, being ignored felt like kindness.

The concert at Rockwell Elementary went about as well as Arlo had expected. After a passable "Largo," the woodwinds got so off during "The Star-Spangled Banner" that the band had to start over. Still, the grade school students were patient and actually seemed interested as they sat on the cafetorium floor.

Merilee then performed a flute solo that was genuinely terrific, with trills and fast finger work. As she was finishing up, Arlo saw the Rockwell principal approach Mr. O'Brien and whisper something to him. It seemed urgent.

As Merilee took her bow, Mr. O'Brien addressed the students. "Unfortunately, we're going to have to cut this short today. Your principal is going to ask you all to stay put, but right now I need the band to quickly pack up your instruments so we can get back on the bus."

"What's going on?" asked Russell.

O'Brien turned his back to the audience. "Apparently there's a fire a few canyons over. They may need to close some roads, so we want to get back to school before that happens."

Arlo quickly disassembled his clarinet. He didn't swab it to get the spit out, but made a silent promise to do it on the bus.

He double-checked that the spirit knife was nestled in its proper spot and shut the case.

In less than five minutes, they were all back on the bus, headed away from Rockwell Elementary. Some of the kids were hanging their heads out the windows, trying to smell smoke.

"Uh-uh! Nope!" shouted Mr. O'Brien. "Keep the windows shut." He then turned his attention back to the bus driver, a heavyset woman wearing a straw cowboy hat. They were talking in low voices, and seemed to be discussing routes. Mr. O'Brien was consulting maps on his phone.

Russell was suddenly sitting beside Arlo. He'd snuck his way up from the back of the bus.

"You know O'Brien's a Warden, right?" he asked. "He was at the Alpine Derby. He's a firecraefter."

"I remember." Arlo hadn't known Mr. O'Brien's name back then, but had marveled at how the bearded Warden had manipulated the bonfire flames.

"I bet he can sense exactly where the fire is," said Russell.

"Like how Christian feels when there's an aberration."

"What are you talking about?"

Arlo backpedaled. "Just that Mr. O'Brien probably got his Bear when he was in Rangers. He would have learned the same things Christian learned."

The bus slowed, then stopped. Up ahead, Sheriff's Department vehicles with flashing lights were parked at the entrance to the highway.

"There!" shouted Dylan Kaddo, an eighth-grader percussionist.

He pointed to the right, where a thick cloud of gray-brown smoke was drifting around the edge of the mountain.

All the kids crowded the windows to watch. The fire itself was out of sight, but based on the amount of smoke it was generating, Arlo suspected it had to be huge. It looked like photos he'd seen of Hawaiian volcanos.

"Everyone back in your seats!" shouted O'Brien. He then stepped off the bus to talk with one of the deputies.

"Are we going to be able to get home?" asked Merilee. Arlo was wondering the same thing.

"The fire's in the opposite direction," said Russell. "We'll be fine."

Dylan Kaddo disagreed. "The fire could go over the pass. If it does, we're screwed."

For the first time, Arlo could smell smoke. It was faint, like a distant campfire, but it tickled the back of his throat.

"Look!" shouted Emma Rodriguez, first-chair clarinet.

Within the dark cloud, Arlo could make out a fan of glowing orange sparks. They looked like fireflies.

"The wind must be picking up," said Russell.

"What does that mean?" asked Merilee.

"It's not good," said Arlo.

From what he'd read in the Field Book, Arlo knew that forest fires had the same basic requirements as campfires: fuel, heat and oxygen. This fire had thousands of acres of very dry timber to burn as fuel, sparks to provide heat and wind to supply the oxygen. Unlike a campfire, there was no stone ring to hold it in. It could spread everywhere, and quickly.

Mr. O'Brien was back on the bus. "Okay, the sheriff says we can take the county road to get back to school. It's going to be bumpy in places, so we need everyone in their seats the whole time. If you understand me, say 'Yes, Mr. O'Brien!'"

Everyone echoed back, "Yes, Mr. O'Brien!"

The bus pulled forward, not onto the highway but rather a gravel access road that ran parallel to it before eventually turning deeper into the forest. Russell showed Arlo a map he'd pulled up on his phone. "This route should work. It takes us way out of the way, but we'll make it."

This road was only a little wider than the bus, with deep grooves from tire tracks. Twice they had to pull to the side to let another vehicle pass them. After twenty minutes, they didn't see any more cars. They were alone on the road, with pine trees towering over them. While glad to be away from the flames, Arlo was eager to see familiar buildings. This road felt very remote.

The brakes squealed as the bus slowly came to a stop, the engine still humming.

"Why are we stopping?" asked Russell.

Mr. O'Brien stood up. He had a puzzled expression on his face, like he was listening for a sound he couldn't quite discern. "Something's wrong."

He held out his hand, slowly rotating himself in a full circle.

Arlo was pretty sure he knew what O'Brien was doing: "He's feeling for the fire."

Russell agreed. "Something must be out there."

On a hunch, Arlo flipped open the latches on his clarinet case and reached inside for the spirit knife. His fingers wrapped around its engraved hilt, revealing the spectral blade.

He turned to the window. From deep in the forest, he saw them coming: hundreds of tiny red lights. They weren't sparks. They were spirits, burning with supernatural heat.

And they were headed right his way.

28
FIREBENDER

"GET DOWN!" SHOUTED ARLO.

He ducked low, bracing for impact. Some kids followed his lead, but most just stared out the windows in confusion. They couldn't see anything unusual. Only Arlo could, because he was holding the spirit knife.

At the front of the bus, Mr. O'Brien suddenly jerked his hand back, as if touching a hot stove. He wasn't able to see the spirits, but he could feel them.

"Everyone!" he shouted. "Down!"

The fire spirits hit the side of the bus like hailstones. *PLUNK PLUNK PLUNK PLUNK.* The blows came faster and faster, growing to a roar, a deluge of invisible strikes.

Some kids screamed. Many slid under their seats as the assault continued.

Shielding his eyes, Arlo looked up at the window, where

ghostly flames slammed against the glass, leaving scorch marks. For all their speed and heat, the fire spirits had almost no mass, no physical presence. The glass was too strong for them to shatter.

"What's happening?" asked Russell.

"Is someone shooting at us?" asked Merilee.

"They're fire spirits. Lots of them." Arlo carefully touched his hand to the metal wall. It was already heating up. *They don't have to get in*, he realized. *They can just bake us like in an oven.* He could already smell burning rubber.

Mr. O'Brien shouted at the driver. "Go! Drive!"

The bus suddenly lurched forward. Everyone screamed again. They were picking up speed, trying to get away from the spirits. It seemed to be working: the rate of the *plunks* slowed, then stopped altogether.

Arlo looked down the aisle and out the back window. The fire spirits were pursuing them like a swarm of bees, but didn't seem able to catch up. *Maybe we can get away*, he thought. And then—

BOOM! The bus swerved but stayed on the road. Arlo heard *thwapping*, like when the washing machine at home got off-balance.

"It's the tires," said Russell. "They're on fire." He pointed to the driver's side mirror. In its reflection Arlo could see orange flames clinging to the bottom of the bus.

BOOM! Another tire blew. This time, the bus slowed. A mechanical scraping sound made Arlo grit his teeth. Worse, the spirits were catching up. He could see them gaining ground.

Russell leaned over to Arlo. "Can you do something?"

"What do you mean?"

"With that knife. Can you fight them?"

"No. I can only see them."

"What about the grisp? You cut it off."

Arlo shook his head. "I cut the string binding it to you. I don't think these things are bound to anything."

They're free spirits, he thought. A grim joke.

BOOM! It was one of the front tires this time. For a heart-stopping moment, Arlo felt the entire bus pitching to the side, but the driver managed to keep it upright. They were still moving, but now not nearly as fast as the spirits chasing them.

Mr. O'Brien made his way down the aisle, rolling up his sleeves to reveal elaborate tattoos on his beefy arms.

"They're fire spirits," Arlo told O'Brien as he passed.

With a screech, another part of the bus failed. Arlo felt something heavy—*an axle? the driveshaft?*—fall away. The bus slowed, then stopped. They were dead in the middle of the gravel road.

"Everyone, keep away from the windows!" shouted Mr. O'Brien. "And don't break my concentration." He then clasped his hands, holding them above his head as he shut his eyes. He took three fast breaths like an Olympic powerlifter about to compete.

Arlo peered out the back. The spirits had nearly caught up to them.

O'Brien lowered his hands, gripping the seat backs on either side of him. His arms were vibrating from the strain.

"What's he doing?" whispered Merilee.

"Firecraefting," answered Arlo. Since the Alpine Derby, he'd wanted to see more of it. Just not like this.

The spirits arrived, but this time, rather than hitting the bus, they split into two streams. Arlo watched as the spectral flames circled the vehicle, unable to touch it. *He's keeping them back*, Arlo realized. *Like a living ward.*

O'Brien was only able to hold them a certain distance away, perhaps thirty feet. *That's why he moved to the center of the bus.*

"It's working," Arlo told Russell. "They can't touch us."

In his Elementary Spirits class, Arlo had been warned about thinking of spirits as having emotions, but these fire spirits certainly seemed angry, or at least frustrated. They slammed against the invisible barrier, determined to find a way through. With each blow, they flared brightly: tiny pops of light, like fireflies on a summer night. Apparently Arlo's bandmates could see this as well.

"What is that?" asked Dylan.

"Fireworks?" someone suggested.

"Maybe they're faeries," said Merilee. "Here to protect us."

Only Arlo could see what they truly were, and what they were doing. One by one, the spirits broke off the attack, drifting down to the yellow grass alongside the gravel road, or floating up into the dry pine needles of nearby trees. Once there, they smoldered until the material caught fire.

If they couldn't reach the bus, they'd burn everything around it. In less than a minute, flames had fully encircled the bus.

"Mr. O'Brien!" shouted a girl in the back, pointing to a flaming tree.

Their teacher didn't answer. Arlo could see sweat trickling down O'Brien's neck. The strain of keeping the spirits away was clearly exhausting him.

Russell whispered to Arlo. "I don't think he can keep it up much longer."

Arlo looked back out the window, where the flames kept growing. But the spirits themselves had disappeared. *Where did they go?* he wondered. *If they're trying to burn the bus, why don't they stay until the job's complete?* He didn't want to break his teacher's concentration, but he needed to make sure O'Brien knew—

"They're gone. The spirits, they left. Can you feel it?"

Mr. O'Brien cocked his head, as if listening for a faint voice. Arlo saw him soften his grip on the seat backs before finally letting go. He shook out his arms. His face was red and slicked with sweat.

"They could come back," Arlo warned.

O'Brien shook his head. "Once they ignite something, they become part of the fire. They're not spirits anymore." He bent down to look out the windows. It wasn't just the area right around the bus that was aflame. The inferno raged in every direction, blazing orange.

"We're trapped!" cried Dylan.

The only thing growing faster than the flames was the panic. Many kids were weeping, or trying to call their parents on their phones. No one could get a signal.

"Everybody, calm down!" shouted the bus driver unhelpfully.

"What if the gas tank blows?" asked Russell.

As if in answer, O'Brien swept his arms outward. The fire bent away from the bus, pushed by invisible forces. But then it slowly crept back in.

Despite the flames, despite their precarious situation, Arlo felt surprisingly calm. Surviving so many near-death encounters had readied him. "How long can you keep the fire back?" he asked O'Brien.

"A while. The smoke is the problem. I can't control that."

"You could clear a path off the bus. We could all go together."

O'Brien shook his head. "No guarantee we can outrun it. Where would we even go?"

"To the Long Woods."

Arlo could feel the familiar tingle: they were close to an entrance to the Woods. It was no more than five minutes away, and would presumably not be on fire. Once safely there, Arlo hoped he could lead the group back to Pine Mountain. But only if O'Brien could protect them from the fire for the first part of the journey.

"I can get us there," Arlo said. "We're not far."

Russell, who had been listening, chimed in. "He can do it, Mr. O'Brien. You can trust him."

O'Brien bent back the flames once more, then took a moment to consider his options. Ultimately, he didn't have any.

"All right!" he shouted. "Leave everything on the bus. We're getting out of here."

The rubber gaskets of the front door had fused together, so they had to evacuate out the back. Arlo and Russell helped kids climb down while O'Brien suppressed the nearby flames.

The bus driver was the last off. Behind her, windows shattered from the heat.

"Which way?" O'Brien shouted.

Arlo pointed left.

Mr. O'Brien swung his arms like he was conducting a symphony, clearing a path through the fire. Charred blades of grass glowed like just-extinguished birthday candles while tree branches swayed from the flames. It was as hot as a hair dryer and as loud as a waterfall.

O'Brien shouted over the roar. "Everyone! We're gonna keep low and stick together!" Then, to Arlo: "Lead the way."

29
INFERNO

EARLIER THAT SPRING, while watching a beetle climb on the rocks around their evening campfire, Blue Patrol had speculated about what the bug was thinking. Could it even understand what it was seeing?

"Maybe it thinks a piece of the sun fell from the sky," suggested Indra.

"Or it's a portal to a different world," said Wu.

Jonas leaned close to the beetle to see the fire from its perspective. "No. It's thinking, 'Man, if I'm not careful, I'm toast.'"

At this moment, Arlo knew exactly how that beetle felt.

He and his bandmates were like tiny insects walking through a blazing campfire. Smoke had blotted out the sun, leaving only the fire itself for light. Trees on either side of them were burning so hot that the bark exploded, sending glowing embers in all directions.

Mr. O'Brien's firecraefting could keep the flames back, but not the heat and smoke. Arlo's eyes stung. His skin was red, his throat raw. They were being broiled. Roasted.

Still he pushed forward, following his inner compass towards the Long Woods. Merilee was holding on to his belt loop. Russell had his hand on Arlo's shoulder. All twenty-five members of the middle school band were linked together for moments like this, when the wind shifted and the smoke became blinding.

"Stay low!" shouted O'Brien.

Arlo squeezed his eyes shut and bent down where the air was cooler.

We're so close, he thought. He could feel that the entrance to the Long Woods was just ahead. But where? As the smoke thinned, he saw it: the cleft base of a giant, broken tree. That opening was the way in. The way *out*.

Then Arlo saw them: four fire spirits floating near the entrance, gently bobbing and weaving.

"What is it?" said Russell.

It's a trap, Arlo realized. *They were waiting here. They want me to go into the Long Woods. This whole thing was planned.*

And who would have planned it? Who wanted Arlo to go into the Woods?

Hadryn.

Arlo searched for any other option. Any alternate route. Fire raged in every direction, a wall of flame and smoke. The only way out was through.

"We're almost there," Arlo shouted, leading the group

forward. The fire spirits parted, circling behind them. Welcoming them.

Arlo ducked down into the cleft at the base of the tree. The wood was rotted and crumbling. The space inside was so dark, he couldn't see more than a few inches ahead. He tucked the spirit knife into his pocket and began crawling blindly on his hands and knees, feeling his way deeper into the tree.

The dirt was wet and cold and smelled like rain. The space was tight—too narrow to turn around—so he had to keep moving forward. After five feet, the point where he should have reached the back of the tree, it just kept going. He was no longer in a world of normal distances. This passage could go for yards or miles and all he could do was keep crawling forward. For the second time that day he knew what it felt like to be a beetle.

Merilee was right behind him, just past his sneakers. "How far does this go?"

"Is this the Long Woods?" asked Russell, further back.

Almost, Arlo thought. The path was curving, a tight squeeze past knobby roots with whiskery tendrils. Merilee shrieked, no doubt mistaking them for bugs. Arlo could hear other kids reacting to pokes and squashed fingers. It was terrifying to be crawling in the dark, but the inferno they'd left was no better.

A few yards further on, Arlo noticed a change beginning: the dirt gradually transitioned to stone, cold and hard under his knees. In place of the tree roots, shimmering veins of silver provided some light. This was now clearly a tunnel, and he was pretty sure it was leading upwards.

He could smell salty air, clean as fresh laundry. There was a glow up ahead, and fine grains of sand sticking to his fingers. He was nearly out.

Pushing back thick leaves, Arlo Finch emerged into sunlight so bright he recoiled. But with Merilee right behind him, he had to keep moving to make room. His eyes slowly adjusted, revealing green fronds and blue sky. To his right, ocean waves gently rolled onto a pale sand beach.

"Where are we?" asked Merilee.

"I have no idea," answered Arlo. He could feel they were definitely in the Long Woods, but none of his travels had taken him to an ocean. Although he couldn't see more than this beach, he suspected this was an island.

Kids kept emerging from the tunnel, panicked and bewildered. Arlo and Merilee shepherded them away, encouraging them to sit in the shade and rest. Mr. O'Brien was the last out. He was much bigger than everyone else and had clearly had a tough time navigating the narrow passageway, resulting in many cuts and scrapes.

"Do a headcount," Mr. O'Brien said, checking his bleeding knees. "Should be twenty-five students."

Arlo counted and Merilee confirmed: everyone had made it out, including O'Brien and the bus driver. They were all filthy, covered in dirt and soot, some coughing from smoke inhalation.

Still, they had survived, and no one seemed seriously hurt. Many were fruitlessly trying to get signals on their phones, for the moment ignoring that they had somehow crawled from a mountain forest to a tropical beach.

"Guys," said Dylan, "can anyone get maps to load? It just keeps spinning."

While everyone compared phones, Mr. O'Brien pulled Arlo aside, out of earshot of the others. "Have you been here before?"

"No. I mean, I've been in the Long Woods a bunch, but never here specifically."

"Can you get us out?"

Arlo pointed. "We can go back the same way we came, but the fire will still be burning."

"Not for long. In two or three hours, it'll have burned past. We can cross back and call for help."

Arlo didn't want to wait that long. "If I scout around, I may be able to find a way to Pine Mountain."

"If you can, you should," said O'Brien. "The way the wind's blowing, that's where the fire's headed next. It could be—"

O'Brien stopped himself, but Arlo imagined he was going to say *bad* or *catastrophic*. Arlo realized he'd been so worried about saving his bandmates that he hadn't considered the danger to his town. His friends. His family.

"What about the spirits?" asked O'Brien. "You have any idea why they attacked us?"

Arlo nodded. "I think I know who sent them." He paused, tears forming at the corners of his eyes. It caught him by

182

surprise. His voice cracked. "It's my fault. None of you should be here. I'm sorry."

Mr. O'Brien took Arlo by the shoulders, which just made it worse. "None of that. You saved us out there. These kids owe their lives to you, Arlo Finch. So do I."

"You did all the firecraefting."

"Only you could get us here. And you did. We're alive thanks to you. Now the question going forward is, how much danger are we in?"

Arlo looked over at his bandmates. Some were crying, some were pacing, some were wandering down to the ocean. They had survived the fire, but had no way of knowing that this was only a temporary respite.

"The guy who's behind this, I don't think he really cares about you or them. It's me he wants. I have to do this part alone."

— 30 —
PARADISE

MR. O'BRIEN TOOK CHARGE, starting with having everyone stand in groups. Arlo recognized what he was doing—it was right out of the Ranger Field Book chapter on emergency preparedness. By assigning everyone a job, you kept them calm and focused.

The first priority was finding fresh water. O'Brien instructed the brass section to scout left along the beach. Percussion would scout right. Woodwinds were to fan out and begin searching deeper in the woods. Everyone was partnered up with a buddy—except Arlo, who had his own assignment.

Once he was out of sight of the others, he pulled the spirit knife from his pocket. What he saw next nearly made him drop it.

This tropical island was teeming with spirits. In every direction, he saw thousands of glowing shapes, as if a crazed homeowner had strung Christmas lights on every square inch of a house. Not since he'd first picked up the blade at Giant's Fist had he seen so many spirits in one place.

Arlo recognized some common classes of spirits—wind, water, tree—but most of them were unlike any he'd encountered. *Is it because it's an island?* he wondered. In biology class, they'd just started learning about Charles Darwin and his discovery of unique animals on the Galápagos Islands. Separated by an ocean, with no natural predators, those creatures had evolved into new species. *Is that what happened here,* Arlo wondered, *isolated from the rest of the Long Woods?*

He knelt down to examine a small fern, its stem spiraling in on itself. A pale green light flitted around it like a moth. The spirit landed on his fingertip with the faintest tingle. It was completely docile. It had no fear of humans.

That's when Arlo realized he hadn't seen any creatures on this island: no bugs, no crabs, no birds. Even for the Long Woods, this was strange. *Is it all spirits?* he wondered.

Setting the tiny tree spirit back on the fern, Arlo stood up to find a small cluster of fire spirits circling nearby. They seemed to be waiting for him to notice them. He waved a hand in their direction—*I see you.* They swirled faster, moving in a line, beckoning him to join them.

The last time Arlo had followed floating lights into the woods, it was two wisps attempting to lure him into a spike-filled trap.

This time, he was already in a trap. It was time to meet his trapper.

The fire spirits led Arlo deeper into the forest. A rumble of thunder announced a light rain, but not many drops made it through the dense foliage.

As Arlo emerged into a clearing, storm winds swayed the long grass. Straight ahead stood a black stone mountain—clearly a volcano, the top of its cone sheared off. A glowing ribbon of red lava curled along its slope. But the fire spirits weren't headed there. Instead, they guided Arlo to a rocky outcropping at the forest edge, where bamboo poles had been lashed together to form a rustic campsite.

Arlo noticed empty cans and brown beer bottles discarded in the grass. Near the lean-to, wafts of smoke rose from a tiny campfire.

On either side of the path, two human skulls were skewered on poles, the bones bleached by the sun. Arlo had seen skeletons in science class, but those were plaster models. These skulls had clearly belonged to actual people. They had cracks and missing teeth.

"The one on the left was Roberts," said a gravelly voice. "Never knew the other one's name. He didn't talk much."

Hadryn. From this angle, Arlo couldn't see into the lean-to, but that's where the voice was coming from.

"What is this place?" asked Arlo.

"I don't think this island has a name. Or at least, anyone who ever knew it is dead."

Arlo moved until he could see into the lean-to. Deep in the shadows, Hadryn was sitting on the bamboo platform. He had his boots off. Spirits floated around him like flies.

"It's paradise, isn't it?" Hadryn said. "Untouched and unspoiled." Then he coughed, wet and throaty. He spit something out.

"Why did you bring me here?"

"Couldn't very well come to you, could I? Eldritch would snatch me right up. So I had to send my little scouts." He gestured to the four fire spirits floating nearby. "Hope they weren't too rough."

"Why are they helping you?"

"Because I saved them. I'm their liberator." Hadryn slid forward until the sun caught half his face. His cheeks were gaunt, his eyes bulging. He was shirtless, revealing the stump of his left arm. It was swollen, possibly rotting. "You see, a few years back, some trappers—Roberts and what's-his-name there—they discovered this island. You've seen how many spirits there are. It's a gold mine. And they're unbelievably tame. They don't know to be afraid of us. You can just pick them right up."

Hadryn was holding his good arm against his side, where he'd been hurt the night before. Blood was seeping through a poultice of leaves and grass. *It's infected*, Arlo thought. *That's why he's so sick.*

"So these men, these trappers," Hadryn continued. "They

show up in Fallpath one day with spirits no one's ever seen before. Naturally, there are questions, but they're not telling anyone where they found them. Week after week, they keep coming back, bringing more and more of these strange spirits. They're making a fortune, and no one can figure out their source."

"So you followed them here," said Arlo.

"I did. And then I killed them." He said it casually, showing no compunction. "I mean, yeah, I've killed plenty of people, but this was for a noble purpose. To these spirits, I am a hero. A savior. They'll do anything for me."

"You just wanted them for yourself."

Hadryn acted offended. "I'm not a trapper, Arlo. I'm not inter-ested in money. I want to change the world, just like your dad."

Arlo felt a shiver: *How much does he know about Dad?* Arlo tried not to react, but his face had already given him away.

Hadryn smiled with his sharpened teeth. "I know you smug-gled your dad through the Long Woods, Arlo. Where are you hiding him? Do you really think you can keep him safe?"

Arlo didn't answer, fearing anything he said would reveal more.

"Look, you're protecting your old man. I'm protecting my-self. We're all just doing what we have to, right?"

It was time to change the topic. "What do you want?"

"Same as last night. Give me the knife."

"How do I know you won't just kill us all anyway?"

Hadryn half laughed. "As you can see, I'm not at my strongest."

"Then you'll have the spirits do it."

"They won't kill for me. The fire spirits, they'll burn things, sure, because that's what they do. But they won't kill, not on this island, particularly not children."

"Then why should I give you the knife?"

Hadryn leaned further forward until his face was fully in the light. "Because I'll keep coming until you give it to me. See, I have nothing to lose. No family, no friends, no possessions . . ."

"No principles," added Arlo.

Hadryn smiled again. "I have one principle: get them before they get you."

Arlo thought back to his bus ride this morning. Indra and Wu had warned him not to pursue Hadryn. *You're not a killer*, Indra had said.

But what if he was? Hadryn was right in front of him, and weak. The spirit knife wouldn't hurt him—the blade would pass right through him—but there was a machete stuck into a nearby stump. There were rocks. Even if it came to a brawl, Arlo might be able to win against a one-armed man with a serious infection.

Hadryn caught Arlo eyeing the machete. He laughed.

"Go on. Pick it up! I don't think you'll kill me, but you might get a swing in. Love to see you try."

Instead, Arlo focused on the knife in his hand. "You can already see the spirits. Why do you even want this?"

"Because for some reason the Eldritch want it. I don't know why exactly, but they're afraid of it. I want them to be afraid of me."

"If this knife is so dangerous, why did they let me keep it?"

"Maybe because they know you don't have the guts to do anything with it. Look at you. You're three feet from a machete and you're too scared to grab it."

"I'm not a killer."

"Exactly. That's why you should give me the knife. All this stuff with the Eldritch? I can end it. I can give you your life back, Arlo Finch. No one else can offer you that. I'm the only hope you've got."

Hadryn extended his hand.

"How do I know you won't just come after me once you're strong again?"

Hadryn shrugged, dropping his hand. "You don't. I mean, if I were in your situation, I probably wouldn't give me the knife, especially given our history. But I had to try. It would have been impressive if I'd talked you into it."

With that, Hadryn hunkered back into the lean-to, dark in the shadows. Their conversation was apparently finished.

Frustrated, Arlo turned and walked back down the path. He was twenty feet away when Hadryn called out: "One thing you should know, though!"

Arlo stopped. Hadryn continued: "This island, there's only one way in and out. And the spirits, they guard that entrance very closely. So if you were to look now, you'd see that the tunnel you came through, it's completely shut. And it's going to stay shut until you hand me that knife."

Arlo's heart sank. He felt stupid. *The island itself is a trap.*

"If you want to leave, if you ever want to see your family again, you've got to pay the toll."

Arlo looked at the knife in his hand. What good had it actually done him? Sure, it allowed him to see spirits and cut their bindings, but how did that help him? From the moment he'd picked it up, the spirit knife had attracted the attention of Hadryn and the Eldritch, endangering him, his friends and his family. It was as much a curse as a blessing.

That was when Arlo considered the unthinkable: *What if I just gave it to him?*

The Eldritch were desperately afraid of Hadryn getting the spirit knife, but why exactly? What were they worried he'd do? The knife wasn't a weapon in any traditional sense, and it didn't seem to have any special powers beyond seeing spirits and cutting bindings. *Are they afraid he might set spirits free, and have them as allies?* That wouldn't be the worst thing. *Maybe it's good to have your enemies fighting each other*, he thought.

And there was the more immediate concern of getting home. Hadryn claimed the spirits weren't going to kill his bandmates, but hunger and dehydration eventually would. No one was going to rescue them. It was up to Arlo. Even if he somehow found another way off this island, he knew Hadryn would keep coming after him. As long as the knife was in Arlo's possession, everyone around him was in danger.

"If I give you the knife, do you promise you'll let everyone leave the island safely? And that you'll never come back to Pine Mountain?"

191

"Oh, you have my *word*." Arlo could hear the smile in Hadryn's voice.

They both knew his promise was meaningless. Hadryn had no principles and no values. Nor did he have friends, family or allies. He was all alone, barely surviving on a hidden island in the Long Woods. In that moment, Arlo realized how pathetic and weak Hadryn was. Like a wounded predator, he was dangerous but also pitiable.

Arlo tossed the knife on the dirt in front of the lean-to, not handing it over as much as discarding it. He watched as Hadryn's good arm reached down to pick it up, his fingers caked with dried blood.

"Don't get attached," said Arlo. "I'll be taking it back."

With that, Arlo walked away.

— 31 —
ASHES

ALL THAT WAS LEFT OF THE SCHOOL BUS was a scorched metal shell. It looked impossibly hollow—windows missing, tires gone, vinyl seats melted down to the springs.

Mr. O'Brien wouldn't let the students go inside it. Instead, he and the driver retrieved backpacks and instruments, passing them out through the back door. Merilee's flute had survived, protected by its heavy case, as had Russell's trumpet. The silver keys of Arlo's clarinet had darkened, but he suspected it could be salvaged. His library copy of *The Lion, The Witch and the Wardrobe* had been almost completely destroyed, the pages flaking away.

Arlo was surprised by how many trees were still standing. They were blackened and bare, thinner branches burned away, leaving just wooden pillars. Everything was covered by a layer of fine ash. Smoke hung in the air like a veil.

No birds sang. There were no leaves left to rustle. It was cold, quiet and still.

Mr. O'Brien got through to the Sheriff's Department. Less than an hour after they'd emerged from the Long Woods, they were aboard a new school bus headed back to Havlick.

On the ride, Arlo listened as kids called their parents to let them know they were okay. None of them mentioned the tropical island or the mysterious passage that led there, which seemed like a big thing to leave out.

"What do you think happened?" he asked Merilee after she hung up. "How did we survive the fire?"

She looked at him, puzzled. "You were there."

"I know, but what do you remember?"

"We hid in the hollow of an old tree," she answered. "And then waited until the fire burned past." There was no trace of deception in her voice. She seemed to truly not remember the details of what had actually occurred and had pieced together the most plausible version of events based on the fragments that remained.

As they got off the bus at school, Arlo pulled Mr. O'Brien aside to ask what he recalled.

"Yeah, it's the Wonder," said O'Brien, keeping his voice low so the others wouldn't hear. "To be honest, I'm having a hard time keeping it all straight myself. I've got sand in my shoes and I can't figure out why. Were we at a beach somehow?"

"No, really, Mom, I'm okay! I'm fine." Arlo was calling from Jaycee's phone, plugging his other ear so he could hear better. "No one's hurt. We just got stuck in the woods for a while."

He'd found his sister in the gym, where the Red Cross had started setting up cots. They were expecting hundreds of people. His mom said that the sheriff had ordered evacuations in Pine Mountain, but now with the road closed, everyone was gathering at the elementary school. The cinderblock building was likely the safest place in town.

"Your uncle thinks he can defend the house, of course. I made him promise to call every hour, and not to do anything stupidly heroic."

Arlo wanted to ask about his dad—was he still hiding at Mitch's garage?—but stopped himself. People might be listening.

"Be careful," Arlo said. "Love you."

He handed the phone back to Jaycee, who kept talking with their mother. Indra and Wu had been waiting for Arlo to finish. They pulled him aside, making sure no one was in earshot.

"We have to do something," said Wu. "We need to get back to Pine Mountain."

Indra agreed. "You could get everyone in town out through the Long Woods."

Arlo wasn't so sure. "It's going to be hundreds of people. Even if I could get them into the Woods, getting them out isn't going to be easy. The quickest path would be at the river, but then we'd go by the Broken Bridge—"

195

"And that means the troll," said Wu. "Can you imagine trying to keep a hundred people quiet?"

Besides, Arlo had another idea. "What if we could put out the fire?"

"How?" asked Wu. "None of us know firecraefting."

"Every fire requires three things: a spark, fuel and air," said Arlo. "We can't control the spark or the fuel. But we know a spirit who can control the air."

Indra's eyes got wide. "Big Breezy! She could probably stop it."

Wu pointed out the obvious flaw: "Except she's up at Camp Redfeather. That's a hundred miles away."

"I can get us there," said Arlo. "We just have to get out of here first."

The school had initiated Code Green protocol. It was the most lenient of the three emergency drills they'd rehearsed at the start of the year.

Code Red was a full lockdown for an immediate threat, such as a shooter in the building. Students had to remain in their classrooms, sit on the floor with the lights off and doors locked. Code Blue was for less-urgent situations, like a coyote in the hallway. (That had happened twice the year before.) For these cases, students just had to remain in their classrooms until they got the all clear.

Code Green, the one they were under now, was mostly used in case of blizzards and other severe weather. No students could leave the building until their parents or guardians arrived to take them home. That meant that Arlo, Indra and Wu would be trapped at school until the road to Pine Mountain was reopened.

"It's going to be hard to sneak out," said Wu. "Everyone has to enter and leave through the front, past the sign-out table. They've got the other doors locked."

"Locked on the outside," corrected Indra. "But you can still push the bar to get out. They have to allow that for fire code. The question is, would the alarm go off?"

"I don't care if we get in trouble," said Arlo. "Just as long as we get out."

As if he sensed what they were plotting, Principal Brownlee looked over from his table near the gym doors. All three quickly averted their eyes.

"He knows we're up to something," whispered Wu.

"It doesn't help that you're whispering," Indra whispered back.

"Let's split up," suggested Arlo, also whispering. "Meet back at the drinking fountain in five minutes."

Arlo made his way into the lobby, wandering over to the trophy case. In it were dozens of awards from the past twenty years. In the 1980s, the school had evidently made it to the state championships in field hockey.

He saw a shape approaching, reflected in the glass. "What are you up to, Mr. Finch?"

It was Principal Brownlee. He'd followed Arlo out.

"Just looking at the trophies."

Brownlee crossed his arms. Arlo noticed the elbows of his

blazer jacket had worn through. "Mr. O'Brien told me about what happened on the bus. What you did."

Arlo wasn't sure what O'Brien had actually said, so he kept it noncommittal: "I did what I could to help."

"Oh, you did more than that. I talked to some of your classmates, and it sounds to me like you tried to take control of the situation. Like you thought you knew more than the teacher."

"I didn't," Arlo said.

"Cut the humble act, it's sickening. Let me make something clear, Mr. Finch. I don't want any of your help or your interference. A student's job is to take instruction. You're supposed to follow, not lead."

"Okay." Arlo wasn't trying to sound dismissive, but that's how Brownlee seemed to take it.

"The thing I can't stand about Rangers is how smug you all are. You think because you tromp around in the woods and tie your little knots, you've got it all figured out. But that's not how the real world works. In the real world, you go to school, you get a job and you contribute to society. I was in the army for six years, and do you know what I did?"

Arlo shook his head.

"I did what I was told. That's a lesson you should learn."

With that, Brownlee headed back into the gym. Indra and Wu stepped out from behind the next set of doors. They'd evidently heard everything.

"Wow, he really does not like you," said Wu.

"We think we've found a way out," said Indra. "But we'll need a distraction."

"I need you to pick a fight with Bryce."

Arlo was talking to Russell Stokes, who was sitting on the gym floor while his phone charged in a nearby outlet.

"Who the heck is Bryce?" asked Russell.

"He's a seventh grader." Arlo nodded towards Bryce, who was bouncing a tennis ball out of boredom while he listened to music on headphones. "The blond kid in the blue shirt. He's my locker partner."

Russell wasn't impressed. "I could take him."

"Don't actually hurt him. Just pick a fight. I need a distraction."

"Why?"

"Because I do. It's important."

That was enough explanation for Russell. He got up and marched over to Bryce, looming over him. Bryce looked up, confused. Russell suddenly grabbed the tennis ball and threw it across the gym. It ricocheted off the back wall.

"Why did you do that?" asked Bryce.

"Because I'm sick of your stupid face and your stupid tennis ball, *Bryyyyyce*." Russell drew out the name, making it sound whiny. Then he reached into Bryce's hair, plucking out a nonexistent bug. "Hey, everyone!" he shouted. "Bryce has lice!"

Bryce stood up and shoved Russell away. It was exactly what Russell had been hoping for.

"You think you can take me, bug boy?"

Bryce charged. Russell deflected, catching him in a headlock. Soon they were on the floor, wrestling. No actual punches were exchanged, but it caught everyone's attention. Principal Brownlee ran up to them and tried to pull them apart, but they were a pretzel of angry limbs and adrenaline.

Arlo felt a pang of guilt. As much as he disliked Bryce, it seemed unfair to pit him against another bully. Still, the distraction worked: with all eyes on the brawl, no one noticed as Arlo, Wu and Indra slipped out the side door.

They dashed down the back hallway, past the gymnastics mats and towel carts. As they reached the outside door, they found Jaycee and Benjy kissing in a quiet corner. Jaycee had her hands in Benjy's back pockets. They were evidently back together.

Jaycee pushed away from Benjy, embarrassed to have been caught kissing. "Where are you going?" she asked Arlo.

"To save Pine Mountain."

Jaycee could have told her little brother to be careful or to share his exact plan. But they were beyond all that.

"Good luck," said Jaycee. "I'll cover for you."

32

FOREST SPIRITS, HEAR ME NOW

THIS IS WHERE IT STARTED, Arlo thought.

He was standing on the shore of Redfeather Lake, at the site of the old Summerland campsite. Thirty years earlier, he'd cut Big Breezy free from Eldritch restraints. The resulting explosion had knocked down giant trees that still rested at odd angles, their exposed roots grasping for earth.

The blast had also changed the trajectory of Arlo Finch's life. It was the moment when forest spirits first became aware of him. Beneath the bark, beetles began writing *brown green eye boy lake moon fox wind knife* not as prophecy, but as history. They were recording what they'd seen: a boy with mismatched eyes had traveled across a moonlit lake with the aid of a fox and the wind. Wielding a mystical knife, the boy had done something remarkable and heroic.

Now the boy was back, but he didn't have the knife anymore.

He didn't have Fox. He wasn't here to save the wind, but to ask the wind to save Pine Mountain.

Arlo, Indra and Wu walked up to the water's edge. To the west, the sun was just touching the tops of the mountains, the long rays sparkling across the ripples in the lake. It would be dark in less than an hour.

"It's so weird to be here when it's not camp," said Wu. "I wonder if anyone's around, like Warden Mpasu."

"I'm pretty sure she's only here in the summer," said Indra. "They close the camp down in September. We could be the only people for twenty miles."

While his friends were talking, Arlo had picked up a handful of dry pine needles, slowly scattering them. They floated away on the water.

"What are you doing?" asked Wu.

"I'm trying to get her attention." At summer camp, Arlo had first encountered Big Breezy during Elementary Spirits, when he and his class had made offerings to her. Breezy enjoyed playing with things she could swirl through. Now, with no feathers or aluminum pie plates to offer, Arlo had to make do with what he had. He scooped up more pine needles, flinging them higher. They simply dropped, unswirled and unnoticed.

Wu cupped his hands around his mouth. "Hey, Breezy!" he shouted. "You here?!" His voice faintly echoed, but there was no answer. Wu shrugged. "Worth a shot."

"Maybe we should go up to Coral Rock," suggested Indra. "That's where you did the original offering, right?"

"It'll be dark before we get there," said Wu.

Arlo looked across the water to the rocky island known as Giant's Fist. While he'd first met Big Breezy atop Coral Rock, she then scooped him up and carried him to Giant's Fist. The island was clearly important to her—and it was close. He began taking off his shoes and socks.

"What are you doing?" asked Indra, concerned.

Wu realized where Arlo was headed. "You're not seriously going to swim out there. The lake is cold in summer. It's going to be absolutely freezing now."

"We can find a canoe," said Indra. "They're probably locked up at the Lake Center. We can break a lock if we have to."

Arlo was already wading into the water. "There's no time. Either this works or it doesn't." He unzipped his jacket, throwing it back to Indra. Then he leaned forward into the water and began to swim.

Indra turned to Wu, exasperated. "When did he get so stubborn?"

"This summer, when you and I were fighting."

She nodded. He was probably right.

Arlo's strokes were strong and steady, but his kicking was another matter. He'd kept his jeans on, figuring they'd help him stay warm, but instead they weighed him down. After twenty yards, he gave up trying to kick, instead fluttering his feet. He thought of videos he'd seen of swimmers crossing the English Channel, or under frozen lakes. If they could do it, he could do it. He tried to keep his mind anywhere but inside his body, which was cold and heavy and straining for oxygen.

He could see Giant's Fist ahead. How far had he gone? Half-way? Less than halfway? He worried that if he stopped to check he wouldn't be able to start again.

Taking a breath, he swallowed some water by accident. He coughed, trying to maintain his strokes. Trying to stay on the surface. Trying to keep moving forward and not . . .

Under. He was surprised to find himself swimming upwards, fighting to keep his head above water. Through clogged ears, he heard someone shouting his name. His heart was pounding.

Treading water, he looked towards Giant's Fist. It was still a considerable distance away. He looked back to shore. Indra was yelling. Wu was stripping off his shoes. Arlo waved back that he was okay.

And then he was underwater again. It happened so quickly that it caught him by surprise. His eyes were wide open. He wasn't even trying to swim. He was sinking, pulled down by the cold and gravity. This was no mystical force. It was simply exhaustion.

Above him, sunlight glowed green. Below him was darkness. *Drowning*, he thought. *I'm drowning!*

He worried about Wu coming to save him. From the Field Book, he'd learned how careful you had to be when trying to rescue a drowning person. In desperation, the drowning person could cling too tightly and drown you as well. Arlo vowed that he wouldn't drown Wu. He would go limp, or help as best he could, but he wouldn't be a burden. *An anchor.*

His mind flashed to the anchor in front of Pine Mountain Elementary. *Why would a school a thousand miles from the ocean have an anchor?*

He thought of the freezer at home, and the rocky road ice cream his mom had bought him last week. *Why think of that?* he wondered. *Is it because I'm freezing?*

More than anything, this experience reminded Arlo of those last moments before sleep, when his mind flittered from idea to idea, never really landing.

The cold began to wrap around him like an icy serpent. *No*, he realized. *Many serpents.* He could feel them writhing, grasping, churning. They were squeezing the life from him.

Suddenly, he was thrust straight upwards. He shot out of the water like a cannonball.

Looking down past his shriveled white feet, he saw the lake swirling. *Water spirits.* They had pulled him up from the depths. But why wasn't he falling? How was he being held twenty feet up?

He pushed his trembling hand against the air. The air pushed back. *Hello.*

⬤

"How do you tell Big Breezy we want her to come with us?" asked Wu.

Arlo was standing on the shore, putting his jacket back on. Like a giant fan, Big Breezy had mostly dried him off, but he was still shaking from the cold. Indra had to zip him up.

Without the spirit knife, Arlo couldn't see Breezy, but it was obvious she was here. Branches swayed. Hair swirled.

Arlo spoke loudly and slowly, as if talking to someone who didn't speak English, incorporating a lot of hand gestures. "*We* want *you* to *come with us.*"

Branches kept swaying. Hair kept swirling. There was no sign Big Breezy understood what Arlo was requesting.

"Where's Fox?" asked Indra. "He could probably talk to her."

"How do you get ahold of him?" asked Wu.

Arlo shrugged. "I don't. He just shows up. Last time I saw him was when he took us to Fallpath."

"That was weeks ago," said Wu. "Months, actually." He paused a moment before asking, "Are you sure Fox is okay? There was that woman in Fallpath who smelled him on you. She could have—"

"I don't know!" Arlo hadn't meant to shout, but the exhaustion and frustration were getting to him. "I don't know where Fox is! I don't know if he's okay or how I would even find out. Right now, we just need to get Big Breezy to come to Pine Mountain, and I don't know how we're going to do that. I didn't really have a plan for this part. I'm sorry."

Indra and Wu backed off, giving Arlo some space.

"Okay," said Indra. "Let's think through it. If Breezy were a dog, how would you tell her? I mean, I know she's not an animal, but she is intelligent. There's got to be a way for her to understand."

Wu continued her thought. "We basically just need her to come with us. For a dog, you whistle and slap your leg. It helps if you have a treat, like peanut butter. But not peanut butter here, obviously. Because of the howlers. That would be bad."

Arlo leaned his forehead against a tree. He was too tired to think and too cold to move.

Brown green eye boy lake moon fox wind knife. Those were the symbols that had been written under the bark. Indra had discovered them while working on her Pinereading patch. She had done a charcoal rubbing in her notebook, then showed it to Arlo.

"How does pinereading work?" he asked, not looking up from the tree. "Can you speak it, like Spanish or Chinese?"

"No," said Indra. "I don't think there is a spoken version. It's just symbols, like hieroglyphics."

"Do you just look it up in a book?"

"Basically, yeah," said Indra. "It's called the Pine Log. It's a list of all the known glyphs."

Arlo turned to face them. "Is there a Pine Log here at camp?"

"Sure. At the dining hall, and also the Nature Center."

Wu sensed they were headed out for a hike. "We better hurry before it gets dark."

Indra stopped them. "Arlo, if you need a Pine Log, I can get it on my phone. It's just a web page with a list and pictures. There's nothing special about the printed book."

It took Arlo a moment to process what she'd said. Indra already had her phone out and was tapping away.

"Can you get service?" asked Wu.

"One bar, but it's loading." A few seconds later, she showed them the screen. The website looked very old, with minimal formatting and borders around all the images.

"Look up the symbol for fire," Arlo said.

It took some scrolling, but Indra found it: two parallel lines crossing an arc.

"It looks like a camel sneaking under a fence," said Wu.

"Help me draw it," Arlo said. "Big. On the ground."

Digging with their heels, the trio scratched back dirt and pine needles to form a close approximation of the symbol on the screen. Then they stood back. Arlo pointed to the ground, hoping Big Breezy would pay attention.

Then, a rustling. Dead leaves flittered up from the ground, tumbling and falling, tumbling and falling, in a seemingly random pattern. Wu was the first to recognize what Big Breezy was doing.

"Flames!" he shouted. "She's trying to show flames. She understands."

Indeed, it even sounded like the crackling of a campfire. Arlo turned to Indra. "Now look up *come*, or *follow*."

Indra searched and scrolled. Meanwhile, Big Breezy kept making the dead-leaf flames.

"There's no symbol for *come* or *follow*," she said. "There basically aren't any verbs. It's all nouns."

"What about *help*?" suggested Wu.

"That's a verb."

"It's also a noun," said Wu under his breath.

"It's not in here, anyway."

Arlo racked his brain, trying to think of some way to describe what he needed with only nouns. *Journey? Forest? Battle? Please?*

"What about *home*?" he asked.

Indra scrolled and scrolled. "Yes!" She showed them the image.

"It looks like a tent," said Wu. "Or an A for Arlo."

With their feet, they quickly scrubbed away the symbol for fire. Then they drew *home*, being careful that none of the old lines got confused with the new.

When they were finished, Big Breezy dropped the fake flame leaves. Although Arlo couldn't see her, he sensed she was reading the new symbol, trying to understand what they meant by it.

After a few moments, he felt the wind rush through his hair. Another blast poked his chest.

"Yes," he said. "My home. There's a fire at my home. I need your help."

The dead leaves began swirling in a tiny tornado no taller than they were. It seemed to be waiting.

"What do you think that means?" asked Wu.

Arlo smiled. "It means yes. She's coming with us."

33

THE LAST STAND OF WADE BELLMAN

NO ONE TOLD WADE BELLMAN HOW TO DRESS, what to say or when to leave.

All a man has is his autonomy. He'd read that sentence in a sci-fi book as a teenager and it resonated with him. *Autonomy* meant independence, self-determination and freedom from being controlled. He'd lost the book—it wasn't very good anyway, a lazy Asimov knockoff—but had held on to that phrase. He wrote it on his arm with a Bic pen and vowed to get it as a tattoo when he turned eighteen.

When that day finally came, the saying had ended up being too long and too expensive to make into a tattoo, so Wade had simplified it to a two-word Latin phrase: *Ego sum.* It translated to "I am myself."

Most people weren't themselves. They were trying to be someone for someone else. Not Wade Bellman. He had been himself his whole life, and had done what suited him. He wasn't about to change just because some sheriff's deputy said it was a "mandatory" evacuation, that he "had to" leave because this house was "definitely" in the fire's path.

Wade Bellman was going to stay and fight.

For the past four hours, he had been alternating between the chain saw and the garden hose. He felled trees, cleared brush and kept the roofs of both the house and his workshop wet. As winds sent glowing embers onto the property, he ran to extinguish each one before it could catch.

When the smoke grew thicker, he put on his respirator and goggles, the same equipment he used for firing glazes on his more elaborate taxidermy projects. He had considered loading up his truck with some of his works-in-progress, just in case the workshop burned. But that felt like giving up, and besides, it was past that point now. The flames were close. If he let down his guard for even a minute, both the house and the workshop could burn.

He'd promised his sister that he wouldn't be a hero. But saving your home and your life's work wasn't heroic. It was just what you did if you were Wade Bellman.

As night fell, the fire became easy to spot: an orange wall quickly approaching from the east. Wade still rushed to stomp out cinders, but now the flames were close enough that he worried they could leap to the buildings directly. The garden hose, as anemic as the flow was, seemed like his best option. He climbed the stepladder to spray down the roof of the workshop again.

The winds shifted, and suddenly the smoke became so thick he couldn't see the house. It was all lost in an orange haze. He carefully made his way back down the ladder, like an astronaut climbing out of a lunar lander, hearing each breath he took.

He could feel the heat on his skin. He sprayed himself down, tucking the hose under his arm as he folded the ladder. The house was only fifty feet away—he'd walked this path thousands of times—yet he was suddenly unsure if he was headed in the right direction. The flames, which should have been on his left, were also now in front of him.

Now, he was confused. Dizzy. Was it oxygen deprivation?

As the water splashed down his jeans, he realized how he could find his way to the house: the hose. It was attached to the spigot by the laundry room door. Still carrying the stepladder, Wade followed the hose until he'd reached the brick wall.

He unfolded the stepladder and carefully climbed. The air grew hotter with each foot he gained in elevation. Then he saw why: the roof was on fire. Flames curled along the edges of the wooden shingles, snaking along the seams. Wade sprayed them with the hose, but some were beyond the water's reach. So he climbed up onto the roof. He knew it was risky and foolish, but it was that or watch it burn.

The wind shifted again, sending smoke in the opposite direction. As the air cleared, Wade could see the workshop again, where a single glowing cinder had landed on the roof. He held his breath, waiting to see if it would die out or catch fire. *Please please please*, he whispered.

The ember smoldered, dimmed and then flared as true flames took hold. Both buildings were now on fire. Wade Bellman had to choose: save his house or save his workshop. One structure was the only home he'd ever known. The other was his refuge and sanctuary, the place where he made his art and his living.

He could picture every item in his workshop: every tool, every sketch, every bit of junk he had gathered knowing that they would become a piece of his art one day. There was a road-killed raccoon he'd collected just that morning, and commissions that were months overdue, with customers in New York and Dubai waiting. The workshop held twenty years of his past, and most of his future.

Wade Bellman chose to save the house instead. It was where he lived with his sister, his niece and nephew. It was his home.

He kept the roof wet, climbing up and down the ladder to extinguish smaller blazes at the base. He cursed the cinders and raged at the flames, but he never stopped. Only once did he look over to see the workshop fully engulfed. It was horrifying and beautiful, a radiant shimmer in the smoky night. He stared long enough to remember it, like the face of a friend he would never see again.

The fire was beginning to encircle the house, and now Wade wondered if he had ever really had a choice between the two buildings. They were both going to burn, and in all likelihood he was going to burn with them.

A shingle slid under his boot. Wade slipped, rolled and fell off the roof, dropping ten feet onto his back. It knocked the wind out of him, and the fight. It was cooler here on the ground. Wade pulled off his goggles and stared up at the sky, which held no stars but only embers, shooting past like comets.

He was going to die here. He had been a fool to stay. But he was Wade Bellman, and he was himself. *Ego sum.*

"Uncle Wade!"

It was a faint voice. Distant. A smoke-induced hallucination.

"Uncle Wade!"

But there it was again. It sounded like his nephew, but Wade knew he was safe in Havlick. Still, just in case . . .

"Arlo?" The respirator swallowed the sound. Wade sat up on his elbows, pulling down the mask. "Arlo?!" he shouted.

"Where are you!?" shouted Arlo.

"Near the porch!"

Wade Bellman sat up fully as the smoke parted and his nephew approached, flanked by his two friends: the girl with the curly hair and the other kid. (He had never bothered learning their names.)

As they approached, strong winds blew the smoke and fire away from the house, pushing the flames back into the areas they had already burned. With surgical precision, the wind snuffed the burning sections of the roof until everything was dark.

Arlo and his friends helped Wade up. "Are you okay?" they asked.

Every part of his body hurt, but he could walk, and he was alive. He watched as the wind continued to drive the flames back from the house, like a supercharged leaf blower. "How are you doing this?" he asked.

"It's an air spirit," said the girl. "Big Breezy, from Camp Redfeather."

"I saved her when we were kids," said Arlo. "You were there."

Wade nodded, although he didn't truly remember or understand. Still, he knew his nephew was remarkable. He'd known that since the day he showed up in Pine Mountain.

⬤•⬤•⬤

From Signal Rock, they could look out over the valley and see nearly all of the town.

Fires dotted the mountainside, glowing lights amid the darkness. On Main Street, several storefronts were burning, along with the church. As they watched, its steeple fell in a crash of flames. Arlo imagined the quartermaster's supply room with Blue Patrol's tents and gear. Everything would be destroyed.

This is my fault, he thought. *Hadryn said he'd hurt my friends, my family, everyone I care about. I should have stopped him.*

Three fire trucks were parked in front of the school, their lights strobing. The building seemed undamaged, with no sign of flames.

"Your mom's gonna be fine," said Wade. "She's probably taking care of a lot of folks, keeping 'em calm."

"What about Mitch's garage?" asked Arlo. "Do you think it's . . ." He trailed off. Indra and Wu still didn't know that his dad was hiding there.

"I'm sure it's fine," said Wade, but his tone wasn't convincing.

Arlo wondered if Big Breezy was powerful enough to fight the fire. Her winds had driven the flames away from his house, but could they really protect the entire valley?

Then, a deep rumble shook them. It seemed to come from all directions, a teeth-chattering quake. Lightning arced across the sky, so bright they had to squint. The resulting thunder was even louder. Was it some kind of freak firestorm?

"Is that Big Breezy?" asked Indra.

"I don't know," said Arlo. "She's never done that before."

"Unless . . ." said Wu, not quite sure how to finish the thought. "Arlo, remember back in the desert?"

"What desert?" asked Indra.

"When we were coming back from China," explained Wu, "we found this ship in a sand dune and a spirit cage. Arlo cut it open and the spirit inside was some kind of storm."

"Why didn't you tell me this before?!"

"A lot happened!"

Rain began to fall. The first drops smeared the soot on Arlo's blackened hands as he rubbed them together, disbelieving. He thought back to that night in the dunes and the spirit he'd unleashed. It had swirled together with the wind to form a storm. *What if it's still mixed together?* he wondered.

Arlo was used to thinking of spirits as individual beings, like animals or people, but it was clearly more complicated. Fox was a fox, but he said he was also all the foxes. From what Arlo had learned in the Ranger Field Book, plants often worked this way; an aspen grove was often a single organism, its shared roots forming new trees. The same thing happened with Japanese knotweed and dozens of other species.

So was this the same spirit he'd set free? Maybe that was the wrong question. But Arlo felt certain this storm's arrival was a result of his actions. He'd freed a spirit, and now a storm spirit was helping him. It was all connected.

Suddenly, the heavens opened and an absolute deluge began. It was like trying to stand in a car wash. Indra laughed at how intense it was. Wu cheered.

The thunderstorm seemed to fill the entire valley. Even as they watched, distant fires dimmed, drenched by the downpour.

As the rain slowed, Wade sat down on the rock beside Arlo. "Did you do this?"

Arlo was exhausted and exhilarated. Smiling. "I guess. Kinda."

"Well done, kid. Proud of you."

"I'm sorry about your workshop. I wish I could have saved it."

Wade waved it off. But Arlo knew what a loss it was: "Everything you had was in there."

Wade shrugged. "Those were just things. They come and go. All a man has is his autonomy."

Arlo nodded like he understood, but then admitted: "I don't know what that means."

"It's an excuse for being stubborn, I guess. Bullheaded." Wade stopped to wipe the water out of his eyes. Arlo couldn't be sure, but he suspected there were tears mixed in with the rain.

"You coming here, with your mom and your sister, it changed me," said Wade. "For the better, I hope. I dunno. Truth is, I have more than my autonomy. I have you all. And that's more than I ever thought I'd get."

Arlo hugged his uncle. Along with Indra and Wu, they watched as the fires surrounding Pine Mountain went dark.

— 34 —
THANKSGIVING

AS MORNING ROSE OVER THE VALLEY, the fire's toll became evident. No one had died or been seriously hurt, but the blaze had reshaped Pine Mountain forever. Not since the Big Stevens River flooded a century earlier had the town been so transformed.

In addition to the church, forty other buildings had been destroyed. Eleven families had lost their homes. Five stores along Main Street had burned to the ground, including Peterson Hardware and the real estate office.

The road in and out of the valley was closed. The bridge had been damaged by the sudden deluge that quenched the fire. Meteorologists were at a loss to explain how the freak thunderstorm had arisen so quickly, but most residents were happy to leave the mystery unsolved.

"Miracles don't need answers," said Mrs. Fitzrandolph. While her house had burned down, her Scottie dogs had survived, and now wore fire department bandanas. They were the official mascots of the emergency shelter at the elementary school.

Parked beside the Pine Valley Garage, the Finch family station wagon had been awaiting repairs when the fire came. The flames had burned or melted everything but the steel. Even the antenna had twisted and curled.

"This car saw us through a lot," said their mom. "Philadelphia, Chicago. Hauling a trailer across the country. Sliding off the road . . ."

Arlo smiled, remembering the previous winter, when they'd gotten stuck sideways in a ditch. It felt like a lifetime ago.

"Rest in peace, little wagon," she said, tapping it with her hand. Arlo did the same.

The fire had come within ten feet of Mitch's garage when the storm stopped it. Arlo's dad had cleared out long before then. Wearing a smoke mask and baseball cap, he had joined Mitch in helping evacuate families around the valley. Arlo worried that someone might have noticed him. "Didn't anyone ask who you were?"

"I guess they just assumed I was a friend of Mitch's," he said. "Everyone was so panicked, I don't think they paid attention."

Clark Finch was now safely back in his little hidden room behind Mitch's office. Arlo had only told his parents the bare minimum about his very long day, omitting Hadryn, the unnamed island and nearly drowning at Camp Redfeather. It was enough to say that the storm spirit he'd rescued had returned the favor.

"No one in this town is ever going to know what you did for them," said his dad. "Anyone can play the hero when there's an audience, when there's glory to be had. The real heroes are the ones who take risks when there's no reward for it other than doing the right thing."

Although the fires were out, there was still a lot to do. With school canceled for the day, the Pine Mountain Rangers went door-to-door to help families with whatever they needed. Blue Patrol delivered food, repaired fences, washed sooty windows and rounded up runaway chickens. Julie was especially good at coaxing them out of their hiding places.

Arlo was happy to see the patrol's newest members, Sarah and Wyatt, so eager to help. They'd never even been on a campout, but already seemed fully part of the group. While the patrol mopped the bathrooms at the elementary school, Arlo taught them his tricks for learning the Ranger's Vow. "First, focus on the rhymes. Second, you have to think about what the words actually mean. You shouldn't just plow through it without understanding what you're saying."

At sunset on the first night after the fire, nearly the entire town gathered on Main Street to cheer the firefighters. Buildings were missing and families were displaced, but Pine Mountain was still standing.

"Figure it's better than sitting around feeling sorry for myself." That was Wade's explanation for why he was accepting an invitation to join an artists' colony in Louisville, Kentucky. "These people'll probably regret asking once they meet me. I'm not the easiest person to get along with."

Arlo and Jaycee looked through the printed pages from the colony's website, and it honestly seemed like the perfect place for their uncle now that his workshop had been destroyed. The other artists had wild beards and beaded skirts, piercings and tattoos. Some were in their twenties, but many were older than Wade. He would have his own cabin and studio, with all meals provided.

Wade announced his decision at breakfast a few days after the fire. By that afternoon, he was gone. He left without saying goodbye. His friend Nacho had driven him to the bus terminal in Denver; Wade had never flown and didn't intend to start now. He'd left the keys to his truck with instructions not to let Mitch mess with the transmission. At least they'd have a car.

That night, Arlo found a cassette waiting for him on his bed. It was a mixtape. The handwritten liner listed fourteen tracks, including most of Wade's punk rock favorites. Arlo sat in Wade's truck and listened to the whole thing in one sitting, then played it again.

The next three weeks passed in a blur of homework and Ranger meetings. The fire had upended all the normal routines. While Arlo was still concerned about his father, and the possibility of Hadryn's return, the days were too busy to let those sparks of worry catch flame.

With the church destroyed, Pine Mountain Company was now meeting in a barn on Russell and Wyatt's family's property, where piglets interrupted patrol planning. At school, normal hierarchies and animosities were temporarily suspended. Arlo's locker partner, Bryce, kept his books on his own shelf and didn't slam the door while Arlo was waiting. It was really the bare minimum of decency, but tremendous progress from a few weeks earlier.

Principal Brownlee said nothing about Arlo, Indra and Wu violating lockdown on the day of the fire. "We're alive, and our parents didn't complain," pointed out Wu. "He probably figures it's better to just ignore it."

Arlo managed to get a twenty-eight out of thirty on his Spanish quiz. When the papers came back, Merilee asked Arlo to help her study for the next one. He agreed, even though he could see she'd gotten the same score.

"She's obviously trying to ask you out," explained Indra. "Do you *like* her?"

Arlo wasn't sure. He certainly didn't want to kiss Merilee or hold her hand. But he found her fifty percent less annoying than he had at the start of the year, which was puzzling, because her actual behavior hadn't changed that much. The situation reminded him of the ongoing drama between Jaycee and Benjy, who were now officially a couple again for no apparent reason. Perhaps *liking someone* mostly came down to finding something endearing about their obvious flaws.

Thanksgiving arrived with the first dusting of snow, just enough to cling to the branches. Arlo and Jaycee helped make dinner: turkey, potatoes, stuffing, green beans, rolls and cranberry sauce from a can. At just after five in the evening, Mitch arrived with a new water heater in its box and, with Arlo's help, he dollied it into the house. Once the curtains were shut, Jaycee cut through the packing tape, opening the flaps to reveal their dad.

For just one night, they could have dinner as a family.

As they sat down at the table, Arlo's mom raised her glass for a toast. "Before we start, I want to thank Mitch for everything he's done for us, and the incredible risks he's taken. We are truly grateful." Mitch smiled and nodded as she continued: "Clark, thank you for coming home, and for reminding us that you never really left. You've been part of this family the whole time.

"Jaycee, thank you for always being yourself and keeping us honest."

"Can I have wine?" asked Jaycee.

"Absolutely not, but thank you for asking." Arlo's mom turned to him. "And Arlo, thank you for bringing this family back together. I can't pretend to understand how you did it, or how this is all even possible, but today isn't about that. It's about giving thanks. So thank you all. Let's remember how lucky we are."

Arlo clinked glasses with everyone at the table and ate until he was well past full.

— 35 —
THE BELL

A BELL WAS RINGING. It wasn't his alarm clock. It wasn't the doorbell. The sound was high and tinkling, like a wind chime, but frantic.

Rolling over in bed, Arlo looked out his window. The sky was purple, just a few stars left. Nearly dawn, but what time exactly? He glanced over at his clock. The screen was dark, showing no digital numbers. Odd.

Arlo sat up, listening to the bell. It was coming from outdoors. *You're dreaming*, he thought. *Or something like it.* He remembered back to the first time he'd seen Rielle reflected in this same window. Was this one of those moments? Would he soon meet up with her in a strange middle place, not entirely real and not entirely imagined?

Except that everything seemed so normal. He could hear the

radiator burbling and feel the texture of his flannel sheets. The only thing strange was the bell. And the clock.

Arlo got out of bed and stepped to the window, looking out over the yard. He saw nothing unusual. Lifting the sash, he leaned out. The air outside was cold and still. The bell was quite a bit louder. *What could it be?* he wondered. And then he remembered: *The wards.* Wade's friend Nacho had set mystical alarms around the property. Some were matched to Hadryn's blood, while others just detected strangers. If a bell was ringing, it meant someone was here.

Hadryn, thought Arlo, with a sudden shiver. *Who else would it be?*

Arlo stared at the dark edge of the tree line. There was movement, shadows within shadows. Someone was out there. If he could see them, could they see him? Had they spotted him opening his window?

He slowly backed towards the door, feeling for the doorknob. He stepped into the hallway. It was darker than he had expected. *The night-light*, he realized. There was usually a night-light by the stairs so they could find their way to the bathroom.

Jaycee opened her door, groggy. "Who's ringing that bell?"

"It's a ward," Arlo whispered.

"Whose award? What are you saying?"

"It's Hadryn. He's back." Before Arlo could stop her, Jaycee flicked the light switch. It clicked, but nothing came on. The power was out.

228

At the end of the hall, their mom opened her door. "Do you guys hear a bell?"

Just then, a crash of wood from downstairs. And another. The front and back doors were being smashed down. At the stairwell, beams of light traced across the wall.

"FBI!" shouted a man's voice. "Stay where you are! Do not move!"

Arlo took his sister's hand. Without a word, they got on their knees, then lay facedown side by side on the hallway carpet, arms outstretched, fingers spread. They had practiced this, too.

Arlo lifted his head and looked back at his mom. He could see her dim silhouette as she got down on the floor.

"Remember: Don't fight!" she said. "Don't resist. We're gonna be fine."

Arlo put his face back down on the carpet. It smelled like dust and wool. He heard heavy boots climbing the stairs and the squawk of walkie-talkies. He wondered how many agents there were. A dozen? More?

"Can you do something?" Jaycee whispered.

Arlo didn't answer. He didn't *have* an answer. He had faced monsters and murderers, but this was a different class of foe. It couldn't be outsmarted or outrun.

A rubber-gloved hand pulled one arm behind his back, and then the other. A plastic zip tie cinched tight around Arlo's wrists.

There was no secret to discover, no knaught to tie, no spirit to offer advice. This was the ordinary world, and Arlo Finch had no idea what to do next.

36
INTERROGATION

"I WOULD LIKE TO SPEAK to my attorney."

Arlo said it clearly and carefully. *Don't sound angry,* he thought. *Or afraid.*

The man nodded. "She's busy with your dad, so it's going to be a bit." He shut the door and sat down across from Arlo at the table. He sighed, as if relieved to finally be off his feet. He set down a cup of coffee and a thick file folder.

It was the agent who had interviewed Arlo at school. Heavyset, with tiny veins showing in his eyes. Arlo had kept the man's business card, but didn't remember his—

"I'm Agent Sanders," said the man. "You and I talked about Rangers a while back." Arlo nodded. "Your wrists okay? Those zip ties, they can bite."

Arlo looked at his wrists. He could see only the faintest red marks. The zip ties hadn't been on for long. The arresting officers had cut them off Arlo and Jaycee in the van. He presumed it was because they were minors; their mom and Mitch had their hands bound throughout the ride to Fort Collins.

In the parking garage of this nondescript office building, Arlo had finally seen his dad. They'd moved him in a separate van, escorted by a rifle-wielding agent. His father looked pale. He had smiled at his family but didn't say anything.

Arlo had been in this small room for nearly an hour now. They'd offered him a soda and Oreos, which were still sitting on the table, untouched.

"May I?" asked Sanders, pointing to the cookies. Arlo shrugged.

Sanders picked up an Oreo and twisted the two sides apart. He didn't get a clean break. Icing clung to both pieces.

"That's bad luck," said Sanders. "Least that's what we said in Indiana growing up. Don't know if that's a thing here. Or a thing now." He ate both halves of the cookie, washing them down with coffee.

"Look, Arlo, I'm not expecting you to answer any questions until your lawyer's in here. That's your right. But I figure you might have some questions for me. So if I can answer anything, I will. I promise I will be as honest with you as I can, and that this conversation is not being recorded. This is just between us."

Arlo didn't answer. He looked at the cookies, the wall, the window. He found it very hard not to look at the man sitting directly across from him. So instead he focused on a tiny splinter in the heel of his right hand. It was painless but deep, a dark speck well below where he could scrape with his fingernail. He'd had it for weeks—at least since the day of the fire.

After nearly a minute, when Sanders was mid-sip of his coffee, Arlo finally asked: "How did you find my dad?"

Sanders seemed to have anticipated that this would be the first question. "On the night of the fire, someone in town thought they recognized him, and called it in. They said your dad was helping Mitch Jansen evacuate people. So we started following Mr. Jansen. Ultimately, it was a thermal camera that let us discover where he was hiding."

Arlo could envision a glowing human shape inside the dark garage as his dad did his nightly calisthenics.

Sanders continued: "You might wonder, then, why we came to your house this morning and busted down the doors. We had to make sure there weren't any devices or government secrets he had hidden there. It's standard procedure, strictly to preserve evidence. Nothing personal."

Arlo considered Sanders's explanation. Something didn't make sense. They had Clark Finch in custody. They already had all of his equipment. *So why does he want to talk to me?* Arlo suspected the answer was inside the folder on the desk.

Sanders followed Arlo's gaze. Smiled. "All right, yeah. I guess it is a little personal."

He opened the folder, pulling out the same grainy photo he had shown Arlo the last time. It was Hadryn staring straight ahead, evidently looking into a security camera. Even on paper, his wicked smile made Arlo shiver.

"His name is Alva Hadryn Thomas," said Sanders. "We know he was born in Texas. Went through Rangers. Joined the Marines, left the Marines, traveled the world. He's a dangerous man. He's killed people, stolen things. But he doesn't seem particularly interested in money." Sanders looked Arlo in the eye. "Mostly he seems interested in you. What we don't know is why, or why he came to visit you in Pine Mountain last summer. What business does he have with a twelve-year-old boy?"

"I'm thirteen," said Arlo.

"I apologize. What business does this man have with a *thirteen*-year-old boy?"

Arlo shrugged. He wasn't going to answer.

Sanders nodded. "I get it. You want to speak to your attorney. I understand." He tucked the photo back into the folder. "The thing is, I don't think you want her to hear any of this. Because it wouldn't make sense, would it? She'd think you're crazy. Because it is crazy. We know it has something to do with an explosion at a summer camp thirty years ago. This guy Hadryn, he's been trying to find you for decades. And it turns out, he's not just a fugitive in *our* world. The Eldritch, they're looking for him, too."

Arlo tried not to react to *Eldritch*. He failed, and both of them knew it. Leaning forward, Arlo asked in a low voice, "What do you know about them?"

"Not much. It's all classified, but it's there. These Eldritch, they can do all the green-light stuff they want, erasing people's memories, but people have cameras now. You can shoot video on your phone. You're too young to remember this, but back when I was a kid, there was all this talk of UFOs and aliens. Visitors from another world. You don't hear that much these days because the Eldritch don't come nearly as often as they used to. Ancient people, they used to think the Eldritch were gods flying on magical chariots. From what I hear, that's not altogether wrong."

"They're not gods," said Arlo.

"You've seen them?"

Arlo nodded. "They use machines. They're just different from ours."

"Have you been to their world?"

Arlo stopped himself before answering. "You said I could ask the questions."

"Apologies. Ask away."

"You said the Eldritch were looking for Hadryn. How would you know that? Do people in the government talk to them?"

"Not directly. We have informal channels. People in the Long Woods who deal with them. Spirit traders, I presume."

He knows about spirits, Arlo thought. *He knows more than he's saying*. Arlo picked his next question carefully. "Do you know why they want Hadryn?"

"Something about a weapon. A knife. They're worried he's going to get his hands on it."

He already has it.

"What's so dangerous about the knife?" asked Arlo.

"We don't know. But from what we've heard, they're equally

concerned about some boy with one brown eye and one green eye. Does that sound familiar?"

How much does he know? Have I already said too much?

Now it was Sanders's turn to lean forward. "We may not know much about the Eldritch, but they are for all intents and purposes our neighbors. And it's not great to have them freaked out right now. So I'm asking you plainly: what is your role in this, Arlo Finch?"

"I don't know." He hadn't meant to say it out loud, but wasn't sure it mattered anymore.

Sanders shook his head, unsatisfied. He closed the file folder.

"I'm serious!" said Arlo. "I don't know what the Eldritch want with me."

Sanders looked Arlo in the eye. "Son, if I were in your shoes, I'd figure it out."

37
FOSTERED

IN THE YEAR THAT HE'D BEEN A MEMBER OF BLUE PATROL, Arlo Finch had slept over at Wu's, eaten multiple meals at Indra's kitchen table and soaked in Connor's hot tub. But he had never been to Jonas and Julie's house. As far as he knew, no one in Pine Mountain had.

The Delgados lived on the same street as Wu, but they didn't interact with many people. The family didn't go to church, and the twins were homeschooled. Arlo had never understood what their parents did for a living. He only knew it was something about a newsletter or a website.

So as the front door opened, he had no real expectation of what he'd find.

"Welcome, you two little birds!" It was Mrs. Delgado. Arlo had seen her at potlucks. She was tall and thin, with graying blonde hair pulled back in a long braid. She hugged Arlo, then

Jaycee. Arlo watched his sister bristle. She didn't like being touched.

Mr. Delgado was barrel-chested with a closely trimmed beard. He had a firm handshake. "I want you to know that you're safe here. We may be looking after you, but we're not fans of the government, either."

Arlo caught a disapproving glare from the social worker, Mrs. Jeffries. She'd driven them from Fort Collins, explaining that since their parents were in custody and they had no other relatives in Pine Mountain, Arlo and Jaycee would need to stay with a foster family. The only one in the area was the Delgados.

"We're usually looking after babies and toddlers," said Mrs. Delgado. "So it's a treat for us to get teenagers, much less ones who are already friends with our kiddos." She motioned to Jonas and Julie. "Come! Show them where they'll stay."

Jonas's wood-paneled bedroom had a small window, a single dresser and bunkbeds. "You can take the top or bottom," said Jonas. "I don't care."

"Which one do you like?" asked Arlo.

"Seriously, I really don't care."

Arlo chose the bottom bunk. He had a suitcase with some clothes—the social worker had taken them by their house on the way—but he didn't unpack. "I don't know how long I'm going to be here," he told Jonas.

"My parents say your mom could get ten years for lying to federal officers and harboring a fugitive."

"I don't think that's . . ." *True? Fair? Possible?* Arlo had worried so much about the charges against his father that he hadn't really considered what his mom was facing.

"But your sister will be eighteen in two years, right? In theory, she could become your guardian then, if your parents are still in jail. Or maybe your uncle could do it."

"He's in Kentucky."

Jonas shrugged. "I don't know if they'd even let him be your guardian. He's pretty weird."

The Delgados' backyard was a massive vegetable garden. It wasn't a hobby; the family grew nearly everything they ate. Chickens ran free, pecking at bugs, guarded by a massive wolf-hound named Freedom. ("Figure if I gotta yell for him, oughta be something I believe in," explained Mr. Delgado.)

At the back of the property was a steel door built into the hillside. Julie explained that it was a bunker. In case of nuclear war or a national emergency, the Delgados could live for three years inside it. "At least, the four of us and Freedom could. I don't know if there's really room for you and your sister. But I guess you could always run away to the Long Woods, couldn't you?"

The thought had occurred to Arlo. Jaycee brought it up that night as they were brushing their teeth. "Is there some way we could live there, if we got Mom and Dad out? Like maybe in that town, Fallpath?"

"I guess," said Arlo. "But I don't know how to get them out of prison. The Long Woods go everywhere, but not inside buildings."

That night, as Arlo stared up at the springs of the bunk above him, he considered his options.

The first choice would be to do nothing. He and his sister could simply stay with the Delgados and wait to see what happened with their parents. It seemed very unlikely that their dad could avoid trial—in all likelihood, he'd spend many years in jail—but there was a chance their mom could be released. They could go back to the way life had been before.

The second choice would be to do *something*. But what, exactly? There was no knaught to tie, no path to find, no spirit to help him. It wasn't simply a matter of breaking his parents out of jail; that would just be a temporary fix. He wanted to bring them home permanently. But how?

Arlo thought back to his trip to Fallpath. In order to use the atlas, they'd had to bargain with Zhang. That was why they had retrieved the upscale from the coatl's cave: they'd needed something to trade, something she wanted.

Was there anything the government wanted, anything Arlo could offer in exchange for his parents' freedom? It certainly wasn't money; the government printed that itself. He had no state secrets or nuclear codes. There didn't seem to be much a thirteen-year-old boy could offer the most powerful nation in the world.

But what about not *in the world?* thought Arlo. On the other side of the Long Woods, there were powerful beings who seemed very interested in this specific thirteen-year-old boy. Arlo didn't know quite what they wanted, but they definitely wanted *something*. Perhaps he could make a deal.

It was time to visit the Eldritch.

— 38 —
TIME AND SPACE

IT WAS A PERFECTLY ORDINARY CAMPOUT.

On the first Saturday of December, the Rangers of Pine Mountain Company returned to one of their favorite campsites: Ram's Meadow. As they were setting up their tents, Arlo cautioned the new members of Blue Patrol to be mindful of wisps, telling them about his first brush with death in these woods a year earlier.

"But don't worry," he said. "Connor will look out for you."

It had been Blue Patrol's turn to organize the afternoon's activities. They planned an elaborate version of Capture the Flag in which the four patrols would compete separately in a densely wooded area of nearly one square mile. Once they were out of sight of the other teams, Arlo, Indra and Wu said goodbye to their patrol.

"How soon will you be back?" asked Julie.

"Hopefully by morning," said Arlo.

"But what if you're not?" asked Wyatt. "What if you get lost, or someone kidnaps you, or there's a monster?"

"That's pretty much guaranteed to happen," said Jonas. "They'll figure it out. They always do." He fist-bumped Arlo. It was honestly the best compliment Arlo had ever gotten from Jonas.

As Wu and Indra were checking their packs, Connor pulled Arlo aside. "If you see my cousin, tell her that her mom isn't doing well."

This was the first Arlo had heard of it. "What's wrong? Is your aunt sick?"

"It's just a cold. But it's good to remind Rielle that she has family here. She's been living with the Eldritch so long she thinks she's one of them."

As they watched Arlo head off with Wu and Indra, Sarah Fitzrandolph turned to Wyatt and whispered, "Do you understand what the Long Woods are?"

Wyatt whispered back, "I was going to ask you."

———————◆———————

It took Arlo less than an hour to find a way into the Long Woods and up to the hillside overlooking Fallpath. Indra, who had only heard Arlo and Wu's description of the town, felt they'd done it a disservice. "You made it sound temporary, like a refugee camp. This is probably what Pine Mountain was like when it was founded. A bunch of people passing through, and then eventually it becomes a real town."

The Owl and the Snake was much busier than when Arlo and Wu had first visited, with a dozen scruffy men and women drinking and gambling inside. The little girl—Zhang's daughter—was sitting cross-legged on the bar, reading an Archie comic. Spotting Arlo, she yelled something in Chinese, then went back to her reading. A few moments later, the swinging doors parted to reveal Zhang herself, a dishrag in her hands. She seemed very surprised to see Arlo again.

Why? Arlo wondered. *Did she think I wouldn't survive the trip to China? Or does she know who I really am?*

"Ar-lo Finch!" she said. *She knows.* "Last time you were here, you said your name was Daniel. What's with the alias?" She approached them. "Are you some kind of scoundrel? A villain? I don't want any disreputable types in my bar."

It was hard to know how much she was teasing, or whether her knowing his actual name would put them at risk. Either way, it was too late to worry about it. "I just need to use the atlas again," he said.

"Did you bring cash this time? Or another upscale?"

"Something else." He nodded to Indra, who unzipped her pack and pulled out a slightly-rusted coffee tin. She handed it to Zhang, who seemed intrigued as she opened the lid, fishing through wads of paper towels to pull out a single conch.

"It's a speakshell," said Wu.

"I know," said Zhang, a little annoyed. "Where did you find this?"

"There was a hag who tried to kill us last year," said Indra. "She had it. When I brought it home, I buried it in the backyard just in case."

"Smart girl. Someone could have been listening to every word you said. Here's a tip: if you ever see a seashell in some fancy executive's office, ask them if it was a gift. I guarantee it's there to eavesdrop."

"Is it worth enough?" asked Arlo. "Will you let us use the atlas?"

"Depends. Where do you need to go?"

"The Realm."

Zhang smiled, amused. She set the shell and the coffee can on the bar. "Let me guess: you think that because *the Long Woods go everywhere*, they must go to the Realm, right?" Arlo shrugged yeah. "Wrong. The Long Woods most definitely do not go to the Realm. The only connection between them was a bridge, and that blew up a long time ago."

"The Broken Bridge," said Indra, under her breath.

"That's right!" Zhang said. "The three of you have been there, haven't you? Word gets around." Zhang stretched the dishrag between her hands as if it were the bridge. "It used to link the Woods to the Realm, but one day the Eldritch were trying to bring back this ancient spirit they'd captured. It didn't just break free—it broke everything."

244

Arlo had heard this part before, from Fox. "It wasn't just one spirit. It was two."

"Exactly. The twins: Mirnos and Ekafos."

Wu recognized that name. "Ekafos! The monster from the lake at camp."

"I've seen it," said Arlo. "It's a giant snake that lives in a void outside of time."

"I hear you've been there. Or *then*," said Zhang. "You're quite the accidental time traveler."

How much does she know about me? wondered Arlo. *And who told her?*

"So if Ekafos is *time*," said Indra, "that must mean Mirnos is *space*, right?"

Zhang seemed impressed. "Give this girl a prize. Mirnos is the reason why the geography of the Long Woods is so messed up. It warps everything. It also prevents the Eldritch from coming in."

"But there has to be a way to get to the Realm," said Arlo. He gestured to the gamblers, who were playing for caged spirits. "These trappers are catching spirits for the Eldritch. How are they getting them there?"

"Like I said, you can't go to the Realm *through* the Long Woods," said Zhang. "You have to go *under*."

39
DARK TIDES

THE DEEP SEA WAS A VAST UNDERGROUND OCEAN, complete with crashing waves and fog. The air smelled of salt, but Arlo wasn't about to put his hand in to taste the water. He suspected there were creatures waiting to chew on his fingers.

They were aboard a small boat called the *Vespertine*. It had no sails or motor, yet it cut through the water at a fast clip. Arlo suspected it was powered by water spirits bound to the hull. The captain was a heavily tattooed woman with large spacers in her earlobes and a brass sword hanging from her belt. Zhang had hired her at the docks after they had descended for what seemed like a mile in a creaky elevator. "Don't be offended if she's not much for talking," said Zhang as they cast off. "She has to keep an eye out for pirates."

But how would she even see them? Arlo wondered. The

darkness was impenetrable. At the bow of the ship glowing lights hung from long poles, but they barely lit the water beneath them. Everything else was lost in inky blackness. Arlo assumed they were in some kind of massive cavern, but he had no idea how high the ceiling was.

Indra tried casting snaplights, but they never sparked. "I don't think we're in the Long Woods anymore," she said.

Arlo was certain she was right. In the Long Woods, he could always feel the pull of familiar locations, but here he felt nothing but mild seasickness.

Wu had it much worse. He was sitting on the deck with a metal bucket between his legs. He hadn't thrown up yet, but had turned his neckerchief around just in case. Arlo and Indra sat beside him. They weren't sure what else to do.

"I'm glad I'm here with the two of you," said Arlo. "It feels right that it's the three of us back together."

"Don't make it sound like it's our last adventure!" said Indra.

Wu just nodded weakly, taking shallow breaths.

Arlo rubbed his back. "The captain says it's a short trip. Less than an hour."

Wu looked up. His skin had the color and texture of sweaty string cheese. "How long have we been in this boat?"

Indra looked at Arlo. "Twenty minutes at least," she said. "We're almost halfway there." Wu moaned. In fact, they had only been on the water for ten minutes, tops.

Out of nowhere, a wave hit the side of the boat, soaking

them. *Definitely salt water*, thought Arlo, spitting it out. The splash left behind a visitor, as well: a ghostly white catfish with glowing eyes. It was bigger than a house cat, with a mouth full of pointy teeth chewing the air. It slipped and slid across the wet deck until its long whiskers suddenly gained traction. Then, like an octopus, it began to drag itself towards the trio.

Arlo and Indra both screamed. Pulling Wu to his feet, they tried to move away, but the catfish was surprisingly quick, snapping at their wet sneakers. Arlo kicked the bucket at it, clipping the edge of its mouth. The steel bucket suddenly began to rust and dissolve, eaten away by the fish's acidic saliva.

Before they could react, the captain pushed past them, pulling the brass sword from her belt. With a single motion, she skewered the fish and flung it overboard. She seemed completely unfazed.

"That's why your sword is brass," realized Indra. "So it won't rust."

"It's bronze," said the captain, wiping the blade with a rag before returning it to her belt. She took Wu by the hair, lifting his head to look into his eyes. Then she suddenly kicked him in both shins. He went limp in Arlo's and Indra's arms.

"Why did you do that?!" demanded Indra.

"Gave him some sea legs." She pushed past them, headed back to the wheel.

Arlo and Indra carefully set Wu down.

"I'm fine," said Wu. "I feel better, actually." Indeed, his color was already improving. He slowly began to stand up. Once vertical, he seemed unfazed as the boat churned and rocked. He jumped. He spun around. His motion sickness was completely gone. "This is great! You should have her do it to you."

"No point," said the captain. She pointed to a glow in the distance. It looked like a trapdoor in the black sky. "We're here."

40
THE KINGDOM OF SHADOWS

IT'S AUTUMN THERE. IT'S ALWAYS AUTUMN.

In conversations with Arlo, Rielle had described the Realm as being unbelievably beautiful, filled with remarkable gardens and architecture. *There are buildings, things we'd call palaces, but everyone has them. Everyone's equal. Everyone's an artist. There's no war, or poverty, or suffering. No one gets sick, or old, or dies. It's basically paradise. You'll see.*

Arlo felt like he could picture what Rielle was describing— a cross between Washington, D.C., and Asgard from Norse mythology—except for the part about it always being autumn. *How could that be possible?* he had wondered. Autumn was a transition between summer and winter, not a permanent state. *Once trees lose their leaves, they don't keep losing them.*

Now that he was standing in the Realm, he understood.

Twin suns hung low in the sky, casting long shadows. The

trees were filled with red and gold and amber leaves, but the colors were oddly muted, as if someone had applied a filter with an app. There was a chill in the air, and a palpable stillness, like a funeral service. Not fear, but mourning.

Autumn wasn't a season. It was a mood. The leaves weren't falling; the Realm was falling. It was on a slow descent into winter. Into darkness.

Arlo was standing with Wu and Indra at the top of a long ramp leading up from the Deep Sea. It had taken nearly twenty minutes to climb, mostly because Wu had had a hard time walking, stumbling with each step like a dizzy toddler. (Apparently "sea legs" didn't work well on dry land.) The captain had stayed behind with the boat. "You don't go into the Realm unless you've got business."

Ahead of them stretched a grand avenue flanked by two massive winged statues. There were buildings in every direction, and of every material: dark stone towers, alabaster theaters and crystal spires wrapped with delicate metal tendrils. There were parks and fountains and boulevards. But the Realm seemed oddly empty. There was no sign of the Eldritch. No sign that anyone actually lived here.

"Where is everyone?" asked Indra. "You'd think they'd have security or something."

The only movement came from flying objects that flitted between distant buildings. "What do you think those are?" asked Wu, pointing. "Drones?"

As if answering his question, one of the flying objects began

251

making its way down the avenue, heading towards them. The device was the size of a skateboard, made of filigreed copper with a swirling shape suspended inside it. *An air spirit*, Arlo thought. It hovered a few feet ahead of them, playing a simple melody like a music box.

There was a scroll of paper beneath it, hanging by a string. Indra carefully untied it, unrolling it to reveal two words written in English. *Please follow.*

The device led them down the main avenue, between the winged statues, to a gold-domed building with square columns. The steps leading up to the doors were designed for much larger creatures; they were triple the height of normal stairs. Arlo and his friends had to really work to climb them, using their hands and knees to make their way.

"It's like 'Jack and the Beanstalk,'" said Indra. Arlo didn't remember the story fully, but knew it didn't work out well for the giants or the land below.

As Arlo reached the top of the steps, huffing from exhaustion, he saw a familiar face waiting for them: Rielle. She was wearing an embroidered robe, a golden tiara and dramatic makeup—most notably, a bright green stripe that crossed her eyelids.

"There's also a ramp," she said, pointing. Indeed, at the left edge of the steps was a stone slope that would have been much easier to ascend.

Wu was the last one to climb up. Arlo introduced him.

"I pictured you spookier," Wu said. "More like a ghost."

"Are you okay?" she asked, noticing his wobbliness and odd gait.

"I just have sea legs," he answered. "It should go away eventually, I think. I hope."

"What is this place?" asked Arlo.

"The Great Hall," said Rielle. "It's where the High Council meets. They're expecting you." She motioned towards the giant metal doors, which hung open. When Indra and Wu started to follow Arlo, Rielle intercepted them. "Just Arlo. You don't see the High Council unless you have business."

"I'm their business," said Arlo. "They're with me."

Rielle shrugged. "They won't understand anyway."

"Wait," said Arlo, suddenly remembering Connor's instructions. "I'm supposed to tell you something. Your mom, she's sick." He watched her expression. She seemed more curious than concerned.

"Who told you to tell me that? Was it Connor?"

"Yeah. He thought you'd want to know."

Rielle gave a slight smile, then turned, leading the way into the building.

Beyond the doors was a single immense chamber. It reminded Arlo of the sanctuary of the now-destroyed First Church of Pine Mountain, only much larger. The walls were white marble. The windows were vertical stripes of stained glass, so tall they seemed to converge. The light had a thickness and texture, as if the air itself was glowing.

The room was so spectacular that it took Arlo a few moments

to realize they were not alone. Fourteen Eldritch were seated on an elevated dais at the far end of the chamber, arranged in a semicircle. They wore robes and featureless masks that covered their faces. Arlo had originally mistaken them for giant statues.

Arlo followed Rielle to the center of the room. Indra and Wu stood a few feet back.

Welcome, tooble.

The voice resonated in Arlo's head. Had he actually heard it, or did the words just arrive in his mind? He looked back at Indra and Wu, who it seemed hadn't heard anything.

We've long waited for you to come.

This time, Arlo could feel his brain processing the words. They weren't English. They were something else, something older. The language wasn't spoken, but rather delivered telepathically.

Arlo turned back to the Eldritch. "Why were you waiting?" he asked aloud. "If you wanted me, why didn't you just kidnap me like you did with Rielle?"

The Eldritch turned to one another, silently conferring. Wu leaned over Arlo's shoulder, whispering into his ear. "Are they talking to you?"

"In my head, yeah."

"Ask them if it's okay that Indra and I are here."

Arlo shushed him. He sensed that the Eldritch were about to respond.

Your place is in the world of men. We believe the spirit Mirnos has revealed itself to you. Its place is here, in the Realm. You are meant to bring it to us.

Arlo looked over to Rielle. *Had she already known what they wanted?* If so, she wasn't letting on.

"Why do you want me to bring Mirnos here?" he asked.

It is necessary to the Realm.

"What if it doesn't want to come?"

Spirits are necessary to the Realm, as water and sunlight are to your world.

Now Indra was whispering in Arlo's ear. "What do they want with Mirnos?"

"They say it's necessary."

Indra turned to Rielle. "Why is it necessary? Why do they need it?"

"Power," suggested Wu. "All their stuff is powered by spirits. And they were trying to bring it here when it blew up the Broken Bridge."

Rielle was losing patience. "You two are not even supposed to be in here!"

Arlo turned his attention back to the Eldritch. "The Realm is dying, isn't it? Or, *dimming*. It's not supposed to be like this, like autumn all the time. That's why you need Mirnos, to power it up again."

Spirits are a resource. They are energy.

"They're living beings. You can't just take them."

They are not like us. They are not like you.

"Yes, but they're alive. They have thoughts and memories."

They have no culture. No art. They build no cities. They are not creators. They are merely tools.

"They want to be free. That's what matters." Arlo surprised himself with his conviction. He hadn't known what he was going to say until he said it.

The Eldritch conferred. Wu and Indra put their hands on Arlo's shoulders, *Well done.* He was glad he'd brought them in.

Then a door opened in the wall to the right. An Eldritch in armor entered, a chain dangling from its hand. A normal-sized person was walking beside it like a dog on a leash. It wasn't until they came closer that Arlo recognized the slender man with an elaborate mustache, sunken eyes and a steel collar around his neck.

It was Fox.

"Arlo Finch! And his friends. We're a long way from the Woods, aren't we?"

41
THE PRISONER

FOX HAD BEEN CAPTURED on the outskirts of Fallpath just minutes after he'd left Arlo, Wu and Jaycee.

"It was a tangleknaught," said Fox. "A tricky snare for even the trickiest of us. The more you struggle, the tighter it gets. By the time the ladies came, I could barely wiggle a paw."

Arlo suspected the trapper had been the old woman who sniffed Fox's scent on him in Fallpath. *I can smell it on you.* He felt sick that he'd played a role in Fox's capture and that his guide was now a prisoner. The skin on Fox's neck was red and raw from the metal collar he was wearing. His eyes had lost their glisten, and his words didn't have the same flourish.

"The ladies sold me to the Eldritch. Didn't get half of what I was worth, which is small comfort for a small beast." Fox said he had been a prisoner in the Realm for weeks. "What I can't puzzle out is what you're doing here, Arlo Finch. If you came to save me, I'm flattered, but I think you're out of your depth."

Arlo didn't know how to answer. Indra spoke for him: "He didn't come here for you. He's here for his family. They're prisoners, too, back in our world."

"I wanted to see if the Eldritch could help," said Arlo, his voice barely above a whisper.

Fox's pale eyes narrowed, suspicious. "And what exactly did you think they'd do, Mr. Finch? Smash through the prison walls? Use their green light so that everything would be forgotten?"

"I didn't know where else to go! I didn't know where you were."

"Now you do! You're lucky I wasn't bound to one of their machines or else we couldn't have this little chat. Still time, though. I think I'd make a great dust sweeper."

"He didn't know!" insisted Indra.

"But he knew what the Eldritch were. What they did." Fox turned back to Arlo. "Your parents may be imprisoned, but we are the ones shackled to machines."

"It's not like that at all," protested Rielle. "We never harm spirits. We protect them. We give them purpose."

Fox bared his sharp teeth. "One of us is in chains. So why don't you say that again, closer."

Arlo assumed the Eldritch were listening to everything being said, but they weren't reacting or intervening. They simply observed, content to let the conversation play out.

He nodded in their direction. "They want me to find Mirnos

and bring it here. They say they need it." Arlo remembered back to his first conversation with Fox, that night in the snowy parking lot of the church. It suddenly clicked: Fox had said that unnamed forces were looking for *something hidden. Something you may be able to find.*

"You knew," said Arlo. "You knew why the Eldritch needed me, didn't you?"

Fox nodded. "They were always fascinated by you. And worried. Remember: their first encounter with you was thirty years ago, when you suddenly showed up with the spirit knife. Then you vanished for decades. When you reappeared, it's understandable they saw you as a threat."

"That's why they hired the hag to kill you," said Wu. "She sent the wisps and the Night Mare . . ."

"But you survived," said Fox. "And after Mirnos showed itself to you, they realized how useful you could be."

"Rielle saw it, too," said Arlo, thinking back to the night by the bonfire. "I'm not the only one."

"But if the girl could find it herself, they wouldn't need you, would they?"

Wu leaned in to Arlo. "Maybe you could get them to free both Fox *and* your parents."

"You can't make that deal," warned Fox. "If Mirnos leaves the Long Woods, there's nothing stopping the Eldritch from coming in. They'd take everything. Every last spirit."

"No they wouldn't," said Rielle. "They just need enough to survive."

"How much is enough?" snapped Fox. "And why should they get to decide?" He stepped towards Rielle, but the Eldritch guard holding his chain yanked him back.

Arlo found himself shivering not from cold but confusion. His thoughts were jumbled. He couldn't untangle them. *I'm the reason I'm in this mess*, he thought. *I'm the reason Fox is here. The reason my parents are in jail. If I hadn't brought Dad back from China—if I had taken him back like they said—if I hadn't joined Rangers . . .*

Bring us the dragon and we will help you.

That Eldritch voice in his head again. Calm but commanding. It was unfair the way they could force their way in and talk over his thoughts. Arlo glared, but it wasn't clear which one was actually speaking. Maybe it was all of them in unison.

We will free the one you call Fox. We will make things as they should be. You will save the Realm.

Arlo squeezed his eyes shut, as if that would help. He had no good choices. If he led them to Mirnos, they could capture not only the dragon, but all the spirits of the Long Woods. If he said no, his parents could spend years in jail, and Fox . . . would he remain a prisoner, or be bound to some device? Would he simply be energy for some Eldritch machine?

How could he possibly decide? In every scenario, he was hurting someone.

"I don't know what to do," whispered Arlo. "Someone tell me what to do. Please."

"You need to bring them Mirnos," said Rielle.

"Never!" said Fox. "Countless spirits would suffer."

Wu started to speak. "Maybe you could . . ." Then he stopped himself. "I don't know, either. I'm sorry."

Arlo found himself staring directly at Indra, the last to weigh in. All his hopes were pinned on her. She had always been the conscience he wished he had. He silently resolved to do whatever she said.

She took his hand in hers. He realized then that he'd never held it before. It was softer than he had expected. "You shouldn't do anything, Arlo. Not now. We should go home."

Arlo felt a weight lift from him. He nodded, then looked at Fox. Could they really just leave him here, a prisoner?

"The girl's right," said the mustached man. "Go. Quickly."

Arlo turned and began walking towards the massive doors. Indra followed, with Wu lagging behind with his sea legs. Arlo expected someone to stop them, or for the doors to magically swing shut. But the Eldritch seemed willing to let them leave.

We are on the same side, Arlo Finch. You'll come back when you're ready.

Was it a prediction? A threat? Either way, Arlo didn't stop. Didn't acknowledge that he'd heard it.

The air outside was cooler, with a gentle breeze that smelled like cinnamon and wood smoke. The sun, already low in the sky, had now dipped halfway below the horizon. Dim rays of light barely reached into the shadows. All detail in the buildings was lost, leaving just a collection of dark shapes. This kingdom was a magnificent graveyard. A ghost town.

"Do you remember the way back to the undersea?" asked Wu. There was no spirit drone waiting to guide them.

"Wait!" called Rielle. They turned to find her walking out of the building. Arlo couldn't read her expression. Disappointed? Angry?

"I'm not doing it," said Arlo. "Not now. We're leaving."

"I know," she said. "But there's a faster way back to Pine Mountain."

———•◦•———

Technically, it was a tunnel. It ran under the city and then beyond it. But it was unlike any tunnel Arlo had ever seen. The chiseled stone walls were perfectly square, rising to an arched ceiling just a foot above their heads.

Rielle was leading the way, carrying a lantern lit by a glowing spirit.

"Who built this?" asked Indra. "It's way too small for the Eldritch."

"Stone spirits," said Rielle. "The Eldritch had them make this for me, so I could get back and forth more easily."

Arlo estimated they'd been walking for twenty minutes when they reached a dead end. The tunnel had collapsed, leaving giant stones blocking the way. Rielle clapped three times and the stones rolled back, clearing a narrow path.

Wu was impressed. "Can I try it?"

Rielle shrugged. Wu clapped his hands three times and the

stones shifted back into place, perfectly sealing the passage. Then he clapped three more times to reopen it. He was clearly ready to spend an hour doing this.

"Seriously, we have to go," said Indra.

Beyond the magical rubble, the walls became rougher and the floor more uneven. Timbers sagged from the ceiling. Arlo spotted bits of steel and trash in the corners.

This must be an old mine, he realized. He knew there were hundreds of these abandoned sites in the Rockies, but had never ventured inside one, nor had anyone he'd met. Both in school and in Rangers, kids were frequently reminded how dangerous the mines were, with deep shafts and poisonous gases.

Up ahead, Arlo could see the night sky.

They emerged through a narrow opening in a chain-link fence with a rusted NO TRESPASSING sign. Arlo spotted Signal Rock. They were on Cunningham family property, less than a hundred yards from his house. He couldn't believe a passageway to the Realm had been so close all this time.

"Thanks for bringing us back," said Arlo.

She shrugged. "I think you're making a mistake. They'll get Mirnos eventually. If it's not you or me, some trapper will eventually catch it. And you'll have missed your chance."

"At least he'll still have principles," snapped Indra.

"Do you want principles, Arlo? Or do you want your parents?"

"You seem to have done pretty well without either," said Wu. "I guess, I don't know. You're kind of weird and mean, so . . ." He let it trail off.

Rielle sniffed dismissively, then squeezed back through the chain-link fence and headed into the tunnel.

The trio was alone again. It was a full moon. The wind was swaying the treetops.

"We should get back to camp," said Indra.

The nearest way into the Long Woods was back by the house. As Arlo and his friends walked past, he looked at the dark windows. No one was living in his home.

"Okay if I use the bathroom?" asked Wu.

"Me too," added Indra.

Arlo retrieved the key hidden under the front steps, then waited outside as Indra and Wu went in. He realized he was standing right where Cooper the dog used to futilely dig with his phantom paws. Arlo scraped at the dirt with his shoe.

Maybe it was the memory, the night or being alone for those few minutes, but the emotion hit him like a wave. His body shook as he cried. By the time his friends came out, he had dried his tears and could conceal his drippy nose.

"Let's go," he said. "It's not far."

42
A GOOD PERSON

AT SUMMER CAMP A FEW MONTHS EARLIER, Arlo Finch had used a slipknaught to sneak past Warden Mpasu. He'd managed to walk right by her, unseen and untouchable. *Incorporeal.* He'd gotten away, but at a steep cost: the experience had stretched out the cord binding his soul to his body. Like a ghost, he was in the world but not quite part of it. He'd collapsed and nearly died. Only after Fox performed a ritual had Arlo snapped back into himself.

Now Arlo felt a similar disconnection from reality. Only this time there was no supernatural explanation. He'd gotten himself entangled in this mess, and there was no one to help him get unstuck.

At school on Monday, he was marked *present*, but that was just his body. In mind and spirit, Arlo Finch was somewhere else, scrambling to come up with a plan to save his family, Fox and the Long Woods. All the while, he secretly suspected it was hopeless.

In Spanish class, he didn't answer the first three times his teacher called on him. In math, he stared at the fractions on his quiz and couldn't figure out how to add them. In biology, he focused on a corner of the whiteboard that hadn't been fully erased, trying to figure out what had been written there.

"Are you okay?" whispered Merilee.

"Not really," said Arlo.

"Do you need to go to the nurse's office?"

He shook his head. There was nothing to fix except everything.

Merilee pulled Arlo's notebook over and wrote on it with her pen: *You're a good person.* He looked at her, confused.

"So you don't forget," she said.

At lunch, Arlo sat with Indra and Wu, neither of whom had new ideas. At least not practical ones. "Maybe we could figure out the kind of spirits who dug the passageway for the Eldritch," suggested Wu. "Then we could convince them to tunnel into the prison where your parents are and get them out."

They all knew it didn't merit any real discussion. The solution wasn't going to be found in *Culman's Bestiary.* Not every problem had an answer.

After school, Arlo headed outside for the bus. That's when he saw a truck waiting by the curb. It looked just like his Uncle Wade's—same dents, same busted mirror. Stranger still, the woman standing next to it resembled his mother.

It took Arlo a full three seconds to accept that it really was Wade's truck and it really was his mom. He ran to her, hugging her tight. She brushed back his hair, then rested her chin on his head.

"What are you doing here?" he asked. "How did you get out?"

"I'm not entirely sure. But I think it's because of you."

⸺•●•⸺

An hour later, they were back at their house. Arlo, Jaycee and their mom sat in the dining room with Ms. Tran, the lawyer who had been representing Arlo's father in his case. Across the table sat Agent Sanders. He was alone, although three other FBI agents were standing outside on the porch.

"So, Arlo. I have good news," said Sanders. "The government is prepared to drop charges against your father, your mom and Mitch Jansen. In exchange, they need you to deliver an item to a third party."

"Is this for real?" Arlo asked Ms. Tran. He didn't know her well, but she had always struck him as very serious.

"The deal they're offering is legitimate," she said. "But it's not clear what specific item they want you to deliver and to whom. I'm uncomfortable with how vague they're being."

"It's a matter of national security," said Sanders.

Arlo's mom wasn't satisfied with that answer. "It's my son's safety. I need to know exactly what you're asking him to do and why."

267

"It's fine," said Arlo. "I know what they want." He looked across the table at Sanders. "What are they giving you in exchange for this? Technology? Information?"

Sanders half smiled. "I have no idea. This was all decided at levels way above mine."

"Did they say anything about Fox?"

Tran checked her notes. "Yes. The deal says that a 'Mr. Fox' will also be released from custody."

Jaycee looked over at Arlo. He hadn't told her about Fox getting captured.

"If you do this, Arlo, your dad can be home for Christmas," said Sanders. "Everyone wins."

No they don't, thought Arlo. *Mirnos doesn't. The spirits don't.* Arlo would get what he wanted, and so would the Eldritch. But the costs would be paid by others completely unconnected to this.

His mom misread his hesitation. "Arlo, tell me honestly: is this dangerous? I can't begin to understand what this is all about, but I am your mother, and I will not let you risk your safety for this."

Looking into his mom's eyes, for just a moment he remembered her as a child, on an early morning when he had led her back out of the Long Woods. She had trusted him then. She had to trust him now.

"It's not dangerous," he said. "I'll be fine."

— 43 —
THE WATERFALL

AS A YOUNG GIRL, Katie Cunningham had wandered away from a family picnic and ended up in the Long Woods with her cousin Connor. Weeks later, Connor returned to his family, but Katie went to live with the Eldritch, where she took the name Rielle.

When he first heard the story, Arlo had assumed she was kidnapped, stolen like a fairy-tale princess. But the reality was more complicated. Rielle wasn't a hostage or a victim. She didn't just live with the Eldritch. She lived *as* one. She was clearly on their side.

You can't trust her, Connor had warned Arlo.

And he didn't trust her. He knew where her loyalties lay. But he had to work with her anyway.

Rielle was standing in a field of blue flowers, the same clearing where Arlo had tested his father's device. A breeze swayed the blossoms, giving them the impression of gentle ocean waves.

Rielle had her back to him. Arlo wondered how long she had been waiting.

As he approached, she turned. Resting beside her in the flowers was a brass spirit cage. It was larger than the other ones he'd seen, the size of two basketballs.

"Is it just us?" he asked. He'd expected Rielle to be accompanied by a crew. Back at Camp Redfeather, he'd seen the Eldritch struggle to cage Big Breezy. And while they couldn't enter the Long Woods, the Eldritch seemed to have no shortage of people willing to do their dirty work. Why had they only sent Rielle?

She tucked a wisp of hair behind her ear. "Honestly, I assumed you'd bring those two friends you're always with."

"I wanted to keep them out of it."

"Good. We don't need them." She lifted the cage, slinging it over her shoulder by a strap.

"How many spirits have you caught?" he asked.

"A few," she answered. "Just for practice. It's not that hard."

"It's not hard for you to imprison a living creature?" He locked eyes with her. "It's hard for me."

"But you're here, aren't you? You're doing this. So save me your lecture about how wrong this all is. It's happening because it needs to happen."

Rielle was right: No matter how much Arlo protested, he wasn't being forced to do this, any more than Rielle had been kidnapped by the Eldritch. He'd come here willingly. He'd made his choice. He knew what he was doing.

"Do you know where we're going?" she asked.

"Not exactly. I think Mirnos lives near a waterfall. The last time I was in this field, I found this golden koi fish. Then I was suddenly standing at a river. There was a big waterfall over there." He motioned with his hands, imagining where it would be.

Rielle remembered. "It was dark where I was. And really loud—that was probably the waterfall. Mirnos was sleeping."

"You could see it?"

"Barely, but I could feel it breathing. It was close." Like Arlo, she motioned with her hand to indicate where the dragon had been in relation to her.

"You know how you can sense the places you've been before?" said Arlo. "The direction you need to travel in?" Rielle nodded. "This waterfall is different. I know it's a real place, but it's not in any one direction. Even for the Long Woods, it's weird. It's like it doesn't connect anywhere else."

"Except to us," she said.

"What do you mean?"

"Just that every time I've seen Mirnos, you've been there. Same for you, right?" Arlo nodded. "I think the connection is us. We're always there together."

It was a simple observation with profound implications. *What if it has to be both of us?* Arlo wondered. He and Rielle were both toobles, obviously. But it wasn't just that. Having been to Fallpath, Arlo now knew that they weren't the only toobles out there. So why did the dragon only reveal itself to the two of them, and always together? *If Mirnos has a plan,* Arlo realized, *it involves both of us.*

"So how do we get there?" he asked.

"I'm guessing together." She held out a hand to him, her silver bracelets jangling. He didn't reciprocate, which clearly annoyed her. "What?! Are you scared to touch a girl?"

"No! Fine." He took her hand.

"Now close your eyes," she said. Arlo didn't ask why, but he waited until Rielle had shut her own eyes. Even then, he checked a few times to make sure she was really keeping hers closed.

Arlo emptied his mind, letting his thoughts slip away unnoticed. A year ago, when he'd first started navigating the Long Woods, he'd struggled to do this. Now it had become second nature. He could easily feel the magnetic pull of familiar locations around him, from Fallpath to the Broken Bridge. But the waterfall existed only in his memory.

He could still picture it, the sunlight filtering through the leaves. He could remember the sound of the crashing water and feel the spray on his skin. He could even smell the algae in the mud. Still, the waterfall was a recollection rather than a direction. He didn't know which way to head.

Then he felt himself stumble a bit, and suddenly realized he was walking. His feet were moving on their own, without any conscious input. *How long have I been walking?* he wondered. His hand was still holding Rielle's. *She must be moving, too.* Arlo listened, hoping to hear his footsteps. He willed his eyelids to open, but they seemed far too heavy to lift. *Am I dreaming?* he wondered. *Sleepwalking?* Just as he started to panic, he heard a quiet voice shushing him. It gradually grew louder.

The air felt heavy. It smelled sweet and ripe. Birds chirped above him.

His feet were suddenly cold. Wet. The chill went up to his ankles. His calves. With all his might, he forced his eyes open.

He was standing beside Rielle in an ice-cold river downstream from a towering waterfall. Brightly colored birds flitted among the trees, while strange insects skated across the water.

"We're here," he said, not entirely believing it himself. It was like waking up to find yourself in a dream.

Rielle opened her eyes, squinting in the light. She let go of his hand.

"This is where I was before," said Arlo. "I was standing there on the bank. Where were you?"

She pointed to the waterfall. "I think I was behind it. That was the noise I heard." She hesitated before adding, "What I don't get is, why would we see different places?"

"Maybe so we'd have to work together."

The base of the waterfall was treacherous, with slick rocks and few handholds. The cliff was easily fifty feet high, with the river coming down as a solid curtain of water. It formed a pool at the base, but on one edge it crashed onto a flat rock, sending up a spray that caught the sunlight in a full rainbow.

Rielle led the way. She was fearless, but her thick sandals were not ideal for this kind of climbing. Ultimately, she decided to toss them down on the bank. Barefoot, she could at least get a grip. As she made her way higher, she suddenly pointed: "There! Do you see it?"

Arlo did. There was a space behind the waterfall. An opening to a cave. The only question was how to get to it without getting swept away.

After a few false starts, Rielle found a promising route. It required shimmying along a very narrow ledge, little more than a crack. Luckily, a thin tree branch provided some support. She was just about across when the branch suddenly pulled loose. Arlo grabbed for her, catching the strap of the cage. That swung Rielle back into the rocks. As Arlo struggled to hold on, she twisted, trying to right herself.

"Grab onto something!" Arlo shouted.

"I'm trying! I—"

Rielle slipped free of the strap and fell twenty feet into the water below with a sickening *thwwwwunk*. Arlo was left holding the cage, staring dumbstruck. He couldn't see her. She hadn't surfaced. *How deep is it?* he wondered. *Should I dive in after her?*

Seconds passed. Arlo hoisted up the cage, awkwardly slinging it onto his back. Still no Rielle. He had just started to figure out how to make his way back down the cliff when he heard a distant voice shouting: "Arlo? Arlo!"

It was Rielle. But the voice seemed to be coming from above him, rather than below.

"Where are you?" he shouted back.

"I'm in the river! I'm . . . wait, nooooo!"

He looked up as Rielle dropped over the top of the waterfall, carried by the force of the river. Her scream whooshed past Arlo as she fell. This time, she barely missed the flat rock at the bottom. Once again, she disappeared underwater.

"Rielle! RIELLE!" he yelled. No answer. Confused, he looked both below him and above. And then . . .

"Arlo?" Distant, and definitely above him. Somehow, this river was flowing in a loop. The bottom of the waterfall was also the top. Rielle was about to go over it again.

"Stay to your left!" he shouted. "As far as you can!" He had visions of her crashing on the flat rock at the bottom.

A few seconds later, he saw her body drop over the waterfall again. This time, she was far from the rock. After she *plunk*ed into the water, Arlo saw her kicking her way to the surface, fighting to swim to the shore. She pulled herself up out of the river, half drowned and exhausted.

"Are you okay?!" Arlo shouted over the roaring water.

"I think so!" she shouted back.

"Do you want me to come back to you?!"

"No! Go in!"

"Are you sure you're okay?"

"I'll be fine! I just can't climb back up there. I'm dizzy!"

Arlo mentally ran through the first aid he'd learned in Rangers. Her dizziness could be a symptom of shock or a concussion. He remembered an assessment he'd seen in the Field Book: "Can you list the months backwards starting with December?"

Now Rielle was just annoyed. "I'm fine! Go in the cave!"

Clinging to a cliff wall above an impossible looping river, Arlo considered his options. He could climb down and check on Rielle, but there was no guarantee she'd be able to make it back up. Or he could forge ahead and try to make it inside the cave behind the waterfall. If Mirnos was there, he'd face the dragon alone, for better or worse.

He tugged on the branch that had come loose. It was in fact still attached, just with a bit more slack. Before he could talk himself out of it, Arlo stepped onto the narrow ledge, digging in with the sides of his sneakers. He inched along, hugging the cliff face, trying not to rely too much on the branch for support. There was one last difficult transition onto another rock. With no handholds, Arlo simply had to leap. He only had one shot.

It was a terrible jump. He landed on one foot, teetering. Yet somehow he found his balance. He was behind the waterfall, at the entrance to a natural cavern. It was dim, with very little sunlight making it through. Everything was wet and dripping.

Wiping his hands dry on his shirt, he sent a single snaplight into the cave. He watched as it arced, catching glistening reflections of red and gold.

Then he heard movement. Scraping on stone.

Arlo took one step back—any further and he'd be in the

water. As his eyes adjusted to the dark, he saw a massive shape shifting in the dim light. He couldn't tell where the shadows ended and the creature began.

He sent in another snaplight. This time he could make out scales and wings and claws. It was moving, its muscles rippling as it stirred to consciousness.

Arlo considered jumping into the water and taking his chances, but he held his ground. As the creature got closer, he could hear it breathing. He could feel it, too: each exhale was hot and moist on his skin. Still, he couldn't get a good sense of its size until it was right in front of him and opened its golden eyes.

This was Mirnos.

— 44 —
MIRNOS

DRAGONS HAVE EYELASHES. In all the books he'd read about dragons, in all the illustrations he'd seen of them, Arlo couldn't recall a single one that included eyelashes—perhaps because no
one had ever stood this close to an actual dragon's eye. But the
lashes were definitely there: a row of tiny dark hairs along the
leathery eyelids, with white grains of sleep clinging to the roots.

Mirnos was just a few feet away, its head lifted off the ground.
The dragon seemed curious but only half awake. It evidently
didn't regard Arlo as a threat.

Arlo reached a hand forward to touch the dragon's snout.
With a loud sniff, Mirnos curled its lip, revealing a fang. *Don't
pet me*, it seemed to be saying. *I'm not a dog.*

"Sorry," said Arlo. He took a careful step forward, away from
the crashing waterfall behind him.

Like Ekafos and Fox, Mirnos was a spirit with a distinct

physical form. It had a body and mass. But it was unmistakably supernatural as well. Its eyes shimmered with radiant color. Its scales *plink*ed like musical notes as it shifted, resting its head on its front legs to study Arlo.

"Do you know why I'm here?" asked Arlo. "Did you want me to come? I mean, I'm assuming you did, because why else would you have shown me this place?"

It wasn't clear whether Mirnos could understand what he was asking. The dragon seemed more amused than interested. So Arlo decided to answer his own question.

"Maybe you brought me here because you want something. Like how Big Breezy flew me to Giant's Fist. Or how Ekafos took me back in time so I could find the spirit knife. Is that right? Is there something you want me to do?"

Mirnos turned its head to face him directly. Arlo could see his reflection in the black pupils of the dragon's eyes. Beyond that, there was another shape: a glowing tangle of light floating in darkness. *A knot?* he wondered. *No, a knaught.* It was more complicated than a slipknaught, but seemed similarly impossible: a coil that grew tighter as it pulled itself apart.

Staring at the shimmering form, Arlo slowly realized that the space around him was changing. He was no longer in the cave with Mirnos, but rather in a windowless two-story room with smooth stone walls. The knaught was floating a few feet off the ground. *Where is this?* Arlo asked himself. It didn't feel like the Long Woods.

Now he was moving, floating backwards through a door.

Down a hallway. Up a flight of stairs. He emerged outdoors in a place he'd been to before: the Realm. To his right, he could see the two giant winged statues. He looked at the buildings around him and the staircase he'd floated up.

"You want me to find this place," said Arlo. "To find that knaught."

The dragon nodded. Arlo was back in the cavern. He'd never really left.

"Why, though?" Arlo knew the dragon couldn't give him an answer, but he had to ask the question. Of all the people on Earth and in the Long Woods, why had Mirnos chosen him? And why Ekafos before that? Surely there had to be someone more qualified, or at least older. If it had to be a Ranger, why not a better Ranger, like Indra or Connor or Christian? If it had to be a tooble, why not Rielle or Zhang—*well, not them specifically*, he thought, but a hypothetical other tooble who fit the requirements?

He couldn't think of any reason why a dragon would pick a thirteen-year-old kid from Pine Mountain for this quest. Like the Pevensie children saving Narnia, it all seemed so arbitrary. Arlo Finch simply wanted to know—

"What's so special about me?"

A man's voice answered: "I've been asking that question for thirty years."

Arlo turned to see Hadryn. He'd just entered the cave through the same passage behind the waterfall, and his clothes

280

were drenched from the spray. He looked skinny and feral, but stronger than he had on the island.

Mirnos can swallow him in one bite, thought Arlo. Yet the dragon seemed completely uninterested in Hadryn. Its eyelids blinked twice before closing for good. With Mirnos evidently not a threat, Hadryn took a few steps further into the cavern.

"How did you find me?" asked Arlo.

"You must have gotten a splinter when you were on the island. Probably didn't even notice." Arlo had noticed: that small sliver in the heel of his hand. "That splinter's from a tree that grows only on that island. With a little woodsense, it's not hard to track you." Hadryn rested his back against the rough wall, guarding the only way out of the cavern. "So when I saw you meeting up with that girlfriend of yours who lives with the Eldritch, I figured out what you were probably up to and followed you here. I can be pretty stealthy."

"What did you do to Rielle?"

"Oh, I didn't kill her! Not yet. Just knocked her out. Figured she could be a useful hostage." Hadryn smiled. His sharpened teeth still unnerved Arlo. "Now, let's get to why we both came here. Time for the old dragon to go into that cage you brought."

"I don't know how it works," said Arlo. It was technically true.

"Kid, you just open it. These fancy Eldritch cages, they're basically automatic."

Arlo lifted the cage from his back, examining it for something

281

that looked like a latch or a lock. He found it near one end: a brass catch that easily flipped open.

The cage began to expand. Startled, Arlo dropped it and backed away, watching as it quickly unfurled spokes and runners that swirled as they grew to fill the space. Metallic roots curled along the rough stone floor, sliding under the sleeping dragon's belly. Tentacles bumped blindly against the ceiling before curling down over the dragon's back to meet on the far side. In under ten seconds, it had completely encompassed Mirnos.

And then it began to constrict. Only now did the dragon awaken. Brass bands cinched tight, sliding between scales and digging into the creature's hide. When Mirnos opened its mighty jaws, Arlo expected a roar, but what came out was more of a long exhale. The dragon's body was collapsing, flesh dissolving into swirling light. The last things to vanish were the dragon's eyes. They stared directly at Arlo as they faded.

Mirnos was gone.

The cage returned to its original size, only now with a mighty dragon stored inside it. Arlo lifted it, surprised to find it was considerably lighter than before.

"Yeah, funny thing," said Hadryn. "Spirits weigh less than nothing, so cages are lighter when they're full. Now bring it here."

Arlo stayed put. "What are you going to do with it?"

"I'm gonna bargain with the Eldritch. They want this dragon so bad, they're apt to give me anything I want. Can't believe you were willing to trade it for just your parents."

Arlo lifted the strap over his head, returning it to his back.

Hadryn shook his head, annoyed. "C'mon, kid. I may have one arm, but I can still take it from you."

"Maybe," said Arlo. "But why make it easy? I know you'll just kill me eventually."

"True," said Hadryn. "But not today if you're lucky."

Arlo shrugged. Smiled. "I'll take my chances."

With that, Arlo ran full speed towards the waterfall, leaping as far as he could. He'd hoped to pass through the wall of water to the air beyond, but the force of the falling river knocked him straight down. He couldn't get his bearings as he tumbled. There was only the noise and cold and pain as he hit bottom.

The impact knocked the wind out of him. He couldn't tell which way was up. Everything was swirling. Churning. But the spirit cage on his back was yanking him in one direction. It was floating.

Kicking his feet, Arlo broke the surface of the water, clinging to the cage. Sunlight. Air. He gasped, trying to fill his lungs. Wiping his eyes clear, he saw trees whipping by. The current was fast. *I'm back at the top of the waterfall*, he realized.

Twenty feet upstream, Hadryn surfaced. With only one arm, he wasn't a strong swimmer. Arlo was counting on that.

He turned to see the edge of the waterfall fast approaching. *Swim left*, he thought. *Get to the bank*. But the river kept pulling him towards the center. He took one last deep breath as he crossed over the cliff.

The drop was terrifying. He wasn't in the water as much as

on top of it, free-falling towards the churning pool below. At the last moment, Arlo managed to get his legs beneath him so that he wouldn't belly flop. It still hurt.

He kicked hard, making it to the surface more quickly this time. Once again, he was back at the top of the waterfall, but with more river ahead of him. Unfortunately, he was tangled in the cage's strap. He struggled to get it over his head, swallowing water in the process.

Hadryn surfaced and immediately locked eyes on Arlo. He swam towards him.

Finally free of the strap, Arlo pushed the cage away from him. It floated towards the right bank, forcing Hadyrn to make a choice: left or right, Arlo or the cage. Hadryn chose the cage, swimming to catch up with it.

He had just about reached it when Arlo passed over the ridge of the waterfall, plummeting into the water below. This time, Arlo surfaced at the far left edge of the pool, at the waterfall's base. The current wasn't nearly as strong here. Kicking hard, he made it to the riverbank, where he climbed out. He was cold and exhausted. He coughed up water.

He looked back at the waterfall, searching for Hadryn. He didn't see him anywhere.

It wasn't until Arlo made it to his feet that he spotted Hadryn lying facedown on the flat rock at the base of the waterfall. He wasn't moving. But Arlo couldn't be sure he was actually dead.

Moving downstream, Arlo found a place to cross the river, then headed back upstream to check on Hadryn. As he got closer, it became clear that Hadryn had landed headfirst on the rock. His skull was crushed. There was no blood; the constant spray of water was washing it away.

Arlo had never seen a dead body before. It unsettled him. As much as he'd feared and hated the man lying on this rock, he'd known him. He'd known him as a boy. They'd told each other secrets and swum in frozen lakes.

Alva Hadryn Thomas had been a friend before he'd been an enemy. He was a Ranger from a small town in Texas who had seen impossible things and spent his life pursuing them. Was he always destined to do evil, or had he been steered in that direction? And if it was the latter, who had the most blame?

That night on Redfeather Lake, Arlo thought. *What if I'd trusted him? What if I'd let him hold the spirit knife? Would he still have become this man?*

Arlo searched the pockets of Hadryn's cargo pants. There he found it: the spirit knife.

He finally had it back.

———•◦•———

Arlo found the spirit cage in the reeds beside the river, the brass glinting in the sunlight. It had survived its fall, slightly dented but still intact. Arlo considered cutting the small glowing cord he could see with the spirit knife, freeing Mirnos like he had freed the storm spirit in the desert.

But was that what the dragon wanted? Mirnos had seemed remarkably unconcerned about being captured in the first place. It had revealed its location to Rielle and Arlo, and put up no resistance. *Did it plan to be captured?* Arlo wondered. *Was that why it wanted both me and Rielle, so that it would be taken to the Realm?*

Arlo decided to have faith that Mirnos knew what it was doing, and he left the cage sealed.

He found Rielle lying in the grass, still unconscious from her encounter with Hadryn. He checked her pulse and her breathing, then rolled her into recovery position on her side. It took a few minutes to wake her, but she seemed okay except for a headache.

"I can't believe you killed Hadryn," she said.

"I didn't. Not really."

She smiled. "I'll tell the Eldritch you did. They'll be impressed."

"I don't care what they think," said Arlo. "They're bad people, and I hate that I'm helping them."

"I know." Rielle kissed him on the cheek, then slung the cage over her back. Arlo watched as she walked away, headed back to the Realm.

Arlo took one last look at the waterfall, then started back to Pine Mountain.

— 45 —
THINGS AS THEY
SHOULD BE

CLARK FINCH WAS RELEASED from federal custody eight days before Christmas. In a written statement, the Justice Department announced that all charges had been dropped in exchange for his assistance in issues concerning national security.

Celeste Finch and Mitch Jansen were also cleared of any wrongdoing. The matter was declared officially closed.

Clark returned home to Pine Mountain on a Saturday afternoon. After the initial hugs, Arlo and Jaycee gave their father a proper tour of the house and property.

"There's no internet," Jaycee warned him.

"Perfect," said Clark. "I think we can do without it for a while."

The government hadn't returned his laptop or the quantum device he'd been working on, but Clark wasn't worried about anyone figuring out his research. "Everything's encrypted. If they try to unlock it, it'll automatically erase." He said he wasn't planning to tackle any work until after the new year.

A more immediate project was finding the perfect Christmas tree. Arlo had spotted one on their property: a Douglas fir with one partially burned side that could be pushed against the wall. Using a folding camp saw, he managed to cut it down by himself. He and his father carried it into the house. In the basement, their mom retrieved ten boxes of her parents' old decorations. It took hours, but they managed to use almost all of them. Arlo finished his homework in the living room so he could admire the tree, the first they'd had in years.

The news that his parents had been cleared of all charges quickly made it through school. Arlo couldn't be sure, but it felt like his classmates were holding eye contact a bit longer. Even Principal Brownlee avoided his usual sneer.

After the winter band concert, Merilee Myers handed Arlo a store-bought card that depicted two doves kissing atop a Christmas tree. It was heavily decorated, and felt expensive.

"She's so into you," said Wu the next day at lunch. "Those birds are supposed to be you and her."

Indra disagreed. "It's from the 'Twelve Days of Christmas': *Two turtle doves, and a partridge in a pear tree.*"

"Then where's the partridge? All I see is two doves making out."

"That's a classic peace symbol!" protested Indra. "And the card even says *Peace on Earth.*"

"Wait, so you don't think Merilee's into Arlo?"

"Oh no," said Indra. "She *definitely* is. But the card isn't literally them kissing. It's more subtle than that." Arlo was looking forward to two weeks of winter break so he wouldn't have to think about Merilee. Although he suspected he would. He increasingly felt like he owed her an apology, not for anything he'd said or done, but for not noticing her kindness. She was always on his side, and he was never on hers.

That afternoon, as they got off the bus in Pine Mountain, Arlo thanked Merilee for the card. "And thank you for being a friend, too."

Merilee smiled. "You're welcome."

<hr />

Pine Mountain Company was still holding weekly meetings in the Stokes family barn, but for the December Court of Honor, they decided to move to the Gold Pan diner so they wouldn't be eating potluck next to cows. Arlo introduced his father to the rest of his friends, and to their parents. "Great to see someone taking on the system and winning," said Mr. Delgado. "You're an inspiration."

When it came time for awards, Sarah and Wyatt both received their Squirrel rank. Arlo collected the patches he'd earned since summer camp: Beast Lore and First Aid. By the next Court of Honor, he'd be eligible for his Owl.

Connor handed Blue Patrol their patches, and also a bit of surprising news: "I'm going to be moving up to Senior Patrol," he said. "You'll need to pick a new patrol leader."

Arlo immediately flashed back to that summer's patrol leader drama at camp, but his fears were misplaced. Blue Patrol unanimously elected Indra Srinivasaraghavan-Jones as their leader. She was beaming and excited to get started. "I have some ideas for changes."

Arlo and his parents were the last ones left in the diner. His mom needed to check that everything was ready for the breakfast shift, and his dad was fixing a problem with the electronic cash register. Arlo offered to go out and warm up the truck.

It was gently snowing, feathery flakes that took their time falling in the moonlight. Uncle Wade's truck was the only vehicle left in the parking lot. As he walked towards it, Arlo noticed a set of tiny paw prints that transitioned into boot prints. He stopped. Smiled.

"Quite a moon tonight." A man came up behind him. He was small for a grownup, wearing a wool jacket, leather boots and a fur hat. His mustache twisted up into points. "That's a hunter's moon if I ever saw one."

Arlo smiled. "What are you hunting for tonight?"

"Answers." Fox's pale eyes looked directly into his. "I think I know why you gave them the dragon. I think I know why the dragon let you do it. But it all seems quite a gamble, and quite a lot to put on your shoulders. Are you sure you're ready?"

Arlo nodded. "Tomorrow night. It's a new moon. It'll be dark."

"Your friends, your family—do they know what you're doing?" Arlo shook his head. Fox took him by the shoulders.

"Even the pine trees are writing about you, Arlo Finch. The humans deserve to know, too."

With that, Fox stepped behind him. Arlo turned to see a small red fox dashing across the snow, disappearing into the darkness. He stood alone in the parking lot, looking up at a sliver of moon.

— 46 —
THE KNIFE AND
THE KNAUGHT

Dear Mom, Dad and Jaycee,

Sorry that I'm writing this in a letter rather than telling you in person. I didn't want you to feel like you had to talk me out of this or solve it some other way. Plus it's hard to explain.

I'm going to the Realm. It's the place beyond the Long Woods. A dragon showed me something there, and I think I know what to do with it. I'm not sure it's going to work, but I have to try.

In case I don't make it back, please give Indra my Ranger's compass, and give Wu my Field Book. Tell Blue Patrol good luck at the Alpine Derby, and also that Hadryn is dead so they don't need to worry about him anymore.

I want to thank you for setting such a good

example for me. Dad, you taught me how important it is to do what's right even when it's hard. Mom, you taught me to be brave when you don't know what's going to happen. Jaycee, you taught me to not be afraid of what other people think. I couldn't have asked for a better family. I love you.

Arlo

PS Tell Uncle Wade I listened to the tape he left me.

Arlo placed the letter on the hearth in the living room. He figured his family would find it in the morning if he didn't make it back.

As he picked up his boots, he noticed that the clock on the mantel showed just after midnight. It was technically Christmas.

———◆◆◆———

He had packed carefully, trying to anticipate everything he might need. In addition to the spirit knife, his gear included a flashlight with extra batteries, a notebook, two pens, a water bottle, two granola bars, a pocketknife with folding scissors, matches, an emergency whistle and ten feet of rope.

For now, he needed only the flashlight. The mine was pitch-black and spooky. Last time, he had been in the mine with his friends, and Rielle's lantern had illuminated everything around them. It was much creepier alone by flashlight. Arlo could see only straight ahead, and had no sense of what might be approaching from behind. More than once, he heard a sound that made him spin around in panic. But it was just an echo. The tunnel was empty.

Approaching a dim glow at the end of the tunnel, Arlo switched off his flashlight, feeling his way with a hand along the wall. This was the spot he'd been most worried about: was the Eldritch side of the tunnel monitored? Arlo hadn't noticed any creature or device guarding it as they left, but he couldn't be sure.

He peeked out of the tunnel to see a night full of stars. It was much warmer than he had expected—summerlike, in fact—and the buildings of the city were brightly lit, thrumming with energy and activity. He could hear distant orchestral music: soaring strings and pounding drums. The kingdom felt transformed. Lively.

The winged statues were off to his right. Arlo quickly got his bearings, deciding roughly where the staircase Mirnos had shown him must be. Now he just needed to get there without being seen.

He pulled the rope from his daypack, twisting the fibers between his fingers until he could feel a small ripple of energy. Then he gently pulled the rope through itself, tying a slip-knaught. He hadn't tied one since his incident at summer camp, but the technique was still part of his muscle memory. With his thumbs, he carefully opened the center of the knaught, revealing a shimmering film. Once he'd gotten the loop large enough, he stepped through with his right foot, then his left foot, then pulled it over his head.

He was now invisible. Intangible. *A perfect spy*, he thought. Most importantly, he didn't immediately die. He'd worried that using a slipknaught again would snap his silver cord, separating his spirit from his body forever. For now, he was still in one piece.

In this form, he saw spirits quite clearly, along with the glowing cords that bound them to various Eldritch devices. Streetlamps were tethered fire spirits. Public fountains were captive water spirits. The flying drones overhead were air spirits fused to mechanical contraptions. The Realm was powered by tens of thousands of individual spirits chained to machinery. The things that made it work also made it cruel.

Arlo found the staircase in less than ten minutes. He made his way down the steps. Everything was exactly as he had seen it in the dragon's vision—until he reached the two-story room.

It had the same bare walls and dim light. But where Arlo had originally seen a swirling knaught, he now saw a massive stone cube. It looked to be ten feet square. Arlo walked all the way around it, finding no entrance, no buttons, no markings. It was as solid as the floor. Arlo could feel it against his hand, cold and smooth.

What now? he wondered. He felt certain this was the same room Mirnos had shown him, so where was the knaught? *Is it inside the block? Am I supposed to crack it open somehow?*

Arlo hadn't brought a chisel or dynamite. *The knife!* Arlo

retrieved the spirit knife from his pack. The spectral blade poked right through the stone until it reached the hilt, where it *clunk*ed and could go no further.

The knife clearly wasn't the answer. At least not the whole answer.

Arlo sat on the floor, staring at the giant cube. It was maddening to have gotten this far only to be stymied by a literal block. Why hadn't Mirnos shown it to him?

As he looked around, Arlo tried to imagine the purpose of this room. Everything he'd seen in the Realm had been ornate and elegantly designed, but this space was oddly featureless. *What if this room is a vault?* he wondered. Perhaps the knaught is so important that the Eldritch encased it in stone so that no one could touch it—or for that matter, even discover it. *Maybe Mirnos showed me what was inside so I'd know what to look for.*

But knowing the knaught was inside got him no closer to reaching it. He couldn't simply walk through stone to get to it.

But the blade can, Arlo realized. It was invisible and intangible, but unlike him, it could pass through stone. Maybe the solution was to make himself more like that. But how could he achieve that level of nothingness?

Another slipknaught. It felt like a crazy Wu idea: *What if you went through two slipknaughts instead of one?* Indra would then point out that using one slipknaught was already incredibly dangerous, so using two slipknaughts was tempting fate. They would bicker, each one arguing their side.

Arlo felt lucky to have friends he knew so well that he could let them debate an idea even when they weren't around.

In this case, he was siding with Wu. He'd try to make a second slipknaught.

Unfortunately, there wasn't any rope available; he'd left the original loop back at the tunnel. Then he remembered his shoelaces. He pulled them out of his boots, tying them into a loop before working on another slipknaught. They were thinner than he preferred, and his fingers felt oddly disconnected from the task. But after only a minute or two, he sensed the energy starting to crackle. He tied the slipknaught and opened it just wide enough to peer through.

Through the lens of the slipknaught, there was no stone block. In its place—in the exact center of the room—floated a glowing shape. *The knaught.*

Arlo could see it, but could he reach it? As a test, he opened the loop wide enough to pass his hand through. Just as with the blade of the spirit knife, his fingers could now enter the space the stone block occupied. He was *double incorporeal*—at least his hand was. But the glowing knaught was still many feet away, well beyond arm's length. To reach it, he'd need to go fully inside.

Tucking the spirit knife into his pocket, Arlo opened the circle wide enough to step through. First his left foot, then his right, then over his head.

He immediately felt cold, dizzy and disoriented. Sounds

were oddly muffled, as if he was underwater. He could hear his heart pounding, but it was coming from outside his body. Arlo turned to see a thirteen-year-old boy standing motionless in a dark void, a loop of shoelaces in one hand. A silver cord ran from this boy's navel to Arlo's own navel.

Arlo Finch was outside himself, floating in a plane beyond the spirits. He had no idea what to call this place, if it even had a name. Maybe it was literally nowhere, the way that Ekafos lived in a dimension outside of time.

What worried him most was the silver cord. Some sections were as thick as a drinking straw. Others were as thin as a hair. That summer, Fox had warned him that this cord was all that connected his spirit to his body, and that using a slipknaught could weaken it. Now he'd done it twice back-to-back. If it broke, he'd be dead.

Careful not to tug on the cord, Arlo turned to see the glowing object behind him. It was a knaught, too, but of a very different form than a slipknaught. This was a fistlike coil wrapped around itself, constantly drawing tighter. It evidently existed in this dimension, too. He didn't know how to get to it—there was nothing to walk on or push against. He tried swimming through the air with his arms, to no avail. But simply focusing on the knaught seemed to slowly pull him in that direction. He was soon right next to it. Even without touching it, he could feel it crackling with energy.

I wish my dad could see this, thought Arlo. Clark Finch would have had an explanation for what it truly was, using terms like *quantum entanglement* and *spooky action at a distance*. All Arlo knew was that this knaught was so important to the Eldritch that they'd hidden it inside a stone block. It was so important to Mirnos that he'd helped Arlo find it.

Arlo took the spirit knife from his pocket and held the shimmering blade to the knaught. He thought of his family and friends.

And then he cut.

There was no explosion, no jolt of mystical energy. The universe didn't divide or fold in on itself. The knaught simply unraveled, dissolving into thousands of tiny glowing fragments.

One of these embers floated close to the silver cord, landing on it. It sizzled and sparked, burning right through the fibers. The silver cord broke in two, each side coiling back on itself.

Arlo looked at his motionless body as it floated away like an untethered astronaut, eventually vanishing.

Is this death? he wondered. In the last year, he'd come close to dying several times. He'd survived fires and drowning and various creatures trying to kill him. He'd found his consciousness bound to a discarded Rubik's Cube in a Chinese park. But he'd never felt *this*, a kind of vast emptiness, like the silence after an explosion.

He watched as his hands began to fade away. It was fascinating, and not unpleasant. He didn't feel afraid or nervous. He felt finished. Like he could stop trying. He could just *be* until he stopped *being*. And that was okay.

He smiled. At least, it was the idea of smiling. He didn't have a body anymore. Or a face. Or a heartbeat. All that was left was the spirit knife he'd been holding. Arlo was inside it, or had become it. He was a knife floating in the void.

Time passed. *Minutes? Days? Centuries?* he wondered. There was no way to tell. His thoughts were slow. He couldn't remember basic things like his name or his phone number or any number or what words meant.

Then he sensed movement—ripples in the ether. He felt himself being tossed by the wake of a massive creature. He could hear the metallic ring of its scales. It was a dragon. It had come for him.

Arlo Finch slowly sat up. It was dark and cold. He felt around with his hands—*I have hands again!*—discovering his flashlight.

He switched it on to reveal that he was back in the room with the stone block. The fire spirits who had provided light had vanished. Getting to his feet, Arlo felt woozy but otherwise intact. He checked everywhere for the spirit knife, but it was nowhere to be found.

Arlo climbed the stairs leading back to the outside. That's when he realized the extent of what had changed.

The buildings of the Realm were dark. The streetlights, extinguished. All machinery had stopped. The only motion was in the sky, where tens of thousands of glowing spirits swirled, no longer bound to their devices. *The knaught*, Arlo realized. *Cutting it freed all of them.* That mystical, extra-dimensional knaught was what had allowed the Eldritch to bind spirits to their machinery. Without it, they couldn't constrain them. Without it, the spirits were loose.

Arlo saw the Eldritch gathering on the avenues, staring up at the sky. Some had armor and spears, but without their devices, they had no way to reach the spirits. They were earthbound, mortal.

Only then did Arlo realize he was seeing the spirits without holding the spirit knife. He was back in his physical body, but something had changed: he had become the knife, and the knife had become him.

Arlo watched as a fiery form rose from the center of the city, unfurling giant wings. It was Mirnos, or at least a form of Mirnos. The other spirits circled it, seeming to wait for its direction.

Is it going to destroy the city? Arlo wondered. The spirits could smash it, flood it and burn it to the ground. And they would have good reason to do so, not only for what they had suffered, but to keep the Eldritch from ever trying to capture them again.

But Arlo didn't want it destroyed. He didn't want the Eldritch dead. He simply wanted the spirits to be free. He had no control over what Mirnos did next, but he hoped for mercy.

Suddenly, the massive dragon flew down straight between

the winged statues, clipping off their heads. The spirits followed Mirnos as it descended the ramp leading to the undersea. He was leading them out of the Realm and back to the Long Woods. They were going home.

Now it was time for Arlo to do the same.

— 47 —
HOME

AS ARLO EMERGED FROM THE MINE, he switched off his flashlight and looked out across the valley. A light snow was falling in tiny silver flecks that caught the moonlight. He could still make out his footprints from earlier that night, but they'd softened to dimples in a white blanket of powder.

He stood there for a long moment, grateful to be out of the darkness. Out of the uncertainty. Out of the Realm.

Back at the house, Arlo quietly shut and locked the laundry room door behind himself. He unlaced his boots, letting the crusts of snow break apart in his fingers. He then tiptoed in sock feet back to the living room, where he retrieved the letter he'd left on the hearth. He tucked it into his pocket.

According to the clock on the mantel, it was nearly four A.M. In a few hours, the sun would be up and they'd begin opening presents. Still, Arlo wanted a few more moments of Christmas

Eve. He sat on the braided rug in front of the tree and let his eyes go unfocused, until all he saw were constellations of tiny colored lights.

As he climbed the stairs, he was careful to avoid the squeaky step.

Once in his room, he changed back into his pajamas. He tucked the letter into the back of his sock drawer. He wasn't sure why he was keeping it, but it felt wrong to throw it out.

He climbed under the covers with his flashlight and his Ranger Field Book. Flipping to the back, he looked through the requirements for Wolf. He'd read them dozens of times, but it was exciting to think about what new skills lay ahead: *Tracking. Wouldcraeft. Disorienteering.*

By the glow of the flashlight, in those words on paper, Arlo Finch imagined where he would be a year from now, what he would know and who he would become.

He was ready.

1. Arlo had a plan for bringing his father home, but hadn't anticipated the consequences. If you were in his situation, what might you have done differently? Would you have shared your ideas with anyone outside of Blue Patrol?

2. One of the promises in the Ranger's Vow is to "defend the weak." How does Arlo do that in Kingdom of Shadows?

3. Fallpath is a settlement located inside the Long Woods. How do you imagine the town functions? Who picks up the trash? Are there laws, and if so, who enforces them?

4. Blue Patrol adds two new members, Wyatt and Sarah. How does their arrival change Arlo's role within the patrol?

5. Rielle and the Eldritch view spirits as a resource, more like energy than living beings. What characteristics do you think make something *alive*? How

conscious must something be in order for it to have rights?

6. Why does Uncle Wade choose to save the house rather than the workshop? If you had to save one building in your life from destruction, what would you pick?

7. Both Hadryn and Arlo's father are fugitives. In what other ways are they alike?

8. Does meeting Jonas and Julie's parents change your impression of the twins?

9. The government makes a deal with the Eldritch to free Arlo's parents. What do you think the Eldritch are offering the government in exchange? Technology? Secrets? Something else?

10. Why doesn't Arlo tell Indra and Wu about his plan to free the spirits? Would you have made the same choice?

11. What do you think happens to the Realm without spirits to power it? To what degree should Arlo consider the well-being of the Eldritch?

12. How does Arlo's relationship with his parents and sister change over the course of the three books?

THE RANGER'S VOW

LOYAL, BRAVE, KIND AND TRUE—
KEEPER OF THE OLD AND NEW—
I GUARD THE WILD,
DEFEND THE WEAK,
MARK THE PATH,
AND VIRTUE SEEK.
FOREST SPIRITS HEAR ME NOW
AS I SPEAK MY RANGER'S VOW.

IF YOU'RE CURIOUS ABOUT HOW THE ARLO FINCH NOVELS CAME TO BE, CHECK OUT THE LAUNCH PODCAST.

Over the course of six episodes, John August charts the journey from his initial idea to the finished book, talking with editors, designers, authors and booksellers about every step of the process. You'll learn about everything from proofreading to printing to Potter.

You can find it wherever you subscribe to podcasts, or at **http://wondery.fm/launchhome**.

ACKNOWLEDGMENTS

The Arlo Finch trilogy is directly inspired by my childhood in Colorado, so I need to start by thanking the scouts and leaders of Troop 177, especially Jason Hicks and Miguel Ramos. Thank you for climbing those mountains with me.

None of our adventures would have been possible without our parents to drive us, feed us and keep us relatively safe by 1980s standards. I want to thank my mom and dad for their endless patience and love. To my brother Bill, thank you for teaching me my knots. Our ties grow stronger every year.

Arlo Finch is equally inspired by all the books I read as a kid. I was lucky to have great librarians. At Burke Elementary, the actual Mrs. Fitzrandolph kept me supplied with fiction and nonfiction, while public librarian Wendy Hall let me stretch the limits of how many books a kid could check out at once.

Writing is a skill that only improves with practice and feedback.

Thank you to all of my teachers, especially my English and journalism professors. You managed to break many bad habits without breaking my spirit.

I wrote the first chapter of *Valley of Fire* during one stormy night in Austin, Texas. (You can hear the details in the *Launch* podcast.) The journey from one chapter to a trilogy came with the help of my remarkable feature agent David Kramer and his colleague Mary Pender. David, thank you for being a friend and advocate for two decades.

My book agent Jodi Reamer is rightfully a legend. At every turn, she understood what was most important and how to achieve it. Thank you for guiding me through the Long Woods of publishing.

Thanks to the whole team at Writers House, in particular Cecilia de la Campa, who found homes for Arlo around the world.

My incredible editor Connie Hsu at Roaring Brook answered all my questions and kept (gently but relentlessly) pushing me to get these books in their best shape, understanding not only what I wanted to say but how readers would experience them. She and Megan Abbate kept the trains running both creatively and logistically. I'd still be finishing book one without their help.

My thanks to everyone at Macmillan Children's Publishing. I'll probably never know everyone who had a hand in getting Arlo out into the world, but I want to personally thank Johanna Kirby, Mary Van Akin, Morgan Dubin, Alexandra Hernandez, Thomas Nau, Kathryn Little and John Nora. Extra shout-out to all the proofreaders.

I'm endlessly grateful to cover artist Vivienne To and creative director Elizabeth Clark for paying such care to what Arlo Finch looks like on the shelf and in your hands. I've also loved seeing the different styles and interpretations that artists around the world have brought to local editions of Arlo.

James Patrick Cronin, thank you for lending your voice to Arlo Finch and to all the residents of Pine Mountain.

I've been lucky to have great assistants who were my first readers as these books spilled out one chapter at a time. Thank you to Godwin Jabongwe, Megan McDonnell and Megana Rao for proofreading (and re-proofreading) these books in their roughest and most inchoate form. The uncomfortable secret is that most authors are desperate to please readers, so I'm forever grateful for your curiosity and enthusiasm in those initial readings.

Nima Yousefi, Dustin Bocks, Quinn Emmett and Alejandro Victorero were incredibly generous with notes and feedback on first drafts. Thank you for helping me see where the story got off-track or confusing.

I've been fortunate to meet and learn from so many terrific authors in this journey. Thank you to Kenneth Oppel, Geoff Rodkey, Jacob Sager Weinstein, Chris Weitz, Julie Buxbaum and Tomi Adeyemi for your early help.

I visited dozens of schools across the country for Arlo Finch, teaching several thousand kids about heroes, bears and how to tie a square knot. Thank you to all the principals, librarians and teachers who welcomed me into their cafetoriums.

Book tours are only possible with the support of local

booksellers. Thank you for inviting me to your towns and stores, and for putting Arlo Finch in the right kids' hands. (Gibran Graham, you're a superstar.)

At the end of every tour, I was lucky to come home to my family. Mike and Amy, I love you to an absurd degree. Thank you for putting up with my odd hours and eccentricities. I can only imagine these fantasy worlds because I have such an extraordinary real life with you.

Finally, thank you to everyone who has read and recommended these books. We're all now part of an exclusive patrol that knows the secret of what lies in the Long Woods. Let's never lose our Wonder.

John August
September 2019